THE SALON & SPA SCANDAL

A WEAL & WOE BOOKSHOP WITCH MYSTERY

CATE MARTIN

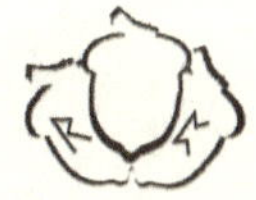

Cover design by Shezaad Sudar.

Ratatoskr Press logo by Aidan Vincent Kise.

ISBN 978-1-958606-49-0

❋ Created with Vellum

CHAPTER

ONE

After a wild first week living in the Square and working in my uncles' bookshop—solving a murder and fighting a woman possessed by some being from the under realms without quite burning down the whole community in the process— the rest of the month of June was pleasantly uneventful.

My life fell into an easy rhythm of having breakfast with my new best friend Audrey Mirken in the teashop she had just inherited, working all day in the quiet bliss of a magical bookshop filled with more wonders than even a voracious knowledge-seeker like myself could ever plow through in a lifetime, and spending nearly every minute of the day with my new companion Houdini.

Houdini, who looked like a little black rat terrier chihuahua, who could speak directly into my mind in English or his own native tongue of Draconic.

To be clear, he wasn't my familiar. First of all, I wasn't enough of a witch to have a familiar. And second of all, Houdini only *looked* like a dog. He was, in fact, a carefully hidden dragon, one who was almost still a baby.

My friend Audrey's grandaunt Agatha, despite her appearance as a doddering old tea-making witch, had actually been a wizard of immense age and power. I know most prosaics think of those two words as gendered, but in the magical community, a wizard is someone who devotes their life to studying magic and finding new sources of magical power. Like a Ph.D. or a grandmaster martial artist. It's your entire life.

Most of us are just witches. We know a few tricks to get by and live within the fabric of a magical society whose infrastructure was laid down over the ages by wizards.

Agatha didn't seek fame or glory. But she was one of the wizards who built the Square in the early days of the city of St. Anthony. I could only guess what else she had done; she had left no hints behind when she died.

But everyone knew she had been a powerful practitioner of magic. And she had used all of that magic to protect the little drag-onet she named Houdini from harm.

In the end, it had cost her her life.

But Audrey, Houdini and I had made sure that her murderess was delivered into the hands of the authorities, and what justice could be done was done.

But anyway, before I came to the Square, I hadn't thought any witch in history had ever had a dragon for a familiar. Dragons were too wise, too powerful, but mostly too rare for such a relationship to work. There were always rumors, of course, of evil wielders of magic who would seek to enslave such sentient beings as dragons, but they were, so far as I knew, only rumors. Cautionary tales.

And yet, Agatha had sacrificed herself to protect her foundling dragon baby for a reason.

Since her death, Houdini and I had been constant companions, and that relationship suited us both just fine. Mostly because I seldom left the confines of the bookshop, except for that morning trip to the teashop and the occasional afternoon repeat trip if I were feeling particularly in need of human company. For my part, running the bookshop took up a lot of time. There was a lot for a single person to do, and a lot more to explore when work wasn't making demands on me.

But after everything that had happened after Agatha's death, Houdini was a little freaked out by the idea of wandering around the rest of the Square. Not that he distrusted the other residents exactly. There were a few he disliked, particularly the cat named Miss Snooty Cat, who lived with Barnardo Daley in the apartment just over the teashop. But he was warier than he had been before Nell Bloom, the co-owner of the Bitter Brew coffeeshop, had channeled an oceanic being from the under realms and attacked Audrey and me while Houdini had been trapped helplessly outside, unable to break in through the coffeeshop windows.

Beings from the under realms aren't exactly demons as religious people use that term. But there's a lot of overlap on the Venn diagram of the two. And just like with demons, making pacts with beings from the under realms was always a bad idea. Only the being from the under realm benefits, no matter what they promise you.

Nell had wanted a better life than running a coffeeshop in a hidden neighborhood in Minneapolis offered her. And the being had wanted access to the power it sensed that Agatha was pouring into protection wards around Houdini.

Neither of them had gotten what they wanted in the end. But they'd still managed to kill Agatha. And Houdini was still grieving. Not that I blamed him. It had been barely a month, and she had been very important to him.

My friend Steph Underwood—who apprenticed with the reclusive Wizard in the ancient-looking Tower that I had yet to see a doorway into from any angle—had assured us both that he had tweaked the magic around the Square to help keep Houdini's growing power hidden from the senses of any who might want to exploit it. And the Wizard had himself sealed the under realms being inside a vessel before casting it back to the watery realm from whence it came, never to return. And Houdini had politely thanked Steph for their efforts.

But I don't think even all that was enough for him to feel safe again.

Of course, the irony in Houdini choosing to stay always close to my side was that I could do absolutely nothing to protect him if Steph's spells somehow failed. Because while I had attended every magical university program I could find and had a vast wealth of knowledge about magical theory, I couldn't actually *do* magic. Not with any kind of control, anyway. It was all random sparks and the occasional accidental conflagration for me.

Maybe that was why I was so miserable and cranky as June rolled into July. My days had fallen into a rhythm, and with no homework assignments to finish or exams to study for, for the first time in my life, my evenings were entirely free.

But while more free time should have meant more time outdoors exploring all the Square had to offer, the thing was, I just couldn't stand to be out there.

Because that summer, the whole world smelled like it was on fire. And not in a pleasant *let's roast marshmallows!* kind of way. No, this was headache-inducing, eye-irritating, miserably thick smoke that hung in a depressing haze over everything. When I woke up in the morning and went to the little balcony outside my French windows, I could barely make out the shops and apartments past the hedge maze on the far side of the Square. The smoke in the air was too dense. Some days, even the trees just below my balcony were obscured by what was very nearly a London-type fog from the Victorian era.

The yellowish-gray tint that smoke lent to the world was irritating enough, day after day. But the smell was the worst. As much as I knew this was all wildfire smoke from burning forests up in Canada that were blowing down over Minneapolis, it didn't smell like wood smoke at all.

It smelled like burning plastic Christmas trees.

It didn't help that most of the Square didn't have any kind of air conditioning. Witches tended to prefer their own solutions to such problems, but, like I said, I wasn't much of a witch. I could keep cool enough with fans, damp towels, and lightweight clothing. But the smell and the irritation of my eyes were making me more than a little cranky.

I was tempted to find an excuse to get inside the one shop on the Square that had air conditioning. But given that this particular shop was the Inanna Salon & Spa, and that the trio of women who worked there didn't exactly take to me on our first few meetings, I was not desperate enough to decide that a ridiculously expensive beauty treatment was worth the short reprieve from the smoke.

Yet.

But worse than the smoke was the fact that my unreliable magical power was starting to spark again. I couldn't control it, but I usually only encountered it when I was stressed out. Like when I had first moved to the Square after spectacularly failing my final interview for my dream job and ending up moving in with an uncle I barely remembered and his husband, whom I had never met before at all.

But after that fight with an under-realms-being-possessed Nell Bloom, I had discharged more power than I had ever known I had. Steph had helped me get rid of it without burning the Square down. Afterwards, I had felt completely empty. Empty, but finally at peace.

It had lasted for a couple of weeks. But that respite was over now. And I kind of blamed the smoke. Because nothing else in my life was stressing me out at all.

You would think the thick humidity in the air would cancel out the way my sparking magic left my hair in a dry, floating cloud around my head. But you would be wrong. Together, they turned my brown curls into some sort of strange chaos that no amount of grooming could bring under control. So that was making me cranky, too.

Luckily, the charms built into the very walls of the Weal & Woe Bookshop kept out the smell of the smoke. And Houdini and I were already used to spending the entire day in the cool semi-darkness of the endless rows of bookshelves. Particularly in the little nook on the fourth floor that had been set aside for my own use.

So that's where the two of us were the morning of the Fourth of July: curled up in my window seat with its view down onto the prosaic Minneapolis street below. The bell over the door downstairs chimed loudly enough for me to hear if any customers came in, but given it was a holiday, I wasn't expecting any.

I loved hanging out in my nook. From my window seat, I could watch passersby without being seen myself. And that was more than a function of the obscuring smoke. Because in the prosaic world, the building I was in stopped after only three floors.

Magic is so cool sometimes.

I had a stack of books beside me, but after paging through them all, I had given up my quest for answers yet again, letting the last book drop with a sigh. Houdini, who had been sleeping between my outstretched legs, opened a single eye to peer up at me.

"Nothing helpful, Tabitha?" he asked, his voice speaking directly inside my mind.

"Not a clue," I told him. "Not that I expected much. I don't even know where to start. Steph never used any words that would give me anything specific to find in an index."

"He would have if he had known which words applied," Houdini said with confidence. Clearly, his initial suspicions of the Wizard's apprentice had shifted to an unshaking loyalty and faith in his skills.

And if held down, I guess I'd have to admit I felt the same. Like Steph could see things that others didn't, and could figure out what he didn't already know. Certainly in the first week I had been in the Square, when all the craziness had been going down, it felt like he was genuinely interested in my strange lack of magical control and what it meant. Like I was a conundrum he was determined to solve and would let nothing prevent him from getting to the bottom of it.

But then, after that first week, I could count on one hand the number of times I had seen him since.

Well, truth be told, I could count it with one finger.

One time. I had seen him one time since the afternoon he had had tea with Audrey, me and Houdini. And on that occasion he had been in the bookshop looking for another rare text for his master, the Wizard, and didn't have time to talk.

I couldn't exactly be annoyed with him for that. I could tell in that brief encounter that he had been very stressed, very exhausted, and very distracted by whatever the two of them were working on. So I had acquired his book for him without pressing him for any details about my own problems.

I mean, I might've still been annoyed with him despite all that, but the grateful smile he had given me when he had that leather-bound book in his hands and could bring it back to the Wizard had been potent enough to set my stomach aflutter.

It was his brown eyes. The way they had sparkled despite the dark circles under them. Like that brief moment of seeing me was enough to recharge his energy, at least for a little while.

But I hadn't seen him since.

And all he had ever really said about my magic was that it was not normal, and that it was interesting.

And also that I wasn't the problem. Which really didn't help me now, since I knew now the problem he had been talking about at the time had been a combination of the magic Agatha had done to hide Houdini from the magical senses of others, and everything that the possessed Nell Bloom had done to find him, anyway.

I mean, try to research *not normal* and *interesting* in magical texts for some time. It's impossible to narrow that down, even considering that those words aren't thrown about by our community nearly as much as they are in the prosaic world.

Prosaic is what we witches call the nonmagical world and the people in it. Sometimes this sounds wistful, like someone longing for a simpler world. And sometimes it sounds condescending. It just depends on the witch who is using the world. It always makes me flinch a little. Like witches and wizards are *so* poetic by comparison or something.

I don't like it. But I grew up in a world where this was just the word we used to describe whatever wasn't us. It's not great, but since we never use it in front of, well, prosaics, I guess it's not actively hurtful.

Anyway, I now knew all about a bunch of *not normal* and *interesting* magics I had never heard of before. Entire schools of magical thought had paralleled certain prosaic developments in the past, and not just the alchemy and biology I was familiar with. There were magicians trying to find ways to turn what prosaics understood about space and time through their studies of physics and chemistry to unlock new powers, and others who were searching for ways to transform DNA and genetics.

The group of five wizards who had attempted to create nuclear-powered magic after the prosaic world hatched the Manhattan Project frankly terrified me. All five were rumored to have died, victims of their own experiments.

But, yeah, that word *rumored* did nothing to allay my fears.

And yet, none of that remotely described whatever was going on with me.

Which is worrying, now that I was starting to spark again. I had felt drained for weeks after my fight with the possessed version of Nell Bloom. I had blasted her with more power than I had even known I'd had. And then Steph had helped me discharge the rest of it. So much of it. It had felt bottomless. But also completely outside of my control. It was a relief when it was gone.

And for a long time after, I was sure I had permanently depleted myself. I would never have to worry about losing control again.

But pretty much from the day the wildfire smoke had obscured the skies over Minneapolis, I had started getting zaps of static electricity whenever I touched anything at all. My clothes crackled when I moved, even in the late afternoon when they were inevitably soaked with sweat.

I didn't know how much longer I had before I became a fire risk again.

And that, really, was what was making me crankiest of all. Because if I was a fire risk, I would have to leave the bookshop. For its own safety. I just couldn't be sure I could reliably make it to the fire-proof rooms on each floor in time. And I would never do anything to put any of what my uncles had built together at risk.

But I needed the sanctuary of the bookshop. I didn't want to think how miserable I would be if I lost that last lifeline. I needed my nook more than I needed clean oxygen.

Houdini was still looking at me with that one deep brown eye. He let it slide shut again, burrowing his nose under my knee.

But then he said, "Of course, you could always switch to researching *my* problem, you know."

"As I've already told you, I never saw you before Agatha made you into a dog. Where would I begin trying to find your family when I don't even know what kind of dragon you are?" I asked. I knew I was speaking too irritably, not quite snapping at him, but not far off. I tried adjusting my glasses, a nervous gesture that was usually calming to the static cloud around me, if not to my mind.

But today it provided me with no relief. And when I followed it up by trying to brush my hair back from my face and ended up with my hand helplessly tangled in a mass of curls that were both at maximum humidity-absorbing curl and dry as straw at the same impossible time, my irritation boiled over.

"We'll never learn anything with that attitude," Houdini said in his most reasonable voice.

But when I'm cranky, the very worst thing for my mood is to be told anything at all in a reasonable voice. I'm not proud of it, but there it is. The only thing I can do is go be cranky somewhere else.

"I'm going to the teashop," I said, swinging my legs out of the window seat without jostling his tightly curled sleeping form too badly.

"It's the middle of the day," he complained. "I don't want to go there now."

"So, don't," I said.

This time it really was a snap, and I regretted it. And I knew I should apologize. But I was still trying to untangle my fingers from my own hair. I pulled my hand free with a yank that pulled out a lot of strands by their roots.

That was the one upside of my terrible mood. I was literally too irritated to feel pain properly. I just looked down at the sizable number of hairs now pulled free from my head but still tangled around my fingers.

I walked away from Houdini and the stacks of useless books, shaking loose hairs from my fingers as I headed for the staircase.

Seeing Audrey usually cheered me up.

But I was going to have to go out into the smoke-filled air to get to the teashop.

It was fifty-fifty, the odds of this plan actually improving my mood. But I decided to take the chance, anyway. My beloved bookshop was offering me no relief that day. At least if I was angry outside, it was only the sky and smoky weather I would be venting at, and not my beloved companion.

CHAPTER

TWO

The Loose Leaves Teashop might not have air conditioning, but being tucked in the southeast corner of the Square, it benefited from all the shade. Plus, Audrey's grandaunt Agatha had cast little spells in each of the windows, minor cantrips that kept a constant movement of air through the open panes. Those cantrips filled the interior of the shop with cool air that smelled strongly of the forests of the Pacific Northwest.

As far as I knew, Agatha herself had come to Minneapolis straight from the British Isles, setting up her shop back in the day when this area was still a separate milling town called St. Anthony, nestled on the bank of the Mississippi opposite from Minneapolis itself, the St. Anthony Falls between them. But I had briefly gone to a magical academy hidden high on the slopes of Mount Rainier, and even more briefly gone to a school hidden deep within the Great Bear Rainforest in Canada. Thanks to my time in both places, I recognized at once the smell of red cedar and Sitka spruce mixed in with more ferny smells.

Such cantrips are easy enough to pull off—for anyone besides me, that is—and Audrey, despite her own magical performance challenges, maintained them with little trouble. But I didn't know how the air got from wherever it originated to the teashop. I suspected somewhere in Oregon, Washington or maybe British Columbia a hiker might be pausing on one of the forest trails, wondering why they were suddenly smelling fragrant teas and fresh-baked scones.

It was nice to smell trees that weren't on fire. Or seemingly made of plastic. Where did that undertone to the smell come from, anyway? I rubbed at my head as I slipped inside the teashop, lingering near the closest window to let the clean, green and growing forest smell wash my headache away.

I had my head down and my eyes closed as I did this, but I recognized both of the voices I could hear speaking. One was Audrey, of course. But the other was Liam Kelly, a prosaic guy of about our age I had met on one of my first days working in the bookshop.

He had helped Audrey and I solve her grandaunt's murder, using his prosaic world research skills to narrow down a long list of suspects. Unfortunately, he had dug too deep and had strayed too close to unearthing the secret existence of the Square. The Square is what we call our magical community, although technically it is more of a rectangle of shops and apartments all built around a central garden, orchard and hedge maze. A dome of magic lets sunlight— and, alas, wildfire smoke—come in but obscures the vision of even satellites and airplanes passing overhead. From any angle, the Square just looks like an entire block of mundane shops like the bookshop, coffeeshop, salon and teashop as well as two floors of apparently empty offices above.

But Liam had realized the property records didn't match what he could see. And he started digging to learn more.

So Steph had had to wipe his memory. Because the secret had to remain secret for the good of us all.

I still felt guilty about that. He had only been trying to help me. He hadn't known that doing so was going to risk his very brain.

But Liam seemed none the worse for it. Sure, he still complained a lot about his lack of employment and his overabundance of room-mates at his tiny apartment.

Five guys sharing two bedrooms; can you imagine?

But he and Audrey currently seemed to be discussing comic books.

For a brief moment, I thought Audrey was only humoring him. But as the conversation went on, it became clear that she wasn't pretending to find it all interesting. No one pretending to like comic books could summon so many character names and long-past plot lines in such a short amount of time as she was currently doing.

I was almost tempted to duck back out again. Not that I hate comic books or anything. I had read a few in my day and had enjoyed them well enough.

It was just that when I finally looked up at the two of them leaning over opposite ends of the same counter so that their heads were close together, their hands almost touching, it felt like too private a moment for me to barge in on. It was only superficially about comic books.

It said a lot that Audrey wasn't using those hands to constantly tuck her long, blonde hair behind her ears. But that nervous tic of hers was currently nowhere to be seen.

And I was a little jealous of her hair just at that moment. It hung sleek and straight down her back, untouched by either humidity or inexplicable static electricity. What must that be like?

Liam's thick blond hair was curling more than usual, which was something, I guess. Only it really only served to make him just that much cuter. That, and the slight pinkish tint to his freckled skin, the last remnants of his walk here through the heat of midday.

I didn't know exactly where he lived, but over the month I'd known him it had become clear that what he considered "walking distance" was skewed a lot by the fact that he had neither a car nor a lot of spare change for public transportation.

Then Liam said something I didn't quite catch, and Audrey

laughed, a completely genuine laughter that burst out of her unexpectedly.

And her hand found his to give it an appreciative squeeze.

Yeah, this definitely wasn't the moment for moody old me to intrude. But at least that breath of Pacific Northwest air had dispelled my headache, if only for a moment.

But before I was more than halfway turned back to the door, Audrey noticed me there and said, "Tabitha! Everything all right?"

I turned back and forced a smile on my face for both of them. "Yeah. There isn't much going on at the bookshop, so I thought I'd get another Arnold Palmer with extra ice if it's not too much trouble."

"Sure thing," Audrey said. She gave Liam a shy smile before turning away to fetch the iced tea and lemonade from the fridge in the back room.

"The bookshop is open on the Fourth of July?" Liam asked me conversationally. He had a bag tucked under his arm, one with the logo for the comic book shop next door on the side of it. That shop was the only one on the Square that didn't actually touch the Square. It was entirely prosaic. And did a surprisingly high amount of business, given that it was both at the end of an alley rather than on the street and stood—unbeknownst to its prosaic owners, I was sure— right next to the Wizard's Tower.

That Tower had powerful magical wards protecting it that kept the likes of me from even being able to try looking at it directly. But the prosaics, being unable to see the Tower anyway, didn't seem to mind the wards.

"The shop is open, but currently customer-free," I said with a shrug. "I closed early."

"Aren't your uncles back?" he asked with a frown, like he wasn't sure he remembered that correctly.

I hated that little frown. Every time I was finally sure the mind wipes hadn't really hurt him, that frown would reemerge. And I hadn't known him long enough before his mind was tampered with to know if he just always frowned in confusion like that.

"They're coming back at the end of August," Audrey told him as she came back to the counter with a tall, frosty glass of iced tea and lemonade and handed it to me. "You always want these super cold, so I've started chilling the glasses in the freezer. Unless the extra ice was about watering it down? Is it too sweet?" She gave me a tremulous but anxious smile as she waited for me to answer her.

"No, this is perfect," I said even before I had taken a sip.

But I turned out to be right. The balance of tea, citrus, and sugar was, indeed, perfection. And, I swear, when it's hot, I can live off Arnold Palmers.

"That does look good," Liam said, eyeing my drink thirstily.

"I'll get one for you," Audrey said, already halfway to the backroom before she was even done with that sentence.

"No, I'm okay!" Liam called after her.

"Too late," I said to him as I took a second sip.

"I just paid my rent and I literally have nothing left over," he whispered to me.

"I've got it," I told him, carefully not looking at the bag of fresh new comic books as I dug into my pocket for cash.

"They're both on the house," Audrey said as she returned with two more frosty glasses and set one in front of Liam. She kept the other for herself, stirring at the contents with an equally frosted stainless steel straw until the yellow on the bottom was thoroughly mixed with the brown on top. Liam copied her gestures before taking a sip of his own.

"Wow. I've had Arnold Palmers before, but never like this," he said. "What kind of tea is this?"

Audrey glowed. "Just a Darjeeling from a family farm my grandaunt has been ordering from for decades."

Knowing how long Agatha had been selling tea from this shop, she'd probably started ordering from that family before Indian Independence in 1947.

Not that I could mention that to Liam.

"Audrey makes every bit of it from scratch," I told him. "The tea, the simple syrup, all of it. I wouldn't be surprised if I caught her growing lemon trees and tea up on the rooftop over her apartment one day."

"Don't be silly," Audrey said. But she was clearly pleased.

I felt a modicum better. And I hadn't even had to vent first. Which, in my book, is the best kind of feeling better.

I took another sip of my drink. The cold liquid felt divine against the smoke-irritated back of my throat. "You know, sometimes, life is pretty good," I said.

"So you're for sure planning to stay after your uncles get back?" Liam asked.

"I haven't talked to them about it yet, but I'd like to," I said.

"She helps in the teashop too," Audrey put in.

"Only a little," I said.

"I've never seen you at the counter," Liam said, then flushed a darker shade of pink. "Not that I stop by *a lot* or anything."

"No, I don't serve the tea," I said. "I just help Audrey with research."

"Research?" Liam said, and that *am I forgetting something?* frown was back on his face.

"With recipes," Audrey said casually.

"I thought your grandaunt left you tons of them," Liam said.

"She did," I said.

"But they are really old," Audrey said. "Some of them are even in languages I can't read. So Tabitha helps me out."

This conversation was starting to freak me out. It was getting too close to territory that would end with Liam's mind getting wiped. Again. I tried to warn Audrey off with my eyes, but that was tough to do with Liam currently looking straight at me.

"What languages do you speak?" he asked.

"I speak a little bit of lots of things," I said with a dismissive wave.

Which was true, if "a little bit" meant a couple thousand words plus a working knowledge of the grammar rules.

And "lots of things" meant about three dozen, give or take.

But most of them were languages Liam didn't even know existed, so I doubted he would be quizzing me.

"Wow," he said. "What did you say you went to college for again?"

I had, in fact, never even tried to tell him that. So it was a little weird that his memory-doubting frown wasn't on his face at the moment. I waited for it for a little too long, though, and now he was giving me a different sort of frown. Like he was worried about *my* memory or something.

"Nothing useful," I said at last, then cast about for anything I could change the subject to. "So, Audrey, you're coming to the big party in the Square tonight, right? We all got invitations this morning."

Her face fell, and she shot a nervous glance at Liam before saying, "Actually, Liam invited me to a block party near his place, and I was thinking I would go to that."

"Oh," I said.

That was all. My brain had no followup. And I wasn't sure why my ears seemed to be ringing.

"You're welcome to come too, of course," Liam rushed to say. And, to his credit, he sounded completely sincere, and not at all like he was being forced to invite a third wheel along to what was probably meant to be a first date of sorts.

"No, I don't think that would be a good idea," I mumbled, looking down at my hands. I still had a few twists of hair wound around my fingers and brushed my hand against the leg of my capris to try to wipe them away.

And it sparked. That motion actually created a spark. It was a brief one, there and gone before anyone else but me noticed. But I could smell smoldering denim.

"What's that?" Liam asked, leaning closer.

"I said thank you for the invitation, but I did promise someone I'd be here," I said.

A total lie. Which I had only meant to give Liam an excuse, but now Audrey was looking at me in a knowing way, and I realized too late what she was thinking.

That I had promised Steph I'd be there.

Which was crazy since, like I've said, I had seen him exactly one time in the last month.

But I really, *really* didn't think it would be a good idea to leave the Square. If my power sparked at the party in the Square, the other partygoers might be annoyed with me, but they wouldn't be surprised to learn that magic was real. They were all better at it than I was, after all. And their help would definitely come in handy if things got really bad.

But a prosaic block party? With just Audrey as magical backup? I loved Audrey, but she wasn't going to be enough help if I started setting things on fire just by walking past them. She may have studied the most challenging branch of magic—ritual magic—back in school. But she had barely graduated.

She had gained a lot of confidence in the past month, with the two of us working together. I didn't question that.

Because all that research I'd been doing to help her out? While our meetings might have technically taken place inside the teashop —and a lot of what I had been researching had indeed been written in languages I could read and Audrey could not—what we'd been working on wasn't recipes for teas or scones.

They had been spells. Ones I could understand but not do. Ones Audrey could do, but only after I researched and then explained them to her.

We had gotten the windows working again, for one. I had tweaked the cantrip chant just a smidge, removing a little out-dated language to make the rhyme something that flowed more naturally for Audrey when she cast it.

And the refrigerator, like my uncle's bookshop and the Square itself, was now officially bigger on the inside.

And, despite Steph's assurances that Houdini was safe from detection, we had put a lot of spells into a collar he now wore to keep him extra safe from magical senses.

Neither of us could do much apart, but my knowledge, together with her actual casting skills, added up to one pretty decent ritual mage.

But being good at research and ritual magic didn't tend to add up to being much use in a spontaneous situation. Especially not a situation that unfolded as rapidly as when my random sparks became a serious problem.

"Are you sure?" Audrey asked.

"Yeah, it's fine," I said.

It wasn't fine. I was positive that Steph would be far too busy working with the Wizard to stop in at a block party. And without Audrey there, the only people in the Square close to my own age would be Thaisa Wolsey—who would be working at her parents' pub all night long and definitely wouldn't have time for more than a quick hello, if that—and Cleopatra Manx's two protégées, Delilah Dare and Cressida Cade.

While neither of them could quite match their employer for dishing out haughty disdain, it wasn't for lack of trying.

Which was maybe unfair to Cressida Cade. I had never had an actual conversation with her, but sometimes when she gave me apologetic looks after I'd been on the receiving end of one of Cleopatra's hurtful digs, I almost thought she might be sincerely sorry to be associating with the likes of Cleopatra Manx and Delilah Dare.

Almost.

"Tabitha?" Audrey said and touched my hand.

I had never sparked before from someone else touching me, and what happened in that instant wasn't precisely a spark, anyway. There was no fire or electricity. But there was a sudden pressure change in the air around the two of us, like a sonic boom, kind of, only it was totally silent.

Well, the compressive blast was silent.

The teacups and saucers and glasses and pitchers and everything else in the teashop around us suddenly bursting into shards and raining down to the floor was the very opposite of silent.

"What the hell?!?" Liam cried out, stepping away from the frosty shards of glass that had previously been the last of his Arnold Palmer.

"It's fine! It's fine!" Audrey yelled, too shrilly for those words to be believed. But she darted out from behind the counter, herding Liam out of the store.

"Audrey?" he said plaintively, but she had already shoved him out onto the sidewalk.

"It's fine! I'll see you at six! Don't worry! This is just... an old building thing," she finished lamely.

Then she closed and locked the door, turned the sign over to *closed*, and slammed shut all the shutters on the prosaic side of the shop with a single frantic wave of the wand she could only take out now that Liam was out of sight.

"Audrey, I'm so sorry," I said.

"I know you didn't do it on purpose," she said, but her voice had a tremor to it. Like she was holding back angry tears. "But Steph probably already knows. Do you think he'll chase after Liam and wipe his mind again?"

"No," I said, with more confidence than I felt. "If he were going to do that, he'd be here already. He's very fast."

She didn't answer, just stood in the middle of all the crockery wreckage and tugged worriedly at her lip.

"I'll get a broom," I said, and moved towards the door in the counter so I could fetch one from the back room.

But her hand on my shoulder pulled me to a halt.

"I've got it, Tabitha," she said. "Please, just go."

"But—" I started to say.

"I know you didn't mean it!" she said, even more shrilly than before. "But it's faster if I just do it myself with magic. I really can't risk letting Steph know that Liam saw this or he'll wipe his mind *again*! And I know you can't lie to Steph, so please just go. Go!"

I wanted to argue. I could totally lie to Steph. I could do anything if it meant keeping her and Liam safe.

But then it occurred to me that what she meant was that Steph wasn't going to believe me when I lied. Which was probably true.

"Sorry," I mumbled, and made myself scarce.

The air outside was still horrid. Too hot, too humid, and far too redolent of burnt plastic. It made no sense why wildfire smoke should smell like *plastic*.

I guess it was weird, how that one strange aspect of it all could make me feel such rage.

But in that moment, the harsh feel of the smoke in my eyes and the way it coated the back of my throat and even felt abrasive against my skin? It all just matched my mood too well.

In a perverse way, I just couldn't *wait* for this party. It was going to be miserable, the weather and the company and all of it.

But unlike the rest of my worries, by midnight the block party would be *over*. And it would be such a relief.

CHAPTER

THREE

My thoughts were all a jumble when I bolted out of the teashop, and I didn't spend any of them plotting a path. When I finally had calmed down enough to look up and around, I realized I was deep within the hedge maze, almost to the magic portal at its heart.

And nothing smelled like smoke. All I could smell was green, growing things all around me.

My mood improved so quickly it was like someone had thrown a switch. I kept walking, but now I was enjoying the world around me, running my hands through the thicket of leaves on both sides of me, listening to the babble of water in fountains that were always just out of sight, around one or the other bends in the maze.

And I could hear voices, the voices of my neighbors in the Square. I followed that sound until I emerged on the far end of the maze, near Cato and Octavia Abergavenny's cornershop on the opposite end of the Square from the Loose Leaves Teashop. There was an open strip of grass here, although it was now crowded with folding tables and little booths still in the process of being set up for the evening's festivities.

As much as the clear air had dissipated my bad temper, I wasn't sure I was up for socializing yet. But then I saw Barnardo Daley spreading a tablecloth over one of the folding tables, his black-haired Persian, Miss Snooty Cat, winding around his ankles as he worked. Barnardo was still a daily visitor to the Loose Leaves Teashop, usually stopping in during the early morning when I was still there, sharing breakfast with Audrey.

I don't know whether it was something different about the way Audrey mixed his medicinal herbs, or just the natural progression of his grieving of his late father finally bringing him to a better place, but he was looking in particularly good spirits this evening. He was dressed nattily in a very fine cream-colored linen suit, complete with matching fedora.

Miss Snooty Cat's dark hairs were clearly visible against that cream, and yet somehow it wouldn't be Barnardo without that little detail.

"Hello, Tabitha," he said when he noticed me walking up. "Are you here to help?"

"Sure, if there's anything I can do," I said. I had never made a public announcement to the people of the Square about my lack of magic, but they all seemed to know about it, anyway. They knew, but they never seemed to mind. That sort of casual acceptance was something I was still getting used to after years in the uber-competitive environment of magical boarding schools.

"I believe that the Abergavennys and the Wolseys have the air exchange spells well in hand, and the Trio are handling the open bar, but I could use help carrying down the food from my apartment," he said as he smoothed his hands over the tablecloth one last time then gave a satisfied nod at its lack of wrinkles.

"I can do that," I said. But something else he said had caught my attention. "What's an air exchange spell? Is it like what Agatha did to the windows in the teashop?"

"Very similar, but on a larger scale," he said. "They are hiding the exchange zones in the trees, I believe, but that just enhances the effect, I think."

"That's why the air smells so good today," I guessed.

"Isn't it a relief?" Barnardo said with a smile. "Hopefully, the prosaics get the situation under control soon. I miss being outside in the summer sun. It's like a second winter, in a way, not being able to go outside comfortably. It's a shame the spells are too draining on such a large scale to keep them up for more than an evening, but by morning, the smoke will be back with us."

"I know what you mean," I said. "Are you going to start bringing the food down now? Isn't it too early and too hot?"

"I have a magical service set," Barnardo said. "Everything hot stays hot, and everything cool stays cool, and nothing goes stale or... what's the opposite of stale? You know, when potato chips sort of melt from the humidity?"

"I have no idea," I said. "There has to be a word for that. Besides just 'disgusting'."

Barnardo laughed and was about to say something else when his eyes darted to something behind me and his whole demeanor just shut down. I didn't have to turn and look to guess what he'd seen. Or rather, who.

The Trio.

They brushed by me and into my view, dressed to the nines, of course, in slinky, sleeveless sundresses and strappy little shoes. Everything about them was glittering, too, from the fabric of their dresses to the details on their shoes to even their very skin.

And that potato-chip-melting humidity wasn't touching the soft blonde curls of their professional blowouts even a little. It wouldn't dare, I was sure.

Cleopatra Manx, the leader of the group and the owner of the Inanna Salon & Spa, swept past me and Barnardo with just enough of a glance to make it clear that she was *intentionally* not noticing us. She made a beeline for the largest of the temporary booths, where a single woman dressed in the black slacks and white dress shirt that is the usual caterer's uniform was stacking crates of alcohol in the back of the booth.

Delilah Dare, dressed all in a brilliant shade of white that was almost painfully bright against her precisely tanned skin, mimicked Cleopatra's dismissive glance almost exactly. But the little sneer she couldn't keep from escaping as she turned away ruined the effect a bit. It was a shade too aggressive, not as coolly unbothered as Cleopatra's disdain always was.

Believe me. I went to dozens of schools in my day, all around the world. I know a thing or two about mean girls. And in that moment, breathing that welcomingly fresh air, I had enough detachment to observe the Trio like an anthropologist studying group behavior. I wasn't taking it personally.

But when Cressida Cade, bringing up the rear in a cream color pretty close to Barnardo's linen suit, almost gave me a smile of recognition as she passed me, it actually threw me a little. She caught herself in a hurry, putting her nose back in the air as she hurried her steps to join the other two at the open bar, but for a minute there she'd been on the verge of an actual friendly hello.

Weird how that made me feel lonely in a way the out-of-hand rejection of the first two had completely failed to.

"Ladies, this is Paula," Cleopatra said to the other two. She enunciated all the vowels separately and distinctly, but that made sense. Paula looked like she was Spanish. "She's the finest bartender in Mallorca. Isn't that right, Paula?"

"I prefer the term mixologist," Paula said. "I do more than serve up the standard fare."

"Of course, darling," Cleopatra said. "Mixologista."

Paula gave her a bright but brief smile, then turned back to whatever she was organizing behind the booth's counter.

"Do you need anything from us, darling?" Cleopatra asked.

"No, it looks like everything I asked you to order is here," Paula said, looking around then nodding.

"Lovely. Lovely. But if something should come up, just let me know," Cleopatra said. Then she took a few steps back, shifting her attention from the mixologist to the banner over the booth's open window. She fussed a little with the satiny folds, poking at the material until the glittery letters that spelled out the name of her business caught the light ever so slightly more intensely.

"Whatever are you attempting to do with your hair?" Delilah asked. I jumped when I realized she was speaking to me. While I had been watching Cleopatra adjusting her sign, Delilah had moved all the way into my personal space and had only spoken when the appalled look she'd been giving me had failed to elicit a response. I would've backed away sooner if I'd noticed. But now that Delilah had spoken, Cleopatra turned to see what she was talking about. Cressida looked over at me as well.

Even Paula, the mixologist from Mallorca, paused in her flurry of activity to look at my hair.

With a huge amount of effort, I resisted the urge to touch my hair. That was never a good idea. Instead, I grabbed the frame of my glasses and adjusted them ever so slightly.

Those glasses had been a gift from my uncle before I had started my first magical academy when I was five. They had grown with me, adjusting to the changes in my vision through the years, but had remained exactly as five-year-old me had wanted them to look: large circular lenses that I fancied made me look wise as an owl. And those lenses and the stainless steel frames both were practically indestructible, as I'd had the misfortune to test on more than one occasion.

But the one thing I hadn't known until I had come to the Square was that my uncle had designed them to mimic some qualities of his own glasses. He had told me it was calming to touch them and adjust them, a gesture I had seen him do on more than one occasion.

I tried to do the same. And sometimes I almost felt like it worked.

This wasn't one of those times.

"What's your impression, Delilah?" Cleopatra asked as she glided closer. They both gave me a gravely serious once-over.

"The heat setting on your blow-dryer is too high for your hair type, dear," Delilah said with mountains of fake empathy.

"I agree," Cleopatra said with a nod.

"I would say the same about your curling iron or flat iron, but I'm fairly certain neither of those tools are in your repertoire," Delilah went on.

"If so, they are definitely being used in an unskilled manner," Cleopatra agreed.

"I'm really not sure why you even care," I said.

"It's a professional interest," Cleopatra said.

"It's hard not to notice when it's so extreme," Delilah said. "We're just trying to be helpful."

"No, you're not," I said.

Then the two of them laughed, as if I had told some perfectly delightful joke. And clean air or not, I just couldn't stand to be there for one more minute. I backed away, then turned to bolt back into the hedge maze.

A hand on my arm stopped me. I was just turning to apologize to Barnardo for abandoning him, when I realized it was Cressida who was detaining me.

She looked back over her shoulder, but Delilah and Cleopatra had already shifted their attention back to the sign over the booth. Even so, she moved closer to me before whispering, "I can help you fix your hair, if you like. The weather here is maybe not what you're used to. I have some products that could help balance the moisture, especially when the humidity is really high?"

"It's not a grooming issue," I said, and snatched my arm out of her grasp. She flinched, as if my words had actually hurt her. But I didn't care.

I fled back into the hedge maze, but its green serenity was marred by the laughter of two-thirds of the Trio that seemed to chase after me long after the rest of the sounds of the party setup faded away.

CHAPTER

FOUR

I wandered through the hedge maze for what felt like hours but was, honestly, maybe fifteen minutes. It was still midafternoon, to judge from the position of the sun in the sky.

I found one of the bubbling water fountains in a little green alcove off the main path. Then I tucked myself out of view on the back of one of the stone benches that flanked the fountain. I sat with my knees drawn all the way up to my chin, hugging my own shins as I watched the sunlight dance over the water. The stone fountain had once been carved to look like... something. But age had worn the edges smooth, and algae had grown up over all but the driest of spots. I thought I was looking at a fish spraying water up into the air, but it might have been a cupid or something else.

I took my glasses off to clean the lenses that had gotten smeared and fogged by my own sweaty cheeks. Then I put them back on with a few extra adjustments.

Which did nothing to calm me. But mostly because I wasn't really angry anymore. I just felt... empty.

Then suddenly Stephanos Underwood was there, sitting on the bench opposite of mine as if he'd been there the entire time. He was in the shade from the hedges that arched over the bench, but he still looked a little uncomfortable being out in the middle of the afternoon. He wasn't wearing his floating cloak of many colors today, as he had been when he'd come looking for that book days before. But dressing all in black, and in long sleeves and tall boots, wasn't a recipe for being comfortable in a Minnesota July.

But to judge from the paleness of his skin, it wasn't a problem Steph dealt with much.

"Hey," he said when he saw me looking over at him.

"Hey," I said back, still hugging my knees.

"What's wrong?" he asked.

I opened my mouth, but then closed it again at once. What was I going to tell him? Him, the Wizard's apprentice, whose workload was both intense in volume and importance and apparently never-ending? That some mean girls had made fun of my hair?

"I'm just grumpy, I guess," I said at last. Which was also true, even in this temporary respite from the constant presence of wildfire smoke.

He looked me over carefully, which triggered memories of earlier when Cleopatra and Delilah had done the same thing. Only when he was done, his empathy wasn't pretend. "Not without cause, I suspect. But if you deal with grumpiness by removing yourself from others, that's usually the kindest choice. Isn't it?"

"You find the nicest way to describe it," I said.

"What would you call it?" he asked.

"Having a pout?" I offered. But I really wanted to change the subject. "Are you here for the party?"

"Party?" he said, as if the word had no meaning for him. "Oh, the Fourth of July. Of course. No, actually, I was just looking for you."

"You were? Why?" I asked.

"I've been neglectful, haven't I?" he said with a wistful smile. "I promised to help you and Houdini both, and I haven't spared you a single moment since."

"Well, you've been busy, I'm sure," I said. But my heart was fluttering strangely in my chest.

He hadn't forgotten, after all.

"You've been sparking again, haven't you?" he said. Then he got up from his bench and circled the fountain to sit beside me.

And touch my hair again. I was so done with my hair being the center of everyone's attention. And yet the look on his face was one of gentle bemusement. Although I didn't quite know what that meant.

"I'm still not the problem?" I asked.

"Not for the Square," he said. Then he let go of my hair to look directly at me instead with those warm brown eyes of his. "That's all I ever meant. I'm sure whatever is going on is a problem for you. Isn't it?"

"I don't love it," I admitted. "Houdini and I have been trying to research what's wrong with me. We've gone through stacks of books every day in the bookshop, but we still haven't found anything helpful."

"I don't think there's anything *wrong* with you," he said sternly. "There's only something we're not understanding. Yet. But once we do understand it, you can find a way to adapt to anything that's not working for you currently. No, there's nothing *wrong* with you."

"Well, it's not like I was afraid I was secretly evil or anything," I said. I absentmindedly tried to push my hair back from my face and accidentally sent a shower of sparks down to the grass below us. Luckily, the spray from the ever-running fountain kept the grass damp enough to where the sparks died out without doing any damage. But I shivered, imagining if I had done that while still inside the bookshop.

"Life has more challenges for some of us than for others," he said. "I've been asking the Wizard about you, and he thinks what's going on with you is likely some rare form of inherited magic. Unless, at some point, you were messing with a cursed or ensorcelled object of some sort?"

"Definitely not," I said. "But back up. Isn't all magic inherited? I mean, witch parents have witch kids."

"To some undifferentiated extent," he said. "Two ritual magicians are as likely to have a daughter who is a kitchen witch as a daughter who is also a ritual magician. It depends on more than just our genetics, what we're drawn to. My parents, for instance, are both nature witches."

"They are?" I asked, surprised. I had just assumed—as he doubtless suspected—that his parents too had been ritual magicians. How else had he gotten such a prime apprenticeship as working with the Wizard, and at his comparatively young age?

But I also didn't know a lot about nature witches. "What do they do specifically?"

"They live on an island north of Canada and west of Greenland, inside the Arctic Circle. There is a community of selkies near there in a village at the bottom of the Arctic Sea, under the ice. My parents help them stay out of sight of the prosaic world and act as diplomats of sorts between their culture and ours," he said.

"And you didn't want to do that too?" I asked.

"Well, I felt a different calling," he said with a shrug. "What about you? Has anything ever called to you?"

"No," I said glumly. "I mean, I find tons of things interesting. I love researching and learning about things. But I've never been good at actually *doing* any of it."

"Interesting," he said. "Because something is clearly trying to come out of you. But you'll never be able to channel it properly until you know what it is."

"And you don't have even a guess?" I asked.

"The Wizard is certain it's something rare, but beyond that?" He ended with a shrug.

"Well, that's not helpful," I said, and put my chin on my knees again.

"I'm sorry. I know it's not helpful when I can't tell you the specifics of our work, but I promise what has the Wizard tied up this summer is very important. In a global way," he said.

"I'm sure," I said, not cheered.

"But when that work is wrapped up, I know he wants to meet you himself," Steph said.

"I'm always here," I said.

"The Wizard seldom leaves the Tower. Very, very seldom," he said. "You would have to come inside to meet him. And that entails... a lot. But we can go into that more when the time comes."

"Okay," I said, feeling a little bewildered.

"In the meantime, I think the Wizard might have found some-thing to help you. We're just waiting to hear back from another wizard as to its current location," he said. "And then the Wizard will have to study it himself before I can give it to you, of course."

Well that was all kinds of mysterious. "Help me how?" I asked.

"It will just help you have a little more control over the power inside you," he said. "Not to channel it. Like I said, without knowing what it is, that's going to be a tough thing to accomplish. But it will help you contain it, and I hope even vent it off in a controlled manner. Like a release valve of sorts."

"That sounds good," I said. And now I was feeling cheered. It sounded very good. Almost *too* good. But if anyone could do it, Steph could.

"The bookshop will be safe," he said as he got to his feet. But then he leaned down to touch one of my curls one last time. "I'm curious what this will look like without your power constantly using it as an outflow antenna. But I hope it doesn't change too much. I kind of like your minion of chaos look. It's cute."

"Very funny," I said, moving out of his reach and flattening my hair down with both hands. My palms were sweaty enough to crush it down. But of course it just hopped drily up again.

"I wasn't kidding," he said. He stood over me for a minute, looking down at me with his hands deep in his pockets. He looked cool and collected, but then I noticed the slightest trickle of sweat running down the side of his cheek from somewhere under that tall mass of black hair.

Talk about having a minion of chaos look.

"Sorry I won't be at the party," he said.

"I didn't think that was your sort of thing," I said.

He chuckled. "No," he agreed somberly. "But all the same, it won't be so long before you see me again as it was last time."

"I hope not," I said.

But then his smile morphed into a worried sort of frown. "Something almost triggered alarms in the teashop earlier this afternoon. You wouldn't know anything about that, would you?"

"Maybe?" I drawled.

Alas, Audrey was right. And not just in the sense that Steph would know when I was lying, although the arch of his eyebrow communicated this pretty effectively.

No, I really couldn't even do it.

"I had a moment, but no one was there to witness it who hadn't seen magic done before. So no harm done," I said. Probably too briskly.

His eyebrow was still arched at me, but he gave in with a little shrug. "Hopefully, my gift for you will help you not have any more... moments."

"I can't wait," I said. Totally not a lie.

"Until then," he said.

And promptly winked out of sight.

Apparently not something he needed his free-floating cape of rainbow colors to accomplish, like I'd assumed. Or the assistance of a portal, like most magic-users relied on.

I sat alone for a moment, but questions were plaguing me. I took out my phone and checked the time. Then I added seven hours.

It was past midnight where my uncles were in rural Spain. From the brief time I had spent in the same apartment as my uncles, I had known them to be quiet night owls. They went to their bedroom at ten or so, but the light would be on for hours and hours after that point. And on more than one occasion, I would hear one of them murmur to the other something along the lines of, "Just one more chapter."

They did own a bookshop, after all.

But did they still stay up late when traveling? Since they'd never had an opportunity to do it until I came along the month before, I doubted even they knew the answer to that question.

There was only one way for me to find out.

I scrolled to my uncle Carlo's name in my contacts and pressed the call button. It rang twice, and then his face was there on my screen. He was in pajamas, but the relative neatness of his hair made me doubt I'd woken him up.

"Tabitha! Everything is going well, I hope?" he asked, and adjusted his glasses.

"The bookshop is fine," I rushed to assure him. "I just had a family question."

"A family question?" he said with a musing frown.

"I don't know anything at all about our family's history, let alone my father's," I said.

"No, I don't suppose you do," he said, and touched his glasses again.

"Is there anything I should know about our heredity?" I asked.

"Do you mean medically?" he asked.

Well, hedged. He hedged. I could tell he was dodging my real question. Even before he touched his glasses for a third time. The whole conversation was making him nervous.

But why?

"That would be good to know too, but I meant more like rare magical gifts," I said. "It's been brought to my attention that what I can and can't do might have a genetic component to it."

"You were thoroughly screened when you started school," he reminded me.

A barrage of flashbacks washed over my mind, and I nearly dropped the phone. I had forgotten about those first weeks. How had

I forgotten? They had been so brutal. I was alone, away from my mother for the first time in my life, surrounded by strangers. And they'd all been grownups. I hadn't seen another kid my age until long after the grownups had given up trying to figure out why my magic didn't work.

I switch my phone to my other hand so I could look down at the faint scars like cat scratches across my right forearm. I had been cut and bled as part of one of the tests.

How had I forgotten that?

"Tabitha?" my uncle called through the phone. I glanced back at him. His glasses were askew, over-adjusted and then left there in his distraction.

"I'm okay," I assured him.

"Do you need me to—"

But there was no way I could let him even finish that sentence.

"No, I'm fine. I promise," I said. "I only asked because the Wizard is helping me figure some things out. Honestly, there's no reason for you and Frank to come home early. There is nothing you can do for me that the Wizard isn't doing already."

Which was way overstating my involvement with the Wizard, but as I suspected, this immediately calmed my uncle. He touched his glasses again, this time setting them straight on his nose. "I'm afraid I can't tell you anymore about your father and his family than you already know," he said.

Which was nothing. Not even his name.

But my uncle was still talking. "When I get home next month, I'll dig out my own records on our family. I'll share every last thing I know with you. But, Tabitha, be warned. It's not a lot. Some families are just like that."

"I would appreciate anything at all," I said. "I should let you go. I know it's very late there, and there's a party here tonight that I should probably clean up for first."

"Oh, that's right! It's the Fourth of July there!" he said.

Technically, it was the Fourth of July there, too. That just didn't mean much in Spain.

"It was good to see you, Tabitha. Please feel free to call again if you need anything at all," he said.

"Good night, Uncle Carlo," I said, then disconnected the call.

So I would get some answers soon, but not many. And the end of August was so far into the future. But as much as I loved research, I wasn't a fan of actually snooping.

And yet I couldn't shake the thought that whatever my uncle wanted to share with me was surely already in the apartment, somewhere. And if I really wanted to, I could find it.

I pushed that thought aside and got up from the bench. After a couple of hours in the July sun, I knew I had acquired a stink, and a cool shower was going to feel divine.

Even if it didn't help at all to tame my hair.

But as I walked back to the bookshop, I realized I was smiling to myself in a way that would look completely ridiculous if I passed anyone in the hedge maze.

Minion of chaos. Why had that sounded like a compliment when Steph had said it?

But it totally had.

CHAPTER
FIVE

Actually, the block party wasn't as bad as I had feared.

At least at first.

Barnardo accepted my apologies for abandoning him in the company of the Trio with total understanding. It turned out the Wolseys who ran the Square Pub had cousins visiting from an island off the coast of Ireland. This included four young lads whose commute back and forth from work to home involved rowing a boat over often rough seas. Carrying trays of food down from a second-floor apartment was a mere trifle for their over-developed arms and shoulders.

And one of them had lingered after, clearly a fan of Barnardo's chili. It was a little mild on spices for my taste, but this Irish Wolsey had a lot of thoughts about the umami flavor that Barnardo had seared into the beef. I was pretty sure the red spots on Barnardo's cheeks were less from the still-hot late afternoon and more from the intensity of the compliments raining down on him. But he didn't even notice when, after finishing off my bowl of his chili, I made myself scarce before the Irish Wolsey could get too far into his discourse on the virtues of grass-fed milk in cheese-making.

The Wolseys themselves were handing out tankards of ale and bottles of beer, but that's never been my kind of thing. I was a little curious about the colorful cocktails Paula the mixologist was preparing. Nibbling on a triangle of cornbread, I stood well out of her way and watched as she muddled leaves, measured out syrups, and poured just the right amount of this or that from a dizzying array of bottles behind her. Everything she served up looked so cool and refreshing. I was really tempted to try just one.

If only the Trio weren't always there, chatting with the crowd waiting to partake of their beverages and flirting with about half of the customers. None of the Trio had noticed me, but I really wanted to keep it that way. The Abergavennys who ran the cornershop were serving nonalcoholic punch and fruit ices, both made from mountains of fresh fruit they were chopping and juicing right there on their own folding table. I grabbed a glass of raspberry punch, delighted to find actual frozen raspberries floating among the ice cubes. But as I backed away from their table, I felt my heel start to come down on someone else's toe.

I held the punch away from my body—because *of course* I was wearing a white top that was just crying out to have bright red liquid spilled all over it—and shifted my body weight to my other foot just in time to avoid a total disaster.

"Excuse me," I said to the man I had nearly fallen over. Even though he had been the one standing way too close behind me. Still, it was the polite thing to do.

I didn't recognize him at all, but there were a lot of strangers in the Square for the party. He definitely wasn't another Irish Wolsey cousin, not with his thick salt and pepper hair and swarthy skin. Too old, and not the right kind of fit. Not that he wasn't in shape, but he looked more like a jogger than a rower.

But mostly, what I noticed about him was his ice-blue eyes. They gave me a chill, and not because of the color. No, there was something in the way he looked down at me that I didn't like, the way that perhaps understandable annoyance shifted to sudden interest. Like he knew just the way to put me to his use.

And then it shifted again to what I'm sure he thought was charming, but which struck me as, really, just smarmy.

Not that I couldn't see he was attractive. For a middle-age man, he was definitely in the top ten percentile of attractiveness. And there was a sparkle of light in his blue eyes that was almost hypnotic.

But he clearly knew it.

And that thing I had seen for just a flash, that look like he could put me to good use? I didn't like that look at all.

"Sorry," I said again. I had sloshed a little bit of sticky punch over my hand, but I had avoided both my own white shirt and his probably bespoke dress pants.

"My apologies. I was standing too close behind you," he said.

I grudgingly gave him points for honesty, but I didn't want to linger in his company. And yet after I had given him an acknowledging nod and attempted to move away, I realized he was trailing behind me.

I tried ignoring him, stepping to the edge of the open field east of the hedge maze to watch a pack of younger kids race past with sparklers. Not prosaic sparklers, but magical ones that only needed a little goosing from the kids' still in development power to explode into brightly colored clouds of dancing light.

But he was right there at my elbow, looking down at my glass of punch with amusement.

"Do you need a little something for that?" he asked. A flask showed up out of nowhere in his hand and he offered it to me with an arch to his perfectly shaped eyebrow.

"No, thanks. I'm good," I said, then turned to head back towards the tables. Bartholomew Bullen, who owned the Potions & Magical Sundries Shop, had set out tiered serving towers of candies. I picked out one shaped like a shamrock that melted creamily on my tongue when I put it in my mouth. It made me feel cooler, even more than the frozen raspberries had done.

But that man was back again, reaching past my shoulder to help himself to a pink bonbon. I would accuse him of over-dramatising his enjoyment of the confection, if I hadn't been pretty sure I had moaned aloud eating that candy shamrock.

Still, why was he following me?

I wished Audrey were there. Not that it wasn't great for her having a date with Liam after almost an entire month of the two of them just chatting and making eyes at each other.

I really wished Steph were there. But that had never felt likely in the first place.

I kind of wished Houdini were there. But I knew he was definitely happier where he was. Wherever he was. He hadn't been in the apartment when I'd gone up to shower and change. I supposed he was still in the bookshop. But he wouldn't want to be around all these strangers, anyway.

Particularly not this one, who was smiling down at me for no apparent reason.

"Have you tried the chili?" he asked me, gesturing towards Barnardo's table.

"I have," I said. How much of an edge would I have to put on my voice before this guy got the message?

"You didn't care for it?" he asked with something like concern.

"It's fine. I just like chili when it's spicier," I said. "Like, way spicier."

"I bet you do," he said with a chuckle, and I felt my cheeks color. I had been trying to imply that I was too fiery-tempered to be bothered with, but he'd clearly read something very different from my words.

I guess it was time to be blunt.

"If you'll excuse me," I said and started to turn away.

"Hey, I was just kidding," he said. He reached out to catch my arm, but changed his mind at my glare, raising his hand as if in surrender. "I think we got off on the wrong foot here. Let's start again. Hello. I'm Taurus Vernon. I'm not a local, at least not of the

Square. I live in the Foshay Tower. The hidden levels, of course. I have a corner apartment with a lovely view of the river. You really should see it sometime; it's amazing. And I work in magical finance downtown."

Then he wiped his hand on the side of his pants as if to be sure no crumb of bonbon had fallen there before offering it to me.

And I just stared at it, not sure where to start with the things I wanted to say no to. Refusing the handshake came well after not wanting to see his luxury apartment.

But mostly I was just confused why he was talking to me at all. It made no sense.

If such things existed in the magical world, I would almost think I was on one of those practical joke reality shows, secretly being recorded to see how I responded to this improbable situation.

But that was strictly a prosaic world thing. And we weren't in the prosaic world.

"Come on. You can at least tell me your name," he said with good humor, even as he retracted his hand and reached for another bonbon. "These are really quite good, you know. Have you tried one?"

"No," I said.

"Here," he said around his mouthful of candy and selected a green one. He held it out for me, his eyes glowing with a warmer humor than before.

Not that I found him charming. Not remotely.

But I did take the bonbon. And it melted on my tongue in a pistachio-flavored cream that lingered cooly long after the candy was gone.

"You're right. That is good," I conceded. Then, with a sigh, I added, "I'm Tabitha Greene. I'm a local."

"Tabitha," he said, and I instantly regretted telling him my name. No one needed to ooze out every syllable like that. "Such a beautiful name," he added, entirely unnecessarily. He had shoved that banal concept into the very way he'd said it.

"Well, it's not like I got to pick it," I said. I drained the last of my punch, then held out the empty glass. "Now, if you'll excuse me, I should really return this to the other table."

"Surely you can just leave that anywhere," he said, looking around.

"We don't have servants to clean up after us here," I said.

"Oh, I'm not so pretentious as all that," he said with a laugh. It was a nice laugh, I suppose, but it was also an ear-catching one. And from over his shoulder, I could see Delilah's head whipping around to find its source.

And then she saw me and her eyes narrowed.

"Yeah, I really must be going," I said and turned away from him.

All of my mind was focused on my arm, and what I was going to do if he tried to catch my elbow again or anything like that.

But what happened instead caught me entirely off guard.

He moved to walk beside me, like we'd agreed to go somewhere together, which was irritating enough. But then I felt his hand resting on the small of my back.

Well, actually, just a little bit lower than that.

He wasn't quite using that hand to steer me around, but there was still something way too proprietary about that gesture. I instantly hated it. In a completely visceral way. Like the one time I'd been tricked into eating durian candy and had spit it out of my mouth with such force it had splatted against a wall a dozen feet away. Just like that.

I heard a sound like splintering glass and felt a sharp pain in my hand. I looked down at the blood dripping from my suddenly empty hand and the shards of glass littering the grass beside my foot. For some reason, solving the mystery of what had just happened there stumped me entirely. It took all of my mental powers to sort it out.

So the screams behind me really caught me off guard. I shook droplets of blood from my hand as I turned to see the Inanna Salon & Spa open bar suddenly on fire. Paula the mixologist dove out of the booth, taking cover under Barnardo's table, but she wasn't the one screaming.

No, the screams were coming from Cleopatra Manx and Delilah Dare as they watched their little booth go up in flames. Bottle after bottle of alcohol exploded. One by one, as if set on a timed fuse, like for a movie or something.

Everything felt so surreal, like I wasn't really there. Like I was underwater, and everything was slow and distorted and hard to hear.

Then Delilah Dare was in my face, her finger jabbing dangerously close to my nose. I had to really focus before I could even hear her words.

"This is all your fault!" she said, probably not for the first time. "You are a menace. A menace! After what you did to Titus Bloom's Coffeeshop, you should've been banned from the Square!"

I looked down at my hand stupidly. I was pretty sure I hadn't squeezed that glass too tightly. The cuts on my hand weren't bad enough for that.

No, I was pretty sure it was my power sparking again that had destroyed it.

And the open bar full of alcohol was probably my fault, too.

At least Taurus's hand had moved off my body. I shifted my attention from my hand to his face and saw him smirking. But not, surprisingly, at me.

No, that look was all for Delilah.

I didn't a hundred percent understand what had just happened, but I thought I had figured out why Taurus had been dogging me all around the party. What better way to irritate Delilah than to pretend to be interested in the one person she considered far beneath her station?

I tried to tell myself that at least I hadn't fallen for it. I hadn't been charmed; I hadn't been wooed.

Sure, I had destroyed something Delilah had helped create, but that couldn't have really been his goal.

Still, the anger was building up inside of me. I hadn't been used the way he had wanted to use me, but I had still been his pawn. And that was making my blood boil.

Metaphorically. My body temperature probably only went up a fraction of a degree, in all honesty.

But it did make my hair stand on end, then spark, then rain those sparks down all around me. I was like a living version of one of the kids' sparklers. One of the kids with oomph to their powers.

I was a fire hazard, for sure.

Delilah was shrieking now, and Taurus was laughing as if this were the funniest thing he'd ever experienced. But I could see Cleopatra gesturing for Cressida to pick up one of the tubs of melting ice and dump it over my head.

As much as I suspected that would actually help, I didn't want to stand there and take it. I turned and fled into the hedge maze.

My sparks sizzled as they landed on the branches of the hedges all around me, but this garden was lovingly watered by more than one user of magic, and like the grass by the fountain, it was in no danger of burning. Still, I felt better when I reached the far side.

But the only way to get upstairs was either to take the stairs inside the bookshop, or to run the long way around level after level of cast-iron balconies to the top.

I decided to find another option. I found a drain spout that ran down past my uncles' veranda above and climbed it. Luckily, this building was more than a century old, dating back to when such things had been built far more solidly than modern aluminum spouts are.

I threw myself over the railing of the veranda, then climbed again, up a trellis this time to my little balcony window. I had left the window open, perhaps the only time I had been grateful to not have air conditioning. I shed clothing as I ran for the shower.

I stood under the cold water long past the point where I had stopped sparking. I stayed there, in fact, until the last of the tears had gone as well. Only then did I shut off the water, towel myself dry, then pull on a T-shirt before collapsing, exhausted, on my bed.

It was still well into the nineties and not likely to get cooler anytime soon. It was full dark now, so dark that the fireworks outside were starting. But I turned my back to the window and tried to just still my mind.

I wasn't sure knowing all this was hereditary was any help at all. It was still a problem I couldn't solve. It just had a different sort of name now.

I was certain I'd be lying awake all night staring at the wall and trying to stop the bad thoughts. But then I felt a presence in my doorway. A familiar presence that, thought it felt like it loomed large there in the shadows, came in on delicate little rat terrier chihuahua feet.

Houdini.

He didn't make a sound, neither speaking into my mind in his dragon voice nor making any kind of dog noise at all. He just turned around and around before flopping down on the bed, his back pressed against the backs of my knees.

But it was enough. Him being there was enough. My mind quieted, and sleep took me before the fireworks outside were even done.

SIX

I don't have a single memory of my mother past the age of five that I can be absolutely certain wasn't just a dream.

Some of those dreams felt absolutely real, except for the bit at the end where I wake up and she isn't there. We have these long conversations while I'm laying in bed and she's stroking my hair, and in the morning I can recall absolutely everything we talked about. It's mostly pretty mundane, "how is school going?" type of stuff, but sometimes it's deeper, particularly when I'm having a bad time. Like right before I changed schools.

I changed schools a lot.

But even when I changed schools, she was never there during the day for that process. Someone from the old school would walk me to the nearest portal, and someone from the new school would be waiting to pick me up and bring me to my new—if doomed to be temporary—home. Those hand-offs always went off without a hitch, no matter how far-flung the schools were. And everyone assured me they had *just* spoken with my mother.

But I never got to see her in the daytime. Only in the middle of the night. Only in a dreamy haze I could never quite be sure wasn't just a very lucid dream.

I kept a journal just for writing down what I remembered after one of these dream visitations. I had read over every entry so many times, hunting for patterns that just weren't there. She came about every three months, except when she didn't. Like when she came three times in one month, or the time when I was ten where I didn't see her for an entire year.

It had been nearly that long again since I'd seen her last. She hadn't been there through my whole process of being pushed out of my last graduate program, forced out of academia, and then failing every single interview I had managed to finagle my way into. And she hadn't been around since I'd moved into her brother's apartment to watch over his bookshop.

I only assumed she knew where I was. I didn't actually know that at all.

But I felt like she knew.

So when I found myself in that liminal place between sleep and wakefulness, aware of the moonlight filling my attic bedroom in a yellowish, smoke-diffused glow, I knew she was near. I was always aware of her approach, although I could never so much as sit up to greet her. It was a sort of sleep paralysis, only without any feeling of panic like most people describe.

Then I could sense her silhouette in the doorway. It wasn't quite like I was looking at it, more that I was just aware of her outline in the hazy darkness. Her hand was on the doorframe and she was looking at me, but I couldn't read her body language well enough to get any sense of her mood at all. Was she happy to see me? Relieved to have found me? Worn out from searching every-where for me?

I didn't know.

But before she could take a step closer, the night stillness was torn asunder by Houdini's most alarmed barks, the ones that rival rooster crows in their intensity. He usually builds up to that level of noise, but this time he went from curled-up sleeping dog to rigid barking monster in the blink of an eye.

And in the next blink of an eye, the feeling of my mother standing in the doorway was gone.

Then I was awake, sitting up with my heart hammering.

"Houdini, hush!" I commanded, even as I fumbled on the nightstand for my glasses.

He barked five or six more times despite my command, as if to be sure. Then he sat back on his haunches to just growl menacingly, still staring at the doorway.

Now, with my glasses on, I could see there was no one there. Worse, that door was closed. When I had sensed my mother, it had been open, and I hadn't heard the sound of it closing. Her visitation had at least something of magic to it, then. So there was definitely no point in trying to run down the stairs after her. She hadn't taken the stairs up to my room in the first place. Whatever arcane means had delivered her here, that was how she had left again.

I was alone again, with no heart to heart moment. No stroking of my hair.

No calming of my sparking powers.

"What did you do that for?" I demanded.

"You were in danger," Houdini said with complete certainty.

"That was my mother!" I hissed at him. I could hear a few doors and windows opening around the Square outside. No one shouted their irritation, but I could sense them waiting to be sure the barking wasn't going to resume again.

I glanced at my phone on the nightstand. It was just past four in the morning.

"Your mother?" Houdini said doubtfully. "She didn't smell like you at all."

"Why would she?" I asked.

"I don't mean soap or perfume or anything like that," he sniffed.

"So what then? You can smell her blood? Our shared DNA?" I asked.

"You're making fun of me," he said. To my surprise, he sounded really hurt.

"I'm not," I sighed. "It's just, I haven't seen her in so long. And I *need* to see her. Aside from the fact that seeing her always calms my random power discharges, at least for a couple of months, she can explain things to me that no one else can. And you chased her away."

"It's my duty as your guardian to keep you safe while you sleep. To chase away danger," he said.

"You know you have that backwards. Legally, I'm your guardian," I reminded him.

He just sniffed. His feelings were still wounded, clearly.

"I don't have any way to contact her, you know," I told him. "If she has a cellphone, I don't have the number. If she has an address, I've never been given it. If she even has any friends or acquaintances who can get in touch with her, I don't know who they are. She just shows up when she can, and I never know when that's going to be. And now she's gone, and I don't know when I'll see her again. Do you understand?"

"I'm sorry for that situation, but I'm not sorry for trying to protect you," he said with stiff dignity.

"You don't have to protect me from my mother," I said.

"I felt her power. I haven't felt power like that since..." he trailed off vaguely, as if words escaped him.

"Nell Bloom?" I offered.

"Nell Bloom? No!" he said with a huff. "No, it wasn't dark other being power that I sensed. It was just powerful magic. No, I was going to say since Agatha died."

"Oh," I said.

"Is your mother not a powerful witch?" he asked conversationally.

"You know, I don't actually know," I admitted. "It's one of the many things I'd like to discuss with Uncle Carlo when he and Frank get back from Europe."

"Or with her if she were here," Houdini said, finally sounding just a little contrite.

"Well, she never answers those questions when I ask them," I said. "Now that I'm older, she might. But I wouldn't count on it."

"But you've been sparking more than usual, and you need her to help fix that," he said.

"That is my hope," I said, and even in the darkness I could see his radar dish ears flatten down around his head. When he was sad or scared, he could alter his appearance to one of such absolute patheticness it tore the heart to look at him.

I think he did it on purpose.

But it still worked. I reached down and scooped him into my lap. He was stiff at first, but then all at once he collapsed against my chest, burrowing the top of his head under my chin as I cuddled him.

"Don't worry about it, okay? Steph is working on something that I'm pretty sure is going to be a big help," I said. I sounded pretty confident to my own ears, despite the fact that I only *hoped* it was true.

But Houdini was heartened at once. "I'm sure whatever he gives you will work marvelously," he enthused. "Would you like to go back to sleep now? I can watch over you again, now that I know your mother is to be trusted."

"No, I don't think I can sleep at all," I said. "Those barks of yours are a very alarming sort of alarm clock. Snooze is not an option."

"You'll thank me when it actually is danger I'm warning you about," he said without irony.

Houdini went back to sleep, but I turned on the light and paged through my mother dream journal. It had definitely been eleven months since I'd seen her last. I really hoped it wouldn't be eleven more before she came again. But I had no way of knowing.

The sun rose, promising another hot, smoky day. Worse than that, because it was barely past the solstice, I still had hours to wait before it was a reasonable time to go down to the Loose Leaves Teashop for breakfast.

Audrey had almost definitely had a better night than I had. I doubted she'd be up so early, waiting for this particular day to start. But there was a limit to how long I could wait to go down to see her.

I still had a better apology to make for breaking everything in her teashop. And I really wanted to tell her about almost seeing my mother. We'd talked enough over the past month where she would understand what that meant to me in a way no one else could.

When it was finally past seven, I got up and attempted to wet down my dry tangles of hair, then get a comb through it. The first part worked out better than the second. The air was so humid I was sure it would never dry, but the ends of course managed it in lightning time. And like lightning, it was all electrical energy looking for a place to discharge that power.

I had to give up on the combing when it became clear that the comb was likely to either break entirely or become a permanent resident in my hair. That wasn't a look I wanted to rock at all.

Houdini was still deeply asleep when I was ready to go. All the barking at four in the morning must have really worn him out. I tiptoed out the door as quietly as I could to avoid waking him, just in case he wasn't playing possum because he still didn't like to go out in public places, not even at such an early hour almost no one was up yet, let alone on the morning after a holiday.

The Square was once more filled with a hazy morning fog that put me in mind of a million Sherlock Holmes movies as I walked from the bookshop to the teashop. It seemed thicker than usual, enough so that sounds were echoing through it in a distorted sort of way. People were cleaning up from the night before, and other people were opening their businesses up for the day. But all those sounds of doors latching and empty crates being tossed together reverberated around me in a sourceless kind of way.

It was a relief to slip inside the teashop and smell that Pacific Northwest air, cool and green. But I only enjoyed a single breath of it before something else put me ill at ease.

Barnardo was there. He came in during the first hour the teashop was open every day, but I couldn't remember a single time I had seen him there before I had arrived.

And I had never, ever seen him without Miss Snooty Cat either in his arms or winding around his ankles.

"Barnardo?" I said, and he turned away from the counter to face me.

"Oh, hello. Audrey is here. She just stepped into the backroom for a moment," he said. He sounded very out of sorts, almost as if he had to justify why he was standing there with no sign of the proprietor anywhere in sight.

"Is something wrong?" I asked. I really didn't want to ask about his absent cat. The idea that something had happened to her was too, too terrible.

"Oh, I'm fine," he said with a completely unconvincing smile. Then he leaned closer to whisper to me, "No matter what anyone else thinks, I know you absolutely didn't do it."

Before I could summon more of a response than a confused blink, Audrey was there as well, a little satchel of what I guessed was Barnardo's usual order in her hands. She saw me standing barely inside the doorway and fumbled handing that satchel over to Barnardo.

"Tabitha, have you heard?" she asked in little more than a whisper. Then she shot a nervous glance over at Barnardo, whose cheeks were in flames. "Not that we think you had anything to do with it, but... well," she ended lamely.

"Heard about what?" I asked, trying not to sound testy, but all the mystery was too much early in the morning before I'd even had any caffeine.

"It's Delilah Dare," Barnardo finally told me. "She was found dead this morning."

I had been bracing to explain about the fire. So much so that it took me a minute to understand what he'd really said.

And why they were both looking at me in equal parts anxiety and fear.

"Dead? What happened?" I asked.

"We're not sure," Audrey said and exchanged another nervous glance with Barnardo.

"People are blaming me?" I asked, my voice picking that moment to crack in an embarrassing sort of squeak.

"No, of course not," Audrey said. "I mean, I heard about the fire. But this was something very different. And anyway, I know how hard you work to keep your power from hurting people. Even people like her."

"She didn't die in the Square," Barnardo said as he took a step closer to me. He had to for me to hear him. He was barely even whispering, as if afraid to be overheard.

But by who? From the way the two of them were talking, it sounded like I was the last to know.

"Where did she die?" I asked. Had she gone back to Mallorca with Paula, the mixologist? Or... actually, I had no idea where Delilah actually lived. I didn't think it was in the Square. Maybe she, like that Taurus guy from the night before, lived in the hidden levels of the Foshay Tower. It felt like her kind of trendy place.

"It was in the alley," Audrey said, pointing with the side of her head towards the alley that ran past the corner windows of her shop, past the comic book store.

Towards, if it had existed in the prosaic world at all, the base of the Tower.

"She was outside the Square?" I asked. I was whispering too now, although I had no idea why.

"That's why we don't know what happened," Barnardo said. "The prosaic authorities found her. I watched them arrive from my apartment windows. I watched them carry her body away. But I don't know how she died. Or why she was even out there."

I chewed at my lip. As distressing as this information was, it paled in comparison to the vibes I was getting off the two of them.

They were both looking at me earnestly, as if waiting for me to reveal what was sure to be an iron-clad alibi.

But it was super disturbing they even thought I needed one at all. Granted, I was more comfortable going into the prosaic world than a lot of other witches. I had traveled across the world that way to come here after leaving my last school, after all. Romania to Minneapolis. It had taken days.

Not that I had been back out in that world since. I had been too busy running a seven-level, bigger-on-the-inside bookshop all on my own every day since. And yet apparently no one had noticed me sticking to magical places, or maybe they assumed I had made an exception for the holiday, or something.

What trouble was I in now?

CHAPTER

SEVEN

The next few moments of awkward conversation sort of ran on without me being mentally present. I mean, I spoke to both of them, answering questions or agreeing with whatever it was that they said.

But I couldn't tell you a single word of what was said, by me or anyone else. It was like my mind was humming a single tone that just went on and on, and I couldn't hear anything else past it.

Then a sudden thought jolted me out of it. "Barnardo, where's Miss Snooty Cat?" I asked.

Barnardo had been about to say something else, but my question brought an expression of horror on his face that quickly morphed into chagrin. "Oh dear. I left her upstairs. I was so upset... Oh, she's going to be so angry with me."

And he scuttled out of the teashop without even saying goodbye.

Leaving me alone with Audrey. Who was still giving me odd looks. But she pulled herself together enough to say, "Breakfast?"

"If that's possible. I know I broke all of your—"

Then I looked around and saw every single plate, cup and saucer that had been smashed all over her floor the day before was back in

59

its respective place. And not a single piece had so much as a chip missing.

"What happened?" I asked. "Did you fix all this yourself?"

"Oh," Audrey said, her cheeks flushing red as she tucked her blonde hair back behind both of her ears. Maximum awkwardness. But then she gave me the smallest of smiles. "Steph stopped in while I was still sweeping up. He took one look around, pulled out his wand, and fixed everything in one big wave of magic. I'd never seen anything like it. And then he just left without a word."

"So you didn't have to explain what happened?" I said.

"Or try to cover up the fact that Liam was here," she said gratefully. "I already have the croissants waiting in a warming drawer. Let me just get the tea started."

I hovered awkwardly for a moment, then finally took a seat at our usual table close to the counter. Audrey came back out with everything on a tray, and within a minute we were pulling apart steaming croissants and sipping her personal blend of fragrant tea. Bergamot and citrus gave the aroma a sense of delicacy that was a startling juxtaposition to the highly caffeinated black tea she always brewed extra strong.

"I'm sorry that happened yesterday, really," I said. "I know it doesn't help to hear that I didn't mean it. You know I didn't. But I am trying to find a way to keep it from happening again. As much as I can."

"I'm sorry if I snapped at you. I was stressed out about Liam," she said.

"I'm sure you were. How was he when you saw him again?" I asked.

She chewed thoughtfully at a bit of croissant, took a long sip of tea, then wiped her mouth delicately on her napkin before answering. "He didn't quite seem to remember it. Or he didn't remember it right."

"What do you mean?" I asked.

"He seemed to remember you knocking over a tray. A tray full of my favorite service set, to be sure, but just a single tray. Not every item in the teashop," she said.

"Was he humoring you, maybe?" I ventured.

"No," she said slowly, shaking her head.

"Do you think Steph caught up with him after cleaning up here?" I asked even more hesitantly.

"No," she said again. "No, I think if anything he has a little residual magic from that mind wipe still in his brain. It might keep wiping smaller incidents forward in time, like ripples from a stone dropped into a pond. A lesser effect each time, and eventually there won't be an effect at all."

"That sounds like a pretty specific impression for him just mentioning a single tray," I said.

"I might've taken a good look in his eyes," she admitted with another blush. "I did learn a couple of things at school, you know."

"I know," I promised her.

We ate in silence for a moment or two, then she wiped her mouth on her napkin again before saying, "So, what is it you're trying to do to control your power?"

"Personally, not much at all," I admitted. "Steph is working on something, and I gather that he's close to bringing something to me that he hopes will help. But we'll see. My own research has been nothing but dead ends."

"I know," she said with a sympathetic smile.

"But I haven't been talking about it with you," I said.

She laughed a little, fond laugh. "Look, not controlling your power is something you've lived your whole life with. I'm sure it's stressful, but it doesn't make you cranky. Not finding what you're looking for when doing research? Now that's a new experience for you. It had to be what was making you cranky. And if it had been about Houdini, I'm sure you would've been sharing it with me all along. So it had to be about you." She ended with a casual shrug.

Like looking directly into my heart and mind and knowing exactly what I hid within them was some everyday occurrence.

"That about wraps it up," I had to admit.

"But something is different this morning," she said, pushing her empty plate aside to lean closer to me over the table. "And I don't mean about Delilah Dare. You had a different demeanor even before you heard about that."

"Oh," I said. "Well..."

And then I told her everything that had happened at four in the morning, about my mother and Houdini and everything I felt about all that.

"And the worst thing is, I have no idea when she'll try to see me again," I said.

"Or why it's always in the middle of the night, or even how to contact her, right?" Audrey said with a sigh. "That's a problem."

"My uncle promised me some answers about our family when he gets home from Europe, but somehow I think that's more about my grandparents and great-grandparents and so on. Not about my mother. He almost never talks about my mother," I said.

"Well, I don't know how we'd implement this, but I do have a thought," she said.

"What is it?"

"You remember I told you that my grandaunt Agatha and I talked together almost every night with our scrying glasses," she said.

"I do, but those are incredibly rare," I said. "Out of all the schools I've been to, I've only seen two of them before. And they both belonged to administrators who also held political appointments. They were on loan from different governments."

"I know," Audrey said. "That's why it feels like such a waste for me to have two of them. Who am I going to call?"

"Wait, you're offering me two scrying glasses?" I asked, getting her point way too late.

"One for you and one for your mother," Audrey said.

"No, that's too much," I said, pushing back from the table as if she were trying to shove those glasses at me right that minute. "I couldn't possibly take those. I couldn't even borrow them. Those are far too valuable! I mean, you saw what happened here yesterday. I'm not sure if Steph could fix a scrying glass if it fell victim to the Curse of Tabitha's Uncontrollable Power."

"They aren't doing anyone any good where they are now, wrapped up in a box at the back of my closet," Audrey said.

"Even if I wanted to take them, I still wouldn't know how to get one of them to my mother. I mean, if I did, I could just write her a more conventional message, right?"

"Just think about it," Audrey said as she stood up. I got up at the same time, desperate to beat her to cleaning up the dishes.

But she was too quick for me. In the end, the best I could do was trail behind her into the back room, then grab a dish towel to dry what she washed by hand.

"I guess you heard what happened at the Square party last night," I said as she handed me the first dripping plate.

"Something about a fire and some exploding spirits," Audrey admitted with the hint of a grin.

"I'm not sure it's funny today with one of the parties involved dead," I said, not quite in a chastising way. But she stopped grinning.

"Nobody is going to think those two things are related at all," she assured me as she handed me a second plate.

"Aren't they? I had two run-ins with the Trio yesterday, and they were both bad ones. With witnesses," I said.

"They also got into a tiff with Barnardo about the distance between their booth and his food table. And another one about the same issue with the Wolseys," Audrey said. "If the list of suspects is going to be everyone who traded words with Delilah Dare yesterday, it's going to be a long one."

"That's not exactly comforting," I said.

"She was killed in the prosaic world. In the sort of place where random prosaic crime happens," she said.

"But she wasn't a prosaic. She was a witch. Her focus might be on beauty and glamor, but no one gets out of any academy without having at least a basic ability to defend themselves," I said.

I didn't have to mention that I was probably the one exception to that rule, because I was the one exception to most rules. I had, after all, been given a special dispensation to study whatever I wanted without ever being required to show my skills in a lab or test.

"From what I heard, she wasn't exactly super drunk either," Audrey admitted. "The booth exploded before anyone had more than two of those cocktails, potent as I've heard they were."

"They *did* look good," I said wistfully. "I didn't get to have any myself. I was barely there at that party, truth be told."

"Everyone remembers you there," Audrey said, and I felt my heart sink. But then it rose again when she turned to look right at me and added, "And everyone remembers the exact minute you left the party. Hours and hours before anyone saw Delilah for the last time."

"That's hardly an alibi, though, is it?" I asked.

"I don't think you're under enough suspicion to need one, really," Audrey said. "Barnardo said that the prosaic police department took her away. That means they will run a whole investigation on their own. The magical authorities will only step in as much as they can without getting in the way of the prosaic investigation."

"That usually means no conviction," I said. "Delilah will be buried there as a Jane Doe whenever they finally give up on identifying her body. And her killer will likely never get caught. It was either some completely random prosaic killer, or it was one of us. And they'll definitely never catch one of us."

"The authorities have ways of nudging things, if they have reason to do so," Audrey said. Which I knew was true.

But a reason to nudge a prosaic investigation would involve an abundance of proof that such nudging was necessary. The authorities would have to have a very strong certainty they knew who the guilty party was, and that the prosaic police could handle it on their end.

"I don't have much hope in that outcome," I admitted.

"Me neither," Audrey said with a sigh. She handed me the last cup, then pulled the plug out of the sink to let it drain.

"Do they have any cameras in the alley? Like CCTV or whatever?" I asked her. "Maybe the comic book store has something over their front door."

"Here's the thing, and it's why Barnardo and I were both pretty sure this isn't the work of a random prosaic killer," Audrey said as she took the towel from me to dry her hands. "The place where she died was right at the base of the Tower."

"Cameras won't work there," I said.

"They'll be too distorted to see anything if they recorded anything at all," she said.

"It *could* be random," I said. "I don't want to say karma came for Delilah Dare, but maybe bad luck?"

"Maybe," Audrey said. But not like she believed it.

Which was fine. I didn't really either.

"There were a lot of strangers here for the party," I said.

"There were," Audrey agreed.

"But Barnardo told you something else," I guessed.

"He did," she said. And now she was grinning at me again, but this was more a conspiratorial sort of grin. "He said that the last time *he* saw Delilah, she was arguing with Cleopatra Manx. And apparently this argument got very heated before the two of them took it into the hedge maze. And he never saw either of them come back out again."

"Has he talked to anyone else yet? Did anyone else see Cleopatra after that point?" I asked.

"I don't think so. It's barely eight o'clock in the morning. But the Inanna Salon & Spa opens early on Fridays, and today is Friday."

"Right," I said brightly. "So let's pop down and see if Cleopatra is around. Either she's there and we can ask her a few questions—"

"—or she's gone, and that definitely tells us something," Audrey finished for me.

We traded one last dry grin, then she scuttled to the front door to switch the sign over to *closed*.

CHAPTER

EIGHT

The lights were on inside the Inanna Salon & Spa, and when I pulled on the door, it opened easily. A blast of frigid air conditioning washed over me, evaporating all the sweat off my skin and leaving behind a rash of goosebumps. It was a shade too intense a feeling, and yet it cleared that smoke smell away and it was like I could breathe freely again.

It was like my mind was suddenly clearer.

But when I stepped further inside with Audrey beside me, we both were surprised to see that no one was there. Everything sat ready for the day, every station with its beauty tools arrayed in easy reach for maximum efficiency, the water baths under the pedicure chairs churning happily, but not a single customer was in sight. And no one in a skimpy sundress and perfectly blown-out blonde hair stood behind the tall counter looking down at us.

It was strange. I had only been inside the store once before, but I walked past it almost daily, and it was always packed.

"Hello?" I called. My voice sounded too loud in the quiet room, and Audrey even flinched a little.

But then I heard a soft sniffle. I looked at Audrey, and she nodded. She had heard it too. She pointed towards the counter, and we approached it from either side. We were both wearing sneakers, and not a squeak of our toes on the tiled floor betrayed us.

But when we both lunged behind the counter, we found only Cressida, who shrieked at our sudden appearance.

"Sorry!" I said quickly. Then felt that word even more deeply when I got a good look at her.

She was wearing an emerald green sundress with little yellow flowers flecked all over it, far too short to sit on the floor in, as I endeavored not to notice. And she had kicked her shoes off. Somehow the bare feet and the redness of the nose she was holding fistfuls of tissue to made her look almost childlike despite the fact that her hair was still completely fabulous. "Sorry," I said again. "We were hoping to see Cleopatra. Is she in today?"

"No," Cressida said with a very unladylike sniffle. "I guess it's safe to be seen now. I've cancelled all the morning appointments." She blew her nose, then struggled up to her feet.

"Have you seen Cleopatra since yesterday?" I asked.

"No, but I've talked to her on the phone. She's going to be in a little late," Cressida said. "She'll probably be mad I didn't try to fit a few regulars in, but I just couldn't."

"You don't look like you're in any shape to be working," Audrey said kindly.

"I know a lot of people didn't like Delilah, but she was still a friend of mine," Cressida said and lifted her chin as if daring either of us to say a word.

"Of course she was," I said. "We didn't come here to disparage her. We're actually hoping to figure out what happened to her, if we can."

"Like you figured out what happened to Agatha Mirken?" she asked, like it was a challenge.

"Well, hopefully we'll figure things out a little quicker this time," I said. I could feel my cheeks flaming.

"I'm sorry," Cressida said, and blotted at her nose again with the completely useless wad of spent tissues. "That was mean of me. It's this place, I think. It brings out meanness."

"That's one theory," I said, and wished I hadn't. Why badger her now? Still, it was a crappy excuse for bad behavior, blaming a place.

"I'm sorry for what happened yesterday," Cressida went on, tossing her used tissues into a trash bin, then pulling out four more in rapid succession from a box on the counter. "But I wasn't making fun of you when I offered to help."

Audrey gave me a questioning look, but I kept my eyes on Cressida.

"Well, like I said, it's really not a grooming problem," I said.

"No, the root cause is likely some deeper magic I have no experience in," Cressida agreed, but she was looking at my hair with a professional's close attention. "May I?" she asked, her hand hovering close to my curls.

I sighed. But in the end, I nodded.

It was tiring, everyone wanting to touch my hair all the time.

But she was gentle with it. Even when she found a tooth from my comb that I hadn't realized I had left behind in there. She worked it free and tossed it into the trash full of tissues without a word. "I can't help with the root cause, like I said, but I think I can help with this particular symptom. I have a rinse. It's sort of a prosaic milk product that I've juiced with just a little magic."

"Your own recipe?" Audrey asked.

"Yes, but I have Cleopatra's permission to use it in the shop," Cressida assured her. "The prosaic part of it is good for the effects of the humidity we've been having. My little something extra is just for the particular needs of witches with certain kinds of magic."

"You've seen this before?" I asked, incredulous.

"Never this bad?" she said with a sympathetic wince. "But sure. Those who channel weather get it sometimes. And when I was in my last year at the magical academy, I had two roommates who were hoping to become Tesla witches. Their hair was always dry and on end. It was pretty funny."

Her eyes were shining brightly, but when neither Audrey nor I shared in her joke, her face grew grave again. "Sorry, you're right. It really wasn't, was it? It was a price they were willing to pay for magic that called to them. I'm a terrible person."

"I don't think I'd go that far," I said. But she was still looking at me expectantly. I looked at Audrey, who shrugged noncommittally. "Fine. Let's try your milky rinsey thing. But I still have some questions for you."

"Absolutely," she said with a wide smile, then directed me to one of the shampooing stations.

I immediately hated how vulnerable it felt, being tipped back in that chair until all I could see were the ceiling tiles overhead.

Then Audrey's face came into view, and I realized I was being silly. Nothing bad was going to happen. I was just getting my hair washed and conditioned. She wasn't even going to come at me with a pair of scissors.

"Let me know if it's too hot or too cold, okay?" Cressida said.

"Okay," I said.

The water that ran over my head was the exact perfect temperature. Then Cressida started working a shampoo through my hair that smelled of mint and rosemary. The feeling of that warm water and the gentleness of her hands as she worked the shampoo through all my hair over my scalp was strangely calming.

Maybe if I came here more often, I wouldn't need anything else to make the sparks go away. I certainly felt more relaxed than I had in longer than I'd care to remember.

"I don't think it was really your fault, what happened to the booth," Cressida said as her hands ran through my hair, rinsing out the shampoo. "I saw that Taurus guy touching you. He comes on strong sometimes, and he obviously took you completely off guard. I would probably do the same thing if my own magic was remotely protective of me at all."

"I don't know. It's not like setting everything on fire protected me from anything at all," I admitted. "If I had better control, maybe? But

I think a single thrust of a targeted elbow would've been more on point."

Cressida laughed as she shut off the water. Then she squeezed an entire bottle of something cold over my hair. It smelled vaguely of vanilla and I guess milk, but mostly it just smelled clean. Then she was massaging my scalp again, and I blissed out for a second time.

I even closed my eyes. So, I guess on some level, I was pretty trusting of Cressida.

Of course, Audrey was still there right beside me.

"Tabitha can't control what happens when she sparks. We all know this," Audrey said.

"Everyone knows that?" I repeated, but they both ignored me.

"Maybe it was a subconscious thing, going after the open bar booth, though," Cressida said to Audrey. "Taurus was only there because Cleopatra had invited him months ago and forgot."

"I didn't know that, not even subconsciously," I put in.

"But you were probably still angry about what Delilah said about your hair before," Cressida said.

"I don't think I was," I said. "I know this is hard for you to understand, given what you do, but I don't spend every waking minute concerned about what my hair looks like."

I mean, it couldn't be more than fifty percent of the time, tops.

Okay, maybe seventy.

It really depended on what I was reading, honestly. If I was evenly mildly engrossed, I didn't even remember I *had* hair.

"None of that had anything to do with Delilah's death, though," Audrey said just as Cressida turned the water on again and started rinsing the goo out of my hair.

"No, of course not," Cressida said, but I could hear her sniffling again. "No, I don't know what happened to Delilah, but I really doubt Tabitha had anything to do with it. I heard she was strangled by someone far stronger than she was."

"Heard from who? Where?" I demanded.

"This morning when I was in the Bitter Brew, but I don't

remember from who. There were a few locals in there when I went to get my coffee, and they were all talking about it," she said.

"Just rumors, then," Audrey said.

"Well, I guess," Cressida said with the air of someone who definitely totally believed that Delilah had been strangled by someone far stronger than she was.

Then the water was off again and she was gently blotting at my hair with a fluffy towel. This felt pretty amazing, too. I wondered how much was just her touch and how much was some kind of magic. Either way, she was good at what she did.

"Let's go over to my station so I can dry it out for you," she said, coming around the sink to help me out of the chair. "Don't worry, it's going to be diffused low heat, I promise."

"Okay," I pretended to reluctantly agree.

I had used a blow-dryer once years ago. I still didn't know exactly how what she said meant anything at all. My knowledge barely went beyond turning the thing on or off. But I knew by then that I was in good hands.

"Barnardo said that Delilah and Cleopatra got into a fight last night," Audrey said. She leaned back against the counter in the station next to Cressida's. Which had to be Delilah's. I wondered if she remembered that fact at all. But her gaze was fixed steadily on Cressida even as Cressida switched on a dryer, testing its temperature against her own hand first before turning it onto my hair.

"Yeah, it was a doozy," Cressida said. Then she seemed to realize how that sounded. "Wait. They have spats all the time. I just make myself scarce until it blows over, because it always does. It didn't mean anything, what Barnardo saw."

"He said neither of them ever came back to the party," I said. "Is that true?"

Cressida thought about this as she used a brush to lift my hair for the blow-dryer. "No," she said at last. "No, Cleopatra came back. I saw her before I went home for the night."

"What did she say?" I asked.

"I didn't try talking to her," Cressida said with a nervous laugh. "Like I said, when they have a tiff, I make myself scarce. She was clearly still raging, so I kind of hid behind some of those tall Irish Wolsey cousins until she was gone."

She laughed a little more, but it died out as she realized, again belatedly, just how that sounded.

"Cleopatra has a fiery temper, but I don't think she—"

Cressida didn't so much trail off as stop dead in the middle of that word. I heard a bell chime and glanced over towards the Square to see Cleopatra herself sweeping into the salon, sipping at the largest size of iced latte that the prosaic chain across the street sold. Then she saw me in Cressida's chair and Audrey loitering in Delilah's station and frowned at both of us in that way she did, where she only moved her face just enough to let us get the message. Not so much that she'd risk a wrinkle.

"What's all this?" she asked. Her voice was even colder than the constantly blasting air conditioning in her shop. I actually shivered.

"I cancelled all the appointments for the morning because I wasn't sure I was up to working alone, but then I felt better, so I took a walk-in," Cressida said smoothly. Then she switched off the blowdryer and finished fussing with my hair with her hands and some sort of wax product.

"I didn't authorize cancellations," Cleopatra said.

"You weren't here to help either," Cressida said.

I saw Audrey quickly put a hand over her face to hide her smile. It was pretty obvious that, as upset as she was about Delilah's death, it had put Cressida in the unique position of being almost unfireable. And she was prepared to exploit it to the max, apparently.

"There, what do you think?" Cressida asked, and spun my chair so that I was facing the mirror.

It was still me, with my honey-blonde curls framing my squirrel-cheeked face.

And yet it was a version of me I'd never seen before. The curls still spun out from my head in random directions, but they were soft, controlled curls. It was an organized sort of chaos.

And when I touched it, nothing happened.

"It's amazing," I said. "I had no idea you could do this."

"You were a little dismissive," Cressida agreed. Then she turned her attention to her boss, still standing with that latte in her hand in the middle of the tiled floor. If Cleopatra were just a little less put-together of a person, her mouth would be hanging open. But all three of us could infer how nonplussed she was. "Now that you're here, I'm going to take the rest of the day off. If you want to handle all the afternoon appointments yourself, that's up to you. I'll see you tomorrow."

And then she was gone.

And Audrey and I were alone with the fiery-tempered Cleopatra Manx.

CHAPTER
NINE

Cleopatra Manx studied me for a long time, or rather she studied my suddenly transformed hair. Then she gave a quick, decisive nod, took a careful sip from her enormous latte, and slipped behind the counter where Audrey and I had found Cressida hiding. She set the coffee aside to tap at the computer keystroke by keystroke with her overly manicured fingers.

"Right, that will be sixty dollars," she said and looked up at me with a cold smile.

"Shouldn't I have paid Cressida if she wanted to charge me?" I asked, not quite choking over the amount, which was a lot, considering all she'd done was wash my hair and dry it for me.

"What she wanted doesn't really come into it," Cleopatra said. "This is my shop, and she works for me. If she wanted to comp your use of her personal products, she definitely should've said so. So I'm charging the full price. You can, of course, take it out of her tip if you're feeling vindictive."

She took another sip of her coffee.

I sighed and dug into the pockets of my capris, emptying the contents onto the counter before Cleopatra. Between the four pockets, I managed a little under seventy dollars. I shoved the final pile towards her and she sniffed at the wrinkled multitude of bills, but took it all the same.

"Rather a light tip. Were you not happy with your service?" Cleopatra asked with totally fake concern.

"I think I rather obviously just gave you everything I have," I said. "I'll make up the difference personally with Cressida when I see her next."

"Suit yourself," she said. She had carefully straightened out each of the bills and stacked them together. Now she dropped them into a drawer I couldn't quite see from my side of the counter, then folded her hands at me as if that concluded our interaction.

"We had a few questions for you," I said.

She rolled her eyes. "Of course you do."

"You clearly have a moment to talk with us," Audrey said.

"Do I? You recently dealt with a death yourself. Didn't you find the amount of death-related activity you suddenly had to deal with a little overwhelming?" Cleopatra asked.

"Agatha was family, and I was her heir," Audrey said.

"Alas, Delilah was on her own in the world. No family to speak of, and I was her dearest friend. So it all does fall on me," she said.

She was simpering, a practiced performance, and the glamor spells she always cloaked herself in were just perceptibly pushing the effect. I could feel myself wanting to respond, despite the fact that I knew it was fake.

And yet, on a deeper level, I felt like behind the layer of performative grief and worried distraction she was shoving in my face, there was something else. Just a glimmer of truth lurked in her words.

Was she truly mourning?

"Have you spoken with the authorities about it, then?" Audrey asked. "I know the local police department in the prosaic world have her body now. I do hope there is a plan for getting her back into our care."

"They promise me they are doing all they can," Cleopatra said.

"Do you know what she wanted done with her remains?" Audrey asked.

"No, actually, I do not. She was far too young to have put any thought into such things. She should've had decades more before facing those sorts of decisions," Cleopatra said.

I glanced over at Audrey. After her grandaunt had been interred in the catacombs under the Square, we had had a rambling conversation late at night where we'd traded our own thoughts about what we might want if we were to die an untimely death. Audrey wanted to be interred in the same wall space as her grandaunt. I had opted to be cremated and have bits of my ashes scattered in every library and bookshop in the world.

Probably an impossible ask, but we'd only been half-serious at the time.

But the point was, we'd thought about it. We'd discussed it. And we were both younger than Delilah by a bit.

Not that I was going to bring that up now. I wasn't heartless. It was just a data point, one that added to the overall impression that Delilah Dare had had a very lonely sort of life. Always in the company of two women who looked almost exactly like her, and yet also always alone.

"Are the authorities keeping you up to date on the prosaic investigation?" I asked.

"No, they didn't even pretend to promise that," Cleopatra said with a careful wrinkle of her nose. "I guess when they either solve it or give up, someone will let me know. But no one from this side of things can track their progress there."

I wasn't sure that was entirely true either, but I had seen for myself how overworked and stretched thin the local magical authorities were. Any work they *could* pass on to others, even if those others were prosaics, they had to pass on.

"That must be frustrating for you," Audrey said, but Cleopatra just shrugged.

"The wait to get her back so I can plan her service is the only really hard part," she said.

"So you don't care what happened to Delilah?" I asked. "Or perhaps you think you already know?"

"How would I know what happened to her?" she asked, almost narrowing her eyes at me. But not quite.

"Weren't you the last one to see her alive?" I asked.

"No, I would gather that whoever killed her was the last one to see her alive," she said coldly. "And that wasn't me. In case that was your next question. You know, rumor has it that it might have been you. You two did have a bit of a moment last night. We all saw it."

"I was seen losing control of my power. Not for the first time," I said, my cheeks flaming.

"In your defense, you did far less damage to my temporary open bar than you did to Titus' coffeeshop," she all but cooed.

I decided to ignore that. "The two of you were seen arguing, though. And then she went into the hedge maze, and you went after her," I said.

"I wasn't *chasing* her, if that's what you're implying," Cleopatra said. "Look, Delilah could be quite hot-tempered in the best of circumstances. But that night had been—as I *know* you know—a bit of a disaster. *Not* the best of circumstances. So when she refused to drop her little tiff with me, I took her far enough away from the rest of the party so that she was no longer making a show out of the two of us. Then I let her speak her piece, and we went our separate ways."

"You left her alone in the hedge maze, then?" Audrey asked. "For the sake of our timeline."

"Oh, you're making a timeline, are you? Little junior investigators," Cleopatra grumbled under her breath. "Poking your nose in when it's your own grandaunt is one thing. But I know no one has asked you to solve this particular murder."

"We're meddlers," I said cheerily. Then I repeated Audrey's question. "You left her alone in the hedge maze?"

"I left her alone in the hedge maze," Cleopatra said. "I wasn't wearing a watch or carrying a phone at the time, but the fireworks had just started. Someone else can probably tell you what time of night that would've been. For the sake of your timeline."

"Thank you," I said, still in my brightest voice. But I wasn't remotely done asking questions. "So, what was the fight about?"

"Barnardo seemed to think it was over a man," Audrey said. Which was news to me, but I carefully schooled my features not to register my surprise.

Cleopatra made her not-quite-nose-wrinkling distasteful face again. "That is *not* how I would put it at all."

"And yet?" I said leadingly.

Cleopatra blew out a frustrated sigh. "Look, I love both my girls. Delilah and Cressida both make working here in the Inanna Salon & Spa a real joy. They are more than my employees. I don't know how to describe it."

"Friends?" Audrey offered.

"No," Cleopatra said, tapping at her chin as she searched for the word.

"Protégées," I offered.

"Yes," she said slowly, clearly still thinking it over. Then she nodded at me. "Yes, that word will do nicely. They both study at my knee, so to speak, learning to emulate my skills and my magic as much as they can. They aren't exact copies by any means, but they aspire to my place in life."

"So, where does the man come in?" I asked.

"I was getting to it," Cleopatra almost growled. Then she forced a bright smile at me again. "You actually met the man in question. Taurus Vernon?"

Audrey looked a question at me. I gave her a nod, then answered Cleopatra, "He'd be hard to forget."

"Yes. Gorgeous, isn't he? Alas, he is not quite the total package he seems to be at first meeting," she said.

"What happened?" Audrey asked, confused.

"It was just before I accidentally set things on fire," I said.

"There was a man who was making me uncomfortable. Then Delilah got angry. And then..." I trailed off with a few exploding hand gestures.

"Oh, that's right. You weren't there," Cleopatra said, clearly implying that whether Audrey was in a place or not was not something anyone like Cleopatra would ever notice. But Audrey didn't take her bait.

"Delilah was mad at you because this man was bothering you?" Audrey asked with a confused frown.

"Oh, that really had nothing to do with you at all, I'm afraid," Cleopatra said with feigned regret. "You see, Delilah had spurned his attentions. He was looking to make her jealous, and you were convenient."

"I had put that together on my own, thanks," I gritted out.

"So it worked? Delilah got angry because she was jealous?" Audrey asked.

"Delilah may be my most apt pupil, but she does miss the point with distressing frequency," Cleopatra said. This time, her regret sounded semi-real as she solemnly shook her head.

"What point did she miss?" Audrey asked.

But at the same time, I said, "Taurus Vernon was there at your invitation. Wasn't he?"

Cleopatra held a hand up at each of us, clearly not liking the cross-talk. Then she took a deep breath before pointing to me. "Yes, Taurus Vernon was there at my invitation. An invitation given weeks ago, which really should've been considered rescinded, but the man can be quite obstinate."

"But he wanted to see Delilah?" Audrey guessed.

"I presume so," Cleopatra said.

I tried putting a few things together in my own head before I said, "So, let me get this straight. You were seeing this Taurus fellow, shall we say socially, some weeks ago. But that's all in the past. Now he was seeing Delilah until much more recently, but that's in the past as well?"

"And the two of you fighting about it is what Barnardo overheard," Audrey said with an air of finality.

"It's a good thing my morning is clear. This conversation is going to take forever, and once this is done, I'm going to have to find Barnardo and set him straight. The rumors he must be spreading! Luckily, no one of any importance puts any stock in his words. But still."

She seethed for a moment, then got her smile back in place.

"I very briefly entertained having a fling with Taurus Vernon. But I found him not suitable to my tastes at all. I was very clear, but he was even more obtuse. He seemed to think that wooing my protégée —" she acknowledged my word choice with a wink, "—would drive me mad with jealousy. Which, of course, it did not. I know what I'm worth, and who is worthy of me, and he most definitely was not. Look into my eyes, both of you. Do you see any hint of jealousy for Delilah Dare in them?"

She gazed at us both, one at a time. Her blue eyes were so startlingly beautiful it was hard to look at her for so long. Okay, that was almost a hundred percent the glamor talking. Her magic might be focused in a way I had never had an interest in mastering, but there was no saying that she didn't have power to spare.

But in the end, I had to shake my head. Whatever her faults were, jealousy wasn't one of them.

Then something else clicked in my head. "That's the point that Delilah didn't learn?" I guessed. "That jealousy is beneath you?"

"Exactly," Cleopatra said, and I briefly felt the warm glow I had missed since my schooldays, of basking in the praise of a teacher well-pleased.

Ugh, sometimes I hated myself.

"But if Vernon wanted you, why was he making Delilah jealous?" Audrey asked.

A very good question. Audrey was handling Cleopatra's waves of mind-fogging glamor better than I was, apparently.

"Force of habit? Or perhaps his affections really had moved on? I have no idea," she said with a dismissive wave. "My point is, the argument Barnardo overheard which he falsely attributed to being *over a man* was, in fact, over Delilah's very bad behavior. The woman she aspires to be would never be so easily manipulated, or descend to such a show of drama in a public place."

"So you shamed her," I said.

Cleopatra shot me a harsh glare, but then relented with a conceding nod. "Basically, yes. She had disappointed me, as her mentor. And I let her know I was disappointed. But only after first removing the both of us from the public eye. And the range of Barnardo Daley's ears."

"Where was Taurus through all of this?" I asked.

Cleopatra blinked as my question caught her off guard. "Goodness, he was nowhere around. He made himself scarce when you started blowing things up, dear. You certainly looked like you would set him on fire next if he so much as looked at you crossways."

"That's what it looked like when I was running away?" I asked. But she just shrugged and took another sip of coffee.

"Barnardo didn't see you come back out of the hedge maze," Audrey said, getting us back on track.

"No, but Cressida did. As I know she's already told you," Cleopatra said. "Now, if you don't mind, despite recent events, I still have a business to run."

"We'll get out of your hair," I said. Audrey nodded her agreement, and the two of us left the frigid interior of the Inanna Salon & Spa and headed back out into the smoke-filled heat of the July morning.

But whatever Cressida had put into my hair repelled the effects of the humidity. My curls stayed soft and bouncy even as a sheen of sweat rapidly formed all over my body.

So I had that going for me.

CHAPTER

TEN

I walked with Audrey back to the teashop, but once inside, she left the shutters down and the signs turned to *closed*. Without a word, we both crossed the room to slump down at our customary table.

"I know I should open for business, but I really don't want to," Audrey sighed.

"That goes double for me," I said. "I'm probably hurting my uncles' business by not being there, but it doesn't feel like the sort of day I can pretend is normal. Is it weird that I feel that way? It's not like I even liked Delilah."

"It's not weird to feel weird about it," Audrey said after a moment's thought. "You were pretty close to her not long before she died. That has an effect. I think we both need a mental health day. And I'm not just saying that because I totally can't handle customer service right now."

"I agree, but I don't think I can just sit here either," I said glumly. "Isn't there anything we can do?"

"I would say comfort the grieving, only..." she trailed off, lifting both hands palms-up in the air. I knew what she meant. The closest to grieving was apparently Cleopatra Manx. And she didn't want any comfort from the two of us.

Only that hadn't really been what I meant. "I was thinking of something a little more magical," I said.

"Us?" she said skeptically.

"We do okay when we work together," I said.

"I suppose. But what were you thinking?" she asked.

"I would like to figure out a way to see the crime scene somehow," I said. "Maybe there's a clue there."

"Well, we don't need magic to do that, do we? Can't we just walk to the end of the alley?" she asked.

"Don't the police have it taped off?" I asked. "We can't just cross that tape. I mean, we aren't supposed to."

"Well, let's see how much we can see without crossing it and then go from there," Audrey said.

Which was far too sensible a plan not to follow through on. So we slipped out the teashop's prosaic door and turned down the alley towards the comic book store. That business was doing its usual small but steady business. Through the windows I could see four people browsing the racks, and a young man came out just as we passed the door. He gave us a brief glance then put down the skateboard he had been carrying and skated away, paper bag of new comics tucked neatly under his arm.

If he had been remotely curious about the abundance of yellow tape at the end of the alley, he certainly hadn't shown it. Perhaps he had investigated before going inside the store.

But as Audrey and I passed the comic shop doorway and headed towards the very end of the alley, I could feel that there was probably another, stronger reason.

The wards inside the Square pushed hard on the minds of the magical passersby to absolutely not notice the anachronistic Neolithic structure dominating one quarter of the building that brought to mind the streets of Paris or the French Quarter in New Orleans. Even when I tried my hardest to focus, I could only occasionally catch a glimpse of it out of the corner of my eye from my French window far above and on the other side of the Square.

But this was in the prosaic world. But it was also just at the foot of the Tower. The spells were subtler here. By the laws of the magical world, they had to be, so that even the most sensitive of prosaics wouldn't consciously notice them.

But they were still there. It was easier here to look around than it was inside the Square, but the pressure to look somewhere else—or better yet, to walk away—was strong on my mind.

And yet, even though I *could* look, there was nothing much to see. There was no hint of Neolithic stone walls on this side of things. It just looked like the perfectly ordinary corner where the end of a Sullivanesque building from the 1880s met the back of a more modern—albeit still quite old—brick building from the 1940s.

It felt strange to be compelled not to look at something that was so blandly unremarkable. But that was probably how the spells had to work on this side of things. Prosaics wouldn't notice they were being manipulated because the effect was so subtle, and as in the case of the police who had been here in the wee hours of the morning, most didn't feel it at all. Having a goal, they could move past the spells to achieve that goal.

So when Audrey and I reached the taped boundary, we were the only people gawking at the crime scene. And we could see everything as well as anyone could expect to. The pinkish granite stained with ancient wood smoke of the outside of the Square on the left, the narrow expanse of crumbling brick wall directly ahead, and the more modern concrete and steel of the building on the right.

No windows overlooked this alley, or at least no prosaic ones did. I knew the windowless stone walls of the Square exterior were a lie. All the apartments on the second and third floors had windows. Although whether they opened up on this alley or some remote overlook in the Rocky Mountains or Europe or wherever really depended on the tastes of the mages who lived inside.

Barnardo's window overlooked the alley. But I wasn't sure that

Barnardo ever did any magic at all. He seemed to prefer a prosaic lifestyle, from his from-scratch cooking to his usually business casual fashion sense.

So no windows meant no witnesses. And if there were any other security cameras in this alley, they, like the ones over the comic shop door, would record nothing usable because of the effects of the Tower.

Someone might have been walking by, but at that hour of the night, unless they'd come all the way to the end of the alley, I doubted they had seen anything in the darkness.

I swept my eyes over the ground in a back-and-forth pattern, but all there was to see was a suspicious moisture that lingered in slick, oily puddles where the pavement was cracked.

And despite the lack of any kind of dumpster, there was still a strong aroma of over-ripe garbage. It was best not to linger on what fluid might be lingering there.

"No flags or markers," Audrey said. "Does that mean no evidence was found?"

"No chalk marks where the body was either," I noted. "Do they only do that in TV shows, do you think?"

Audrey just shrugged. What we didn't know about prosaic police investigation methods could fill a book. But it probably wasn't one we had in the bookshop.

"If they already took photographs, maybe they don't need to leave the markers?" I said. But I wasn't remotely sure. "At any rate, I don't see any blood anywhere. Do you?"

"No," Audrey said at once and with confidence. So we'd both been scanning the scene pretty thoroughly.

"I guess there wouldn't be if the rumors are true and she was strangled," I said with a sigh.

The air in the alley was close, and the dumpster smell was strong enough to overwhelm the toxic smell of wildfire smoke, but that absolutely was not a good thing. "Let's go back," I said.

"Agreed," Audrey said, and we walked briskly back to the cool darkness of the closed teashop. We both lingered by one of the windows, smelling the green smells of Oregon and enjoying the chill air that carried those scents to us.

"We know rumors from inside the Square, but we don't know what rumors the prosaics are sharing," Audrey said.

"What do you think we should do? Go out and ask around?" I asked. I had a vision of the two of us trying to strike up conversations in local bars.

I definitely had seen too many prosaic films. But even so, the idea of the two of us doing that was a little bit funny. We absolutely would not fit in there. And I doubted anyone would talk to two such strange young women asking even stranger questions.

"There's always the internet," I said, digging for my phone.

"Yes, but there's also Liam," Audrey said.

And I felt really stupid. She couldn't have been hinting any harder, but I'd missed it entirely.

"Do you think it's a good idea getting him involved?" I asked. "It wasn't last time when I asked him to do a little prosaic world digging."

"But he was good at it, right?" Audrey said. "And this time, there's no reason why he should start digging into the history of the Square."

"But the crime happened practically inside the Square," I pointed out.

"Yes, but last time you asked him to research property records. That was where the trouble started. This time, we'd just be asking for a little local scuttlebutt. I'm sure it will be fine. And he *is* really good at it."

While it was true that Liam had uncovered more information than I had hoped for the last time I had given him a research assignment, it was a little weird the way she pointed that out twice.

"Does he remember doing any of that?" I asked sharply.

"No," Audrey said. But her cheeks were flaming red.

"What *has* he said?" I pressed.

"He doesn't remember you asking him to do anything, I swear," she said, pressing her hands together earnestly. "I think it's just because he enjoyed doing research in college is why he brings it up all the time. But he really has it in his head that what he wants to do with his life is something that involves that sort of thing."

"Like what?" I asked.

"The thing he keeps bringing up is being a private investigator," she said, and gave me a look that was almost like a wince.

"Well, maybe you're right, and he doesn't remember what he did for me. Because after that, he was fired up to write a secret history of the neighborhood. Like a book or something," I said.

"Yes," Audrey agreed, but too quickly.

"I feel like you know something you're not telling me," I said. "Or you suspect something."

"Okay, sometimes I think he might remember a little, but not like a remembered experience. And certainly not remembered facts! Steph destroyed all the evidence of his notes. Without something to refer to, nothing is triggering that memory," she said.

"But?" I prompted.

"But I think sometimes he remembers what it felt like to be useful in that way, and that emotional memory is pushing him towards this path he wants to take. Maybe," she said. "I'm not as intuitive as some people, and he can't really explain what he means when he's talking about it. It's just my gut sense."

"This could be dangerous, asking for his help," I said.

"I know. But I think he can handle it," she said.

"And you really want to give him another dopamine hit of discovering something useful," I sighed. I threw up my hands. "Fine. Ask him. But if it all goes wrong, you're the one who's going to be explaining it to Steph this time."

"Nothing is going to go wrong, I swear!" she said.

I watched her thumbs fly over her phone's screen as she texted Liam.

And I really hoped she was going to be right about that.

CHAPTER

ELEVEN

As eager as he was to help, Liam texted back that he needed time to do the digging we had asked him to do. So in the end I went back to the bookshop and opened it for business for all the afternoon.

But no customers came in, and neither Houdini nor I felt like getting back to our own fruitless research pursuits. We just sat behind the tall apothecary desk that was the bookshop's checkout counter and stewed silently together.

About the middle of the afternoon, Houdini lifted his head to look at me. "Did you wish I was there yesterday? When you were at the party?"

"No, not at all," I assured him. "I know you feel safer staying out of sight, and I understand that. And if you'd been there, what could you have done? I still would've set fire to everything and run away, I'm sure."

"Maybe that man wouldn't have bothered you if I had been there to put him off," Houdini said.

Which actually was quite likely. Small as he was—he didn't quite top ten pounds soaking wet—he had a fierce bark. Well, fiercely annoying. But someone looking for a random target to make his girl-friend jealous would be plenty motivated to find their target elsewhere.

"How about I just don't go to parties alone from now on?" I said instead.

"Parties are overrated," Houdini said huffily.

I couldn't exactly argue with that.

Just as it was getting close to closing time, I got a text from Audrey that she was closing her own shop and she and Liam were on their way over.

Which wasn't a great idea, but would probably be okay so long as we talked around the desk on the first floor. That was prosaic-friendly space, surrounded by shelves of bestselling paperbacks and an extensive children's books area. Nothing that Liam hadn't seen before. Nothing magical in sight.

But there was no way I was bringing him up to my special nook. *That* was definitely a bad idea.

Audrey came in the door first, smiling a little apologetic smile as the chime over the door tinkled merrily. Then Liam came in behind her, cheeks flushed more from excitement than from the July heat.

"I have so much to tell you both!" he gushed as soon as he was in the shop's darkened interior. "But Audrey said to wait until we were all together."

"I could've come over there," I said.

"This felt... better," Audrey said as she turned my sign to *closed* for me. Then she gave me a significant look, but what she was trying to communicate to me was beyond my ability to decipher.

I would have to remember to ask her later.

"I don't have more chairs here. Do you want to go back to the nook in the children's section? There are beanbags there," I said.

"Here is fine," Liam said, clearly eager to get started. He unslung the backpack from his shoulder and dug out a new Moleskine note-book, then slipped off the elastic strap to open it.

As new as the cover looked, as he flipped through the pages, I could see they were nearly all filled with his jagged writing. And some of the pages were dogeared.

Someone had clearly had a far more productive afternoon than I had.

"Right, so Audrey said the victim was a Jane Doe, but that's not true," he said when he had finally found the page he wanted to start from.

"It isn't?" I said in surprise.

"No. She had no ID on her when she was found, because her wallet and jewelry were all missing. But as soon as they brought her in, they verified her identity by her fingerprints pretty quickly. She was never classified as a Jane Doe. So the rumors you heard were a little wrong on that score."

"But who is she?" I asked. Then I braced to hear the answer. Letting the prosaic world know her magical name would have been very foolish indeed for Delilah Dare. And potentially dangerous to the rest of us. If Liam said her name now, I was going to have to run immediately to let the authorities know. And find a way to get ahold of Steph.

Why didn't I have a way to get ahold of Steph?

"Her name was Deborah Jean Taunt," he said, reading from his notes. "And she has... well, they don't call it a police record exactly. She was never suspected of a crime, but she's reported a few."

"Really," I said, flabbergasted. How much time had Delilah Dare spent in the prosaic world, anyway?

"Really," Liam said. "She had five restraining orders on various men, and she had reported more than that for stalking, although no one was ever charged. There was an investigation of an assault at some man's apartment, which was when she was originally finger-printed, apparently. But nothing came of that either."

"So are they assuming one of her boyfriends did this?" Audrey asked.

"Well, since everything she had on her was missing, it might just be a mugging," he said. "Or it might be an ex who took her stuff to make it *look* like a mugging. Strangling like that is kind of a crime of passion sort of thing."

"So she *was* strangled," I said. I wasn't sure why that made me feel so suddenly sad. Was there a *good* way to snuff someone's life out?

"Oh, yeah. That was very clear," Liam said, scanning through his notes. "I didn't see the crime photos myself, but the police officer I was talking to had been one of the first on the scene, and they were positive that's what had happened."

"So you didn't break any laws digging up this information for us?" Audrey said with a worried look.

"Oh, no. Just good old school investigative reporting," he said. At my sharp look, he colored a little. "I might've implied to a few people that I worked for the newspaper. But no one asked to see any credentials, so I never technically lied."

"What else did you find out?" Audrey asked.

"Let's see," he said, paging through his notebook again. "If you want me to type this up so you can read it, I can. It's mostly information on each of the stalking cases, names of the men involved, that sort of thing. I don't know if that's useful."

Neither did I. While I had no trouble believing Delilah had lead a double life, seducing prosaic men and then discarding them—if that was indeed what she'd been doing—I wasn't sure how any of them could ever have known where to find her.

Unless they'd lured her out. But any sort of text or phone call would be on her cellphone, which had likely been inside the purse that had not been found with her body.

"Ah!" Liam said, stopping on one of the pages of notes. "There is a camera over the comic book store door that should've recorded the entire crime. The angle it has covers the entire alley with no space to slip past it, and while the end of the alley is quite dark, they can tell from the recordings from previous nights that when raccoons are moving around that end, their motion is detected on the camera."

"Only nothing is on the camera for last night at all," I concluded for him.

"Well, yeah," Liam said, a little crushed that I had ruined his big reveal.

But I had already known that would be true. Raccoons wouldn't trigger the wards around the Tower, but any human being, even a prosaic, even Delilah herself, would.

And yet, it did narrow down the list of suspects, I suddenly realized.

"It covers the entire width of the alley in front of the shop, right?" I said, a shade too eagerly.

"Yes. There's a light over the door that reaches to the wall of the next building," he said. "No one crossed that area all night long. No one knows how Deborah Taunt got there at all, let alone how her killer got in and out. The camera's recording is flawless for the entire night, not a single moment of distortion or missing bit of time."

"But surely such things can be tampered with," Audrey said. I presumed in a desperate attempt to make sure Liam had something to blame that wasn't the Square itself.

"Oh, sure," he agreed. "And the men Deborah had been reporting to the police had all been very wealthy, every single one of them. A few might know how to hack such things themselves, maybe, but every single one of them had access to the money and connections to find someone else who would. The police are working on that angle right now."

"Well, that's a relief," I said with an exaggerated sigh. "It sounds like they'll have it all buttoned up soon enough. Not that I ever go down that alley after dark myself. But it's good to know they'll have someone in custody soon."

"Well, I *hope* so," Liam said, biting his lip nervously. "But sometimes these things take time. Or there isn't enough evidence to prosecute. Or a bunch of other stuff might happen or not happen. It's an imperfect world."

"I don't go down that alley either," Audrey assured him, and he gave her a grateful smile.

"Thanks for all this," I said. "You'll let us know when they catch someone?"

"Sure. I have a bunch of notifications set up on the keywords I'm watching," he said smugly. But if he wanted me to ask what that meant, I didn't bite. I just waited until he took the hint and put the notebook away. "Audrey, are you free now that the shop's closed?"

"Oh, I'm sorry, Liam. I promised Tabitha I'd help her with some inventory that arrived this morning," Audrey said. So convincingly, I started to wonder what inventory arrival I was blanking on at the moment.

"Oh, sure," he said, flushing again. "Well, I'll be in touch."

"Thanks again," Audrey said as she walked him to the door. He nodded, still flustered, a situation in no way improved when she pressed a grateful kiss to his cheek. But she somehow herded him out the door, turning the key in the lock once he was gone.

Then she turned to me with a happy smile.

"That was certainly interesting," I said. "But you do realize most of what he had for us wasn't actually useful now that we know the murderer had to have been a magical person."

"Sure," Audrey said with a shrug. "No one else could get through that circle of light on camera without detection. Unless they were a ninja or something. But Occam's razor and all that."

"Exactly!" I said.

Admittedly, deciding that something *had* to have been done by magic was almost exactly what William of Ockham *hadn't* meant.

But then again, he had been, like the majority of prosaics, quite convinced that magic wasn't really a thing. His logic was sound, given what he knew about the world.

But Audrey and I knew just a little bit more.

"Liam's list of stalkers isn't going to be any good, but I think it's still the right track," Audrey said.

"I agree. Delilah was probably behaving the same way in magical communities that she was in the prosaic neighborhood around her," I said. "The problem is, with the portal in the center of the Square, it's likely she was—acquiring stalkers, shall we say?—all over the world. So where do we start? With Taurus Vernon? Because he was seen leaving the Square party just after I did."

"I think I know that one too," Audrey said, looking even more smug than Liam had minutes before.

"I'm eager to hear what you have to say," I said.

"Barnardo Daley, of course," she said. "You're there when he comes into the teashop every morning. For someone who would like us to believe he almost never leaves his own apartment, he *always* knows all the gossip."

"You're right," I said. "Cleopatra and Cressida might know Delilah better, but they aren't going to divulge information like that willingly. But Barnardo, on the other hand, might divulge a little *too* willingly, if you follow me."

"Sure," Audrey admitted with a shrug. "He's prone to exaggeration. But that's what followup investigation is for. If we get a list of potential names from him, we can research all of them ourselves and see if there are any likely candidates."

"That sounds like a plan," I said. "Let's go see if he's home."

"I'm *not* going with you," Houdini said from his dog bed under the desk. I'd quite forgotten he was still there. But that probably wasn't the reason he sounded so sullen now.

No, he truly despised being around Barnardo's Miss Snooty Cat.

"Understood," I said. "I'll be back in time for dinner, but I'll understand if you don't want to wait for me."

"I can fetch my own kibble, as you well know," he said, even more sullen than before.

I traded a frown with Audrey. I was beginning to sense that Houdini, as much as staying inside the bookshop made him feel safer, was starting to go a little stir-crazy always being inside the same space. Even as immense as that space was.

But Audrey just shook her head at me. A problem for a different time. And I nodded then led the way to the back door that opened out onto the Square.

"I'm still going to ask Barnardo about Vernon Taurus, though," Audrey said as we stepped outside. "Cleopatra said he left the party, but Cleopatra isn't entirely trustworthy in my view."

"Mine either. Ask away," I said.

And we headed up the stairs to the cast-iron balcony of the second floor of the Square.

CHAPTER

TWELVE

Barnardo wasn't exactly surprised to see us when he opened the door to our knock.

So much so, the first thing he said was, "I hope you're hungry for leftover chili, because I warmed up the whole pot."

Well, I wasn't one to turn down free food. Audrey and I followed him into the little table in the corner of his kitchen where three places were already set.

"Barnardo, do you see the future?" I asked teasingly.

"No more than anybody else," he said almost wistfully. "We've all had all day to do our various digging, and I just knew you'd want to compare notes."

"What digging have you done?" I asked, but he was already shaking his head.

"Oh, no, Miss Tabitha. You're telling me first what *you* found out. Don't act like I don't know the two of you were out in the prosaic world looking for clues," he said.

So Audrey and I filled him in on what little we had gleaned from the crime scene, and then on what Liam had discovered.

Not that we mentioned Liam by name, of course. As much as I

trusted Barnardo, some secrets really needed to be kept... well, secret.

Barnardo must have had a greatly inflated sense of my internet searching skills by the time Audrey and I were done spinning our tales, but that was better than knowing we had a friend on the outside who just might know too much about the inside.

"So definitely someone from inside our community. Really, that is a pity," Barnardo said, pushing away his now-empty bowl of chili with a sigh.

"Better that than a cross-worlds crime, surely," Audrey said.

"No, I agree. It's just, one magical person killing another magical person, but going into the prosaic world to do it? That's very bad business," he said.

"I take it you no longer think I'm a suspect, then?" I said.

"Hm?" he said, as if I had pulled him out of other thoughts. "Oh. No, not at all. And no one else in the Square does now either, not after a day of talking it over."

"Any idea how they came to that conclusion?" Audrey asked. "I mean, what changed from this morning?"

"Mostly just giving it a little thought, honestly," Barnardo said. "The only reason to suspect our Miss Tabitha in the first place was motive. But it wasn't like she was the only one of us to get rubbed the wrong way by the Trio. And while setting fire to their little booth felt like a tiny bit of overkill, it was within the realm of being understand-able. But there is a big leap from that to murder. And most didn't think you were the kind to make such a leap." He ended with a careless shrug.

As much as I knew I should be relieved to have been cleared in the court of public opinion, I was mostly still hurt that I had been thought so little of for even as long as I was. Did I *look* like someone who could strangle a woman who had four inches' height on me?

Although I definitely outweighed her. Still, when strangling someone in an alleyway, it felt like height would matter.

"As nice as that is, I'm sure it's more that once word got around how she was killed, they all concluded it must have been a man who did it," I said.

"Oh. I hadn't thought of that. But yes, that does make sense," Barnardo said, still irritatingly casual about it all.

"But do you agree with what the two of us were thinking? That Delilah was stringing men along here as well as in the prosaic world?" Audrey asked, clearly just to redirect the conversation into less fraught territory.

"Oh, most definitely," he said. "But is that a surprise? Look at whose feet she's placed herself to learn."

"Cleopatra does this too?" I asked, kind of already knowing the answer.

"Yes, but it's not the same," Barnardo said with a little frown. "Cleopatra, I think, is just looking for a certain sort of fun. She's picky about who she associates with. She wants a partner she considers her equal. And unfortunately, she measures that in money; there's no getting around that. But I think it would be very wrong to think of her as a gold digger."

"Really?" I asked skeptically.

"She doesn't want to be whisked away by some rich man to live out her days in idle luxury in his fancy palace or anything remotely like that," Barnardo said, giving me a look like he wasn't even sure if I was joking.

"She likes running her business," Audrey guessed.

"And owning her own property and managing her own finances. All of that," Barnardo agreed. "She wouldn't give that up for anyone, I don't think. No, I should be very surprised to ever hear she was marrying at all. But if she did, I suppose it would be to a rich man. But one she was sure wouldn't try to control her. And I think she's pretty sensitive about how much anyone can ask of her before she finds them too controlling."

"So she's not a gold digger. But what about Delilah?" I asked.

"Cleopatra did tell us that Delilah keeps getting the wrong

message from her, right?" Audrey put in. "What if this is part of that?"

"Cleopatra said what?" Barnardo laughed.

"We talked to her this morning," I said, then gave him a very brief summation of how that interview had gone.

He was still chuckling to himself when I finished. Then he carried his bowl to the pot still on the stove to get another few ladles-full. He gestured at Audrey and me with the ladle, but we both politely declined.

Apparently, Audrey didn't like spice-free chili any better than I did. We'd have to compare notes later.

"That's all very interesting," Barnardo said as he slid back into his chair then added cheese, sour cream, and a generous sprinkling of green onions to the contents of his bowl. What had been half-full was now a heaping mound as he dug his spoon into it. "Here's what I can tell you. Cleopatra has no stalkers. I'm sure she's never even gone out into the prosaic world looking for men, as none of those would ever be someone she'd consider her equal. But she doesn't burn relationships here either. She told you she doesn't deal in jealousy, but I think it's more than that. All of her split-ups have been amicable. Which isn't to stay some of these men like this Taurus Vernon fellow don't leave with bad feelings. They just keep those feelings to themselves if they know what's good for them."

"Is Cleopatra really that powerful?" Audrey asked skeptically. And I was immensely grateful that she had been the one to ask that question when Barnardo just gawked at her.

"Is she really that powerful? She's more than that powerful," he said. "Her people are one of the oldest magical families in the United Kingdom. Her particular branch has been in the United States since the Gilded Age and is considered equally prominent. Neither of you have heard of the Manx Family *at all*?"

Audrey and I traded a glance, then both shook our heads.

"Sorry," I said. "Society stuff has never been one of my interests."

"They aren't just drivers of society. They are wealthy beyond reckoning. And they are all powerful wizards. Granted, many of them find silly little enterprises to pursue in their younger years. By which I mean their first century or so," he added in a conspiratorial whisper. "But they always take up the family business in the end. And no one knows how old the oldest of them are, since no one even knows which ones of them are still alive. Their birth and death records are held in complete secrecy inside their own vaults."

"That's insane," I said.

"Well, crossing her in any way would clearly be insane," Audrey said. "Can you imagine what that sort of family would do to a stalker?"

"Not that Cleopatra would need them to," Barnardo said. "She might not seem to be using her magic for much, but I assure you, since Agatha passed, she is the most powerful wielder of magic in this Square after the Wizard."

I felt a shiver run up my spine. But I didn't doubt his assessment. Not a bit.

"But what about Delilah?" Audrey asked. "Is her family old too?"

"She claims to be descended from Virginia Dare, but I assure you no one has ever believed that," Barnardo said almost cattily. Then he seemed to remember she was dead and flushed a little. "Well, as Cleopatra told you, she had no family to speak of. She came here fresh out of the academy, much like the two of you did. Cleopatra had hand-chosen her to be her apprentice in the magic of glamor as well as the running of her beauty shop. And she certainly seems to have taken to the magic readily enough."

"But is she... was she a gold digger?" Audrey asked.

"It's hard to remember she's gone, isn't it?" Barnardo mused. "I'm the only person in the Square who saw her body as the police carried it away, and yet it still doesn't feel real to me."

"I wasn't trying to police your verb tenses," Audrey said.

"I know, dear. I was just speaking my heart, I guess," he said. He ate in silence for a moment, then pushed the bowl away for a second time. "Delilah Dare wanted to be the next Cleopatra. But she didn't have that level of power, I don't think. Not enough to attain the extended lifetime of a true wizard. I very much doubt she expected to ever inherit the ownership of the Inanna Salon & Spa ever. Even if she outlived Cleopatra by some twist of fate, the Manx family would just claim the property and do with it what they would. So I suppose she had two choices before her. Open her own salon, which I doubt Cleopatra would look kindly on, or marry well enough that she could afford to walk away from her dead-end career path."

"Not everyone needs to have an always ascending career path," I said.

"No, of course not," Barnardo quickly agreed. "Look at me. I barely even have a job at all. And I'm definitely not looking for any more of one, I assure you."

I desperately wanted to ask just what his "barely even a" job was, but he was still talking.

"But Delilah wanted more than she had. That was pretty clear. And what she wanted, short of actually becoming Cleopatra, which was quite impossible, was any cast-off from Cleopatra she could catch hold of."

"Like Taurus Vernon," I said.

"Well, yes, but more than that," he said. Then he sat forward in his chair to dig into the back pocket of his trousers. He took out a scrap of parchment and unfolded it. Then he scanned the contents as if to be sure he had the right thing before flattening it out on the top of the table, then sliding it over to Audrey and me.

"He has a list of names," Audrey said to me with a grin.

"That is what we were hoping for," I agreed. "These are all men who dated Delilah?"

"Those men all dated *Cleopatra*," Barnardo clarified. "I think Delilah had a separate identity to hit the prosaic world of rich men because she had struck out with every single one of these first. But if you're looking to followup on her dating history, this would be where to start."

I looked over the list of five names, all written in Barnardo's showy cursive. None of the names were familiar to me.

"One last question," I said as I refolded the list, then slipped it away in my own pocket. "Taurus Vernon. Cleopatra said he left the party after I did?"

"Oh, he definitely did," Barnardo said. "He wasn't subtle about it. His plan to use you had backfired in such an explosive way—"

I guess I must have flinched at his word choices, because he suddenly came over all apologetic.

"Sorry, Tabitha. I know that wasn't your fault. But you have to agree, from an outside perspective, it was kind of the perfect end to his little jealousy scheme, right?"

"Maybe," was all I would concede.

But that was enough to put a smile back on his face. "Well, after all that went down, Taurus took one look at Cleopatra as she stood over the burning remains of her fancy mixed drinks booth. And she clearly blamed him for the whole thing. And she was very, very angry about it. In the end, she vented her spleen on Delilah, sure enough, but only because Taurus Vernon had already fled the scene. No, he was most definitely gone from the Square. Although the secret floors of the Foshay Tower have concierge services. If he went home straight away or not, someone in the building probably could tell you for sure."

"We'll check up on that," I said. "Thanks for dinner and especially for this list."

"I hope it helps," he said. "Because from what I've heard, our authorities won't touch anything dealing with this case until the local police department rules out every possible prosaic perpetrator. And knowing the prosaics, that could take months. Or forever."

"Even though this took place right at the base of the Tower?" I asked.

"Unless the Wizard makes a special request, I don't think they care," Barnardo said with a sad little shrug.

Yet another reason I wished I had some way to contact Steph.

And why didn't I? Just waiting around until he popped into existence in my airspace was no way to have any kind of friendship.

But I'd have to wait until the next time he popped in to even ask about it. Which was a little frustrating.

"What now?" Audrey asked as we emerged into the no-cooler July twilight.

"I think asking a bunch of questions is going to have to wait until tomorrow," I said. "Plus, I'm a little worried about Houdini. I think he's spending too much time alone. And here I've gone and eaten dinner without him when I told him I'd wait."

"You should definitely go see him," Audrey said. "I'm going to check in with Liam real quick to see if he's learned anything more. If he has, I'll let you know. Otherwise, I'll see you at breakfast?"

"Breakfast and investigation planning," I said. "See you then."

We walked together up to the third floor, but there our ways parted. And as soon as she was no more than five steps away from me, she broke into a light jog. Eager to hear from Liam, in what I was sure was going to be more of a call than a text.

Strange that should make me feel lonely. But I had a sort of dog waiting for me. Despite the heat, I hurried my own steps to the narrow stairs that led up to the veranda of my uncles' apartment.

CHAPTER

THIRTEEN

As soon as I was inside my uncles' apartment, I went into the kitchen. I always left a light in there for Houdini, and it was still on, but there was no sign of the dog. His bowl was still sparklingly clean from when I had washed it last, and the water bowl was full. I rinsed out the water bowl and refilled it with fresh, cool water. Then I sat down in the little nook where the dining table was tucked in between two bench seats like a booth in a particularly tiny restaurant. I rested my chin on my hands and mulled things over.

My own feelings were so conflicted. Every encounter I'd ever had with Delilah had been deeply unpleasant, and if all her interactions with men had been as self-interested as they seemed, it was hard to imagine she might be a good person on the inside if I just put myself in her shoes. There wasn't enough empathy in the world for that, I was pretty sure.

And yet I still felt kind of sad that she was gone.

Maybe it was just the way she had been killed that was so upsetting. Had anything she'd done been so terrible that she deserved that ending? I mean, her interest in the men she pursued had been decid-

105

edly selfish. But she had never pretended otherwise, had she? A rich man looking to date a woman who put so much energy into being pleasing to the eye couldn't exactly be surprised that she was only looking that way to land a rich man.

Not like Cleopatra, whom I had to admit I was seeing in a different light now. I still didn't get going all-in on one narrow idea of what being beautiful meant, but she was clearly just doing it to reflect to the world how she felt about herself. I both got it and didn't get it at the same time.

I mean, the world was full of more books than I would ever have time to read. Giving up reading time for anything else was always hard for me to understand. And yet other people did it all the time.

Even more puzzling, though, was Cressida. How did she fit into everything?

Because she really didn't seem to fit. Not for lack of trying, of course. She had pursued mimicking Cleopatra with the same level of success as Delilah, at least as it came to outward appearance. I had no idea what her relationships with men were like, if she even had any.

I reached up to touch my hair again. It was still maintaining its composure despite the humidity. I hadn't been sparking so badly that day, but only because I still felt drained from all the fire I had created the night before. I wondered if its properties would fade before I got a chance to really test it.

I was still twisting a curl around my fingers when I suddenly noticed Houdini standing in the doorway between the kitchen and the living room. He was shivering. Not a strange thing for a rat terrier chihuahua to do.

Only he was also dripping wet. And it hadn't rained in days.

"Houdini! What happened? Why are you all wet?" I asked as I bolted out of the booth to scoop him up. He jumped to meet me half-way, shivering in my arms and pressing close against my chest. The smell coming off of him was so intense I nearly put him back down again. "Why do you smell like the river?"

"I can tell you everything, but please clean me up first," he said miserably.

I carried him up to my bedroom and brought him into the shower. He let me wash him all over, although it took three repeats of the shampoo to get the fishy algae smell out of his hair.

Now he smelled like lavender, like everything in my uncles' apartment generally did. But he didn't complain. He just let me towel him off until he was mostly dry, then ran into the bedroom to curl up on the bed. He curled up so tightly his head was hidden under his own back knee, eyes well out of sight.

I had gotten more than a little wet in the process of his shower, and was starting to smell like the river myself. I had a quick rinse, then towel off and got dressed in clean clothes before joining Houdini on the bed. He uncurled from his tight ball to move onto my lap, but curled up miserably again once he was there.

"Did someone hurt you?" I asked as I stroked his head, careful not to touch his ears. He hated to have his ears touched.

"No, this was all my doing," he said.

"What happened?"

He took a moment to collect his thoughts. Then he said, "After you left, I thought I would do a little exploring. So I went out into the alley. My earliest memories were there, you know. From when Agatha found me, just out of my egg, when I was still a dragonet."

"I remember," I told him, keeping my voice calm, although inside I was panicking a little. He had gone outside the Square? Without telling me first?

But this wasn't the time to chastise him. "She found you at the base of the Tower. Very close to where Delilah was murdered. Is that why you went?"

"Sort of," he said. "You were talking about that spot, and I remembered Agatha finding me. But I had never been back since, and I wanted to see it again. I wasn't really thinking I would find anything to help you catch whoever killed Delilah. I just wanted to see."

"Okay," I said. "But how did you get wet? It's not raining, and what puddles there are in that alley are too small to drench even you."

"No, I avoided those puddles, thank you very much," he said testily. "I went down the sewer access point in the back of the alley."

"The sewer access point?" I said. "I didn't see anything like that."

"It's right at the base of the Tower," Houdini said. "You know the Tower is round, although the wall in the alley appears to be straight. If you aren't past the widest point of the Tower base, all you see is what the warding spells are telling you is there."

"We should've crossed the tape," I mumbled to myself.

"I knew it was there from before," he said, as if trying to make me feel better about missing it.

"So there's like a manhole cover back there?" I asked.

"No, it's more like an open grate for runoff. But I could fit through it," he said.

"Houdini! That was incredibly dangerous! You absolutely should not have been doing that alone!" I said. "What if you'd gotten hurt? I'd have no idea where you even were. How could I have gotten there to help you?"

"I know! I know!" he wailed in my mind. "I quickly realized I had made a very foolish mistake. My only excuse can be that my dragonet mind, which should be equivalent to a human your age, is trapped in the body of this dog, who is still technically a puppy. I was too impulsive. It won't happen again."

"So you fell?" I asked.

"Through the grate, into an underground stream. There's been no real rain in weeks, so I guess that stream is always there," he said.

"There are a few like that in Minneapolis," I told him. "They built streets over them back when the city was young, and after decades of building higher and higher, a lot of people don't even know they're down there. But they are. Did you end up in the river?"

"No, I climbed out of the stream at a sort of quay," he said. "Then I was in a dry tunnel, but I could smell that someone had been by there recently. So I followed it. I followed it for what felt like forever. But I didn't follow it to its end. It was just too far. I wonder where it goes?"

"I wonder too," I said. "Maybe I should go check it out. You're sure someone had used it recently?"

"I could smell alcohol and a sort of fire smell," he said. "But yesterday the whole Square smelled like alcohol and fire."

"That's probably my fault," I admitted. "But if someone left the party through that tunnel, now I really want to know where it goes."

"I'm afraid I can't show you," he said, trembling all over again. "I had to swim against the current to get back. It was so tiring, I didn't think I would make it. And then I had to scramble up a moldy old rope to get back out through the grate. I don't even know how I did it. I think I unleashed a little of the dragon in me to do it. All I know is that I found myself standing in the back of the alley, dripping wet and no wiser than when I had gone down that hole in the first place."

"Oh, I think you're a little wiser," I said. "Don't worry about it. Audrey and I can take it from here. Probably not at night, though."

"I'm sorry, Tabitha," he said, still shaking like a leaf. I hugged him tighter, pulling a blanket up and over him in case he really was cold.

"I don't know what I'm going to do with you," I said. "It's not like I can give you a cellphone to take with you for emergencies. We're going to have to figure some other way out."

"I bet Steph knows something that will work," Houdini said with complete confidence.

"I bet he does too," I said. "The only problem is, he doesn't have a cellphone either. So far as I know, anyway. And there are no doors into the Tower that I can see. I have no idea how to get his attention if I need it."

"He generally tends to show up when he's needed," Houdini said.

"I'm not going to fling myself into danger just to have a conversation with him," I said.

Although I was half-tempted to do just that.

But it was late, and Houdini was exhausted. Everything could wait until morning.

Or past that, actually. Because the first thing I was going to do in the morning was find my way downtown and talk to the authorities. Maybe they knew about the tunnel already. And maybe they knew about Delilah Dare's prosaic alter ego.

But maybe they didn't. And if they didn't, they really should.

FOURTEEN

agical communities are scattered all throughout the prosaic world, but they are always hidden. The Square looks like a hulking granite building from the outside, mostly windowless and uninviting. Only magical people can get inside and see the wonders of the Square, with its hedge maze and gardens and apartments set behind cast-iron railings that would put the French Quarter to shame.

I had lived in a lot of places like that, all over the world. But since coming to Minneapolis the month before, I had yet to actually leave the Square. I knew there were several hidden levels in the upper third of the Foshay Tower where magical people lived, and it was always described as a very posh neighborhood, even by magical standards, but I had never been there.

And I knew that the authorities who regulated our magical communities were located in a hidden building under downtown, but I had never been there either. Audrey had gone there a few times to speak to the advocate about the legal matters pertaining to her great-aunt's death, but I had always stayed behind in the Square with Houdini.

I held onto that last fact pretty tightly—that Audrey had been there and back multiple times on her own—as I left Houdini still sleeping on the bed and headed out into the early morning in the Square. Audrey could do more magic than I could, but that still wasn't much. If she was traveling back and forth on her own, she hadn't been teleporting or even using the portal at the heart of the hedge maze.

So there had to be another way.

Only I didn't exactly know what it was.

But I wasn't worried. I just wandered from storefront to storefront until I found one that was open. It just happened to be the Bitter Brew Coffeeshop, but that was all right.

If anyone owed me a favor, it was Titus Bloom. Not that I blamed him for what his wife had done. He had certainly done his part to save Houdini and me from her in the end.

But I hadn't forgotten how he had tried to push Audrey out of the teashop business. He might have been gently persuasive, but it still irked me that he had done it at all.

As I pushed my way into his shop, I could see his balding, olive-skinned head bent over something behind the counter. But he looked up at once at the sound of my footsteps approaching, his warm brown eyes registering surprise.

"Well, good morning, Tabitha," he said, putting aside whatever he had been focusing on. "I must admit, I never expected you to come in my door. Can I get you something? Anything you want, on the house."

"I was just hoping you could tell me how to get to the authorities downtown," I said. "I've never been. There must be a way to get there without going through the prosaic world, right?"

Because traveling through the prosaic world was going to involve a knowledge of bus schedules and street corners that I definitely didn't have.

"Of course," he said, but I could see my question had caught him off guard. It was taking him a moment to formulate what he wanted to say next. "You know she's not there anymore, right?" he said at last.

"She who?" I asked, confused.

He blinked at me in even more confusion. "Well, Nell. She's been moved to a different facility out east," he said.

"Oh, this isn't about Nell," I rushed to assure him. "No, I need to talk to them about Delilah Dare, actually. I might know some things that could be helpful."

"That sounds like you," he said, almost fondly. Then he turned to fuss with something on the shelf behind him. When he turned back, he was holding a blue plastic card out to me. "This is like a Metro card, but it works in the witches' underground. I don't need it anymore, but it still has a few uses on it."

"What do I do with it?" I asked as I took it from him. It was shaped like a credit card, only featureless with no writing of any kind on it. It was also a little bit heavier than a credit card, like the core was something other than plastic, maybe. I put it in my back pocket.

"Just tap the turnstile, same as a prosaic metro," he said. Then he gave me a considering look. "I seem to remember you were in school in Manhattan for a time?"

"That's right," I agreed, although I had no idea where he would've acquired that information. It had only been for a few weeks, and it wasn't like I talked to anyone in the Square about my past besides Audrey. Who definitely wasn't chatting and catching up with Titus Bloom.

"So just like there," he said. "Of course it's not a train. We don't have New York City's abundance of disused subway tunnels to take advantage of."

"So what is it?" I asked.

"It's a boat," he said. "Don't worry. You'll get used to it. It's a little nerve-wracking the first time you go under the falls, but I assure you those spells have been up for generations. You'll be fine."

I dry-swallowed. Just the image his words evoked was setting my heart to racing. I couldn't wait to experience it for myself.

"Where do I catch a boat?" I asked.

"There's a quay under the pub," he said. "That's why the door there is always open."

I had never tried to get into the pub after-hours, so I didn't know it was always open. But my mind was already charting a mental map between the pub basement and the location I had in mind from what Houdini had described to me the night before.

I didn't think the two would overlap. But they likely ran parallel.

"Here," Titus said, and filled a small to-go cup with coffee from an urn behind him. He snapped on a cover and handed it to me. "French roast. Because you look like a young woman who enjoys a rich dark roast."

"I'm afraid I'm completely out of cash," I said, hands up to refuse the drink.

He glanced up at my hair and sort of chuckled, but then thrust the cup out at me again. "Like I said, it's on the house. It'll settle your nerves on your first trip downtown."

That wasn't the effect that caffeine usually had on me, but I opted not to argue. I thanked him for his help and the coffee both, then headed back out into the Minneapolis dawn to cross the Square towards the pub.

The door was indeed unlocked. There was no sign of any of the Wolseys, but the minute I hesitated in the middle of the open space a magical arrow illuminated before me, directing me through the darkened kitchen, down into the cellar, and out a door at the back.

I was grateful the arrow was guiding me. Without its light, I would be underground in total darkness. But it patiently showed the way down a narrow passage of stone walls that looked like part of a castle from the Middle Ages. The passage opened up onto a quay of similar stone that looked like it should be slick underfoot but was surprisingly grippy to the bottoms of my sneakers.

That was a good thing, as the stream that ran past that quay was all swiftly moving murky water of unknown depths. That stream emerged from total darkness and returned to total darkness a few feet to either side of me. But judging from the echoes, it ran on forever in both directions.

And there was no one in sight anywhere. It was more than a little spooky.

The arrow ended its journey by pointing out the turnstile, and I dutifully took out my card and tapped it on top of the structure.

This wasn't a modern turnstile with any kind of reader. It looked like it had been down here since the 1930s. And maybe it had. But when a boat emerged from the darkness to my left to dock itself neatly at the quay, I pushed at the bar in front of me and it turned nicely. It might be as old as it looked, but if so, it was very lovingly maintained. Because all the damp in the air just had to be a rust-causing nightmare.

I stepped down into the boat, then settled on the bench without spilling a drop of that coffee. The minute I was properly seated, the boat moved away from the quay, out into the middle of that roaring stream. We quickly plunged into the inky black beyond the quay, and for a horrible instant, I was terrified this whole journey was going to take place in total darkness.

But then a lantern I hadn't even noticed that was hanging over the prow of the boat slowly started to glow, starting as a dark black-ish-green, then building to a bright but familiar light. It was like the light that came from the phosphorescent fungus that lined the caves in the weird woman Volumnia's place. She had some of it in a lantern as well.

It was possible this was some local magic I hadn't read about before coming into town, but I kind of doubted it. Volumnia had spoken of times long past at Agatha's wake, and I had gotten the sense that she, like Agatha, had measured her life in centuries more than decades. And there was just something about the green glow that felt like ancient nature magic. Not modern flashy magic.

I took a sip of the coffee, mostly because the air underground was damply chilly and the warmth in my belly was a comfort. But the caffeine, as I had predicted, did *not* calm my nerves.

And then the stream took a sudden downward plunge, not quite a waterfall but pretty close. This went on for nearly ten seconds. My panicked brain distracted itself by trying to guess at the math of how far down I was going, but with nothing to gauge my speed on, all it could do was guess.

Then the stream flattened out again. Only what was overhead was no longer an arching stone structure. No, this was all water. Water that passed overhead as if I were in one of those walk-through aquariums. Only I could tell there was no glass between me and all that water.

There was nothing but magic between me and the mighty Mississippi. And not just any part of the Mississippi either. I could tell by the churn that I was under the St. Anthony Falls. And not its current incarnation. No, this was the falls as they'd been before a collapsing tailrace tunnel underneath it had permanently altered its form.

The morning light was diffuse and brownish-green through all that water, but I almost thought I could make out the sky far above.

Then I was back in a tunnel, only this time I was climbing a water flume back up to a level equal to the river behind me.

The pace was slower here, and I could hear the sounds of the water sloshing against the walls of the tunnel and the sides of the boat. The rushing roar was gone, and it was actually a relaxing ride. I sipped my coffee, mostly looking up to catch the occasional glimpse of a manhole cover far above me. I could even see a car or two driving over those covers through the holes in the center.

The boat bumped up against another quay, but this one was far larger. It ran the length of a city block, and all under the same street to judge by the light filtering down through those manhole covers. There were still only a few other people around, and they all looked to be in a tremendous, nervous hurry. But once I was out of the boat, it was simple enough to fall into step with the others and let the flow of the crowd carry me across what looked like a sort of waiting area with benches and even vending machines until I reached a set of double doors.

I was in a building atrium, although being still underground, there was no sign of any windows. The crowd that had swept me through the doors was parting ways now, some heading for staircases and escalators, all going down, and others waiting at a bank of elevators. I looked around for a help desk but found myself instead standing in front of a massive wall of different colors of granite.

The granite was cut so that the different colors formed an art deco sort of image. It reminded me a lot of the aluminum mural in the Empire State Building depicting that skyscraper with beams of light emanating from the top of it. This was like that, but of a Richardsonian Romanesque skyscraper I actually recognized from my research before moving to Minneapolis.

It was the Metropolitan Building, originally known as the Northwestern Guaranty Loan Building. There was no mistaking it.

Only it had been demolished decades ago in 1961.

And, of course, it, unlike the building in the mural I was looking at, had never been upside down.

FIFTEEN

Once I found the help desk on the far end of the atrium, it only took a few moments to get from there to Sheriff Jane MacMorris' office on the fourteenth floor.

Fourteen floors *below* the atrium, of course.

But every room I passed was lined with magical windows. Some showed what likely would be the view of Minneapolis if the Metropolitan Building was still standing upright on the surface. But others showed desert landscapes, or forest scenery, or beach views of a blue ocean and even bluer skies. The offices I passed were all light and airy and marvelously spacious, and the people working there were rushing about industriously, but they all seemed happy in their work. Not a one of them passed me in the corridors without at least giving me a smile if not a full "good morning!"

So it was a little surprising to open the door to the sheriff's office to find an extremely cramped and scruffy space. There were no windows, and the one light that hung from the ceiling above had a very unpleasant yellowish tinge to it. The room itself could barely contain what furniture was crammed within it.

A reception desk stood between the two closed doors on the

opposite side of the room, but no one was sitting there. There was a stack of folders and papers in the wire inbox on the corner of its battered wood surface, but no sign that anyone ever actually sat there. No name plate, no sign of a coffee or tea mug, no jacket or umbrella hanging from the hook on the wall behind the chair.

There were two hard-backed chairs against the wall beside the door I had entered from. Presumably a waiting area. But what good would it do to sit down and wait if no one knew I was even here?

"Hello?" I called uncertainly. How much trouble would I get in if I just tried one of the closed doors? Neither was marked in any way.

But then one of them opened, and a familiar head of pale blond hair poked out. It was Deputy Eric Fluellen, so far as I knew, the sheriff's only deputy. His eerily dark brown eyes blinked at me.

"Oh, Tabitha..." he trailed off, unable to recall my last name.

"Greene," I told him. "I was hoping to speak with the sheriff. Is she in?"

"No, and I don't expect she will be today," he said with a nervous cluck of his tongue.

"Nothing bad, I hope?" I said. Which, on one level, was completely true. I *did* hope that nothing bad had happened.

But if something had, I really wanted to know more. Like was it at all related to what had happened to Delilah? Had her killer struck again?

Because that would change a lot about what Audrey and I were digging into in Delilah's personal life.

But Eric was already shaking his head. "No, just a lot of meetings with the ruling council. Politics," he said, rolling his eyes. But then they lit up with a sudden thought. "Although, if you had something important to report, I could call her away from those meetings to deal with it. If it were urgent?"

"No, I'm afraid not," I said. "I just wanted to talk to her about the Delilah Dare case."

"Well, technically, that's not a case in our docket," he said. "Not until the prosaic investigators abandon it or pass it on to us."

"That's something they can do? Like, they literally ask you to take over?" I asked.

"Not as such, but close enough," he said. "Why don't you come into my office? I'll try to answer your questions, as much as I can."

"Thank you," I said, and followed him into a room that was surely the same size as the one I had just left. Losing one chair and having only the single doorway gave it a sense of being larger than the last. But there was still no window, and the light was, if anything, even more sickly yellow in hue than the other.

"How can you stand to be in here all day?" I asked with a shudder.

"Hmm?" he said distractedly. Then he looked around the room as if noticing it for the first time. "Oh, I'm never here *all* day. I'm usually out with the sheriff doing on-scene work. But even when I'm doing reports and paperwork, I usually take it to the cafeteria on the twelfth floor. They have better coffee."

"And light, I'd imagine," I said.

"The windows there are currently set to a view across the plains of Antarctica. I feel cooler just looking at all that blue and white," he said with a little smile. "Now, what's your first question?"

"Actually, I had some information to provide to you," I said.

"Do you?" he said, and slid his chair to one side to fight a sticking drawer in the side of his desk open. Then he pulled out a digital notebook and woke it up with a tap of his stylus. It lit up to a blank page, but Eric quickly scrawled the date and time in the corner, then added my name underneath it. "Greene with an 'e'?"

"That's right," I said.

"All right. What do you have to report?" he asked, stylus poised.

"If you're in contact with the prosaic police investigation, you probably already know about Delilah's alias?" I guessed.

"Deborah Taunt, yes," he said, but wrote it down anyway.

"And you also know that the camera in the alley didn't pick up anything," I said.

"Because of the Tower," he said as he wrote.

"Yes, but not just," I said.

He looked up at me and raised an eyebrow, but said nothing.

"The camera in front of the comic book shop covers the width of the alley directly in front of its door. That is perpendicular to the Tower and its obfuscation effects," I said. "It ran all night long without interference or time gaps or any kind of glitch. But no one crossed in front of it the entire night. Not Delilah, and not her killer."

Instead of writing this down, the deputy sat back in his chair and absentmindedly tapped his stylus against his teeth. Then he gave me a conspiratorial look. "I don't speak to the prosaics myself. I'm not sure how Jane—I mean, the sheriff—gets the information herself, but I'm curious now whether she saw the entire tape herself, or if she just had the lack of findings presented to her. Am I to believe that you have seen it yourself?"

"Oh, no," I rushed to say. "No, like the sheriff, I just had it described to me. But someone who knows what to look for should definitely check it out, don't you think? I got the story from a prosaic who was certain the tape wasn't tampered with. But he meant not tampered with by prosaic means."

"Well, very few mages could fool that level of technology without leaving some sort of trace," he said. "Few, but not none." He made a note on his tablet, then marked it with a large star. "Please bear in mind these are not the first notes that the sheriff and I have made about the Delilah Dare case, but that doesn't change the fact that, officially, there is no case until the prosaics hand it over, or we have real proof that a user of magic was involved."

"So you can't look at the tape yourselves without having it be an official case? Even though the tape might be the proof you need that someone was using magic?" I asked.

He lifted his hands palms-up in frustrated surrender. "That's the way it goes sometimes."

I nodded, chewing at my lip.

I wondered how hard it would be for Liam to find a copy of that tape. Or how hard it would be to find someone who knew what to look for to find signs of magic use on it. Would I have to get the Wizard himself involved somehow?

But maybe it wouldn't matter after I told the deputy the rest of what I was there to report.

"There is one more anomaly in the alley that I don't think the prosaic police investigators are aware of," I said. "There's a storm drain in the back corner of the alley, one that is large enough for a human to get in and out of if they removed the metal grate. It's tucked behind the curve of the Tower, so someone standing at the point where they taped off the alley wouldn't see it at all. Not even if they were magic-users. And I believe it hides itself from casual investigation by prosaics as well. I think they missed seeing it all together."

"The Tower does make a lot about this case problematic," he said as he scribbled on his notepad. "But if you're thinking the killer escaped through the storm drain, that doesn't make it any more likely to be our problem than theirs."

"I think someone should check out that drain, though," I said.

And here's where things got sticky. I hadn't been down there myself. Houdini had. But there was no way I was going to tell the deputy or even the sheriff that my dog—who wasn't my familiar—could tell me things like what he had seen on his little adventure. They would want to know how he could talk, which would lead to questions of what he really was.

And Eric was looking at me a little skeptically.

"I didn't want to go down there," I said. "But I could see from the angle it ran that it wasn't connected to the stream that runs from the Square to here. But it does seem to run somewhere. The whole underground system is mapped, isn't it?"

"The parts in official use are," he said slowly. Which was the answer I had been afraid of.

But it wasn't remotely strange. Most cities I had lived in had parts of their underground structures magically hidden for our use from the prosaics. But there was always far more that was hidden from us as well.

The truth was, most magical places contained their own magic. They arose through their own means. Witches didn't create them. They just found and exploited them.

Some people knew how to find more secret places than others. And a lot of those people liked having secret places to do fairly anti-social things.

Like running away from the scene of a murder. Or a spree of murders.

"I can go down to the records department and review the maps myself," he said, putting another star on the tablet. "That doesn't involve any paperwork if I go when my friend Lee is on duty, so the fact that this isn't an open case won't matter."

"Then what?" I asked.

"Then it depends on what the maps show," he said. "If there is a tunnel, and it goes somewhere interesting, that might be enough to start an investigation. But in all likelihood, if I find anything at all, it's just going to be more details to add to these notes, which won't technically exist until the investigation is open."

Behind me, I could hear the sound of someone coming into the reception area from the corridor. They shut the door behind them, then coughed loudly. It sounded like a man.

"I'm afraid that's all the time I have for you right now, but I promise to contact you if I learn anything at all that I can share," he said. "You're at the bookshop in the Square, right?"

"That's right," I said, getting up from the chair just in time for him to almost physically shoo me out of his office. The middle-aged man waiting in front of the reception desk with his fists planted on his hips started to speak, but stopped when Eric held up a single finger.

"I would tell you to leave the rest to us, if only I thought you'd listen," he said as he opened the door to the corridor to escort me out. "We're doing all we can."

I bit my tongue to keep from saying, "which is nothing." I just nodded.

"Right. Please stay out of trouble. I'll be in touch."

And then I was standing in the corridor, staring at a closed door.

But at least the light in the hallway was a more pleasant shade of white.

I made my way back to the elevators and up to the atrium, not quite sure what I was going to do next. Explore the tunnel, or interrogate everyone from Delilah's previous love life?

Or see if Liam could find out who or what was passing information from the prosaic police force to the magical one? Only that felt a lot like thrusting him back into mind-wiping danger. As curious as I was, there was no way I could ask him to do that.

Because he was far too likely to succeed.

CHAPTER

SIXTEEN

When I got back to the Square, I went straight to the Loose Leaves Teashop to talk to Audrey. It was a little too late in the morning to expect to meet Barnardo picking up his daily supply of medicinal tea.

Still, when I went inside, Audrey wasn't alone. Liam was with her.

And it kind of looked like I had stepped into an argument in progress. There was a tension to the air, and his cheeks were heated. Granted, it was warm even with the Pacific Northwest breezes blowing through the open windows. And he had the kind of peaches-and-cream complexion that flushed really easily.

But his body language was tense with frustration as well.

And, for her part, Audrey looked more than a little freaked out. Even as she met my eyes, she kept tucking her hair behind her ears over and over again, like she was caught in a loop she couldn't break.

"What's going on?" I asked, stopping three steps inside the shop and half-turning back to the door. If they needed a private moment, I would make myself scarce in a heartbeat.

"You've been here before, right?" Liam said to me, a little too loudly in clear exasperation.

"Almost every day since I came to town," I said, but slowly. I wasn't sure what he was driving at. I should probably be extra careful with my answers.

"So you know there's only ever been one of these teapots," he said, gesturing towards the tray sitting on the counter between the two of them.

It was, indeed, one-of-a-kind. It had been Agatha's favorite, and we had always used it with the matching single pair of cups and saucers for our breakfast together. And now Audrey and I used the same set. They were amusing, from a distance looking like antique China, but up close the blue drawings on white porcelain depicted scenes of death and destruction. I thought they were illustrations from an old edition of the book *The War of the Worlds* with alien spaceships destroying an English village, but I had never asked where Agatha had gotten them.

"Yeah?" I said, even more slowly than before. My danger sense was off the charts, but I still wasn't sure what had him so upset.

Audrey was shaking her head at me over and over again. I was clearly stepping in it.

"Why do you ask?" I said to Liam as Audrey buried her face in her hands.

"I mean, you broke this the other day," he said. He gestured at the tea set again, with the air of someone who was afraid to touch what they're talking about. "On the Fourth of July, you smashed this whole tea set."

Oh, right. Audrey had said that was how he had remembered me smashing every single breakable thing inside the shop. Seeing everything in the shop put to rights hadn't tripped him up.

But that single tea set that he clearly recalled seeing broken, that was tripping him up hard.

"Of course I had to replace it," I lied smoothly. "It was my mistake. You saw what happened." My voice lifted at the end of that sentence despite my best efforts to keep it level. I couldn't help it. I wanted to ask what he remembered. How could I respond if I didn't know what was in his head?

"Audrey said it was one-of-a-kind, hand-painted by a woman who died a decade ago!" he said.

"When did she say that?" I asked.

Audrey, behind her hands, squeaked a little, miserably.

"Weeks ago!" he said.

"Agatha had a second set in the storeroom that Audrey didn't know about?" I offered. He just shot me a furious glare.

"I can tell when I'm being lied to," he said. "Never mind. I don't care. Something weird is going on here, but no one is going to be honest with me. I'm just going to go."

"Liam, wait!" Audrey finally lifted her face out of her hands to say. But he was already out the door.

"Sorry," I said. "I wasn't prepared to lie. I mean, I was *willing* to. I just wasn't prepared. And, like you said, I'm not very good at it."

"Me neither, apparently," she said, blinking back angry tears. "And I'm twice stupid for not hiding this tea set away. I just avoided him asking me about it yesterday by dragging him to the bookshop. I should've remembered it triggers his memory. What if he remembers everything?"

"I don't know how that spell works," I admitted. "I could ask Steph, if I had a way of getting ahold of him."

"In the meantime, I'll just put this away," Audrey said, carrying the tray to the back room and dumping out the tea. She filled the skin with soapy water, and I grabbed a towel to dry.

As we washed and dried the tea set and wrapped the pieces in clean paper to store well out of sight, I told Audrey all about Houdini's adventure and my trip to the sheriff's office that morning.

"Do you think we should go look at that tunnel?" she asked as we went back out into the teashop. She filled the electric kettle and switched it on.

"I think the deputy really didn't want me to, but he didn't quite tell me *not* to," I said.

Audrey was reaching for our usual canister of tea, but changed her mind at the last minute and hopped up onto the counter to reach a different canister sitting on the highest shelf. Apparently, if we breakfasted at nine instead of eight, that called for a different variety of tea? Not that it mattered to me. Anything Audrey brewed was always good.

I went out to our usual table, but stopped when I saw a familiar backpack sitting on one of the chairs. "This is Liam's?"

"Yes, he had more information to share with us, I think," Audrey said with a sigh.

"He has to come back for this, right?" I said, picking it up and putting it in the office behind the counter. "That's something."

"I still don't know what to tell him when I see him again. Only I really wish it could just be the truth," she said glumly.

"There must be a way to do that," I said. "My uncle is married to a prosaic. There must've been a point before they were married when he could tell Frank everything. I mean, there *had* to be, right?"

"It's so rare, though," Audrey said. "And Liam is worse than the two of us at digging in places no one wants you to be looking. I think whatever the standard protocol might be for dating a prosaic, they're probably going to have extra precautions for someone like Liam."

"Our law enforcement has a way of communicating with theirs," I said. "Why can't Liam be something like that?"

"Because he's unemployed, and he's only helping us? Who aren't supposed to be doing this, anyway?" she said with a shrug.

"There must be a way he can take a vow or something," I said grumpily. "Or there ought to be."

The kettle whistled and Audrey poured steaming water into the teapot, then wrapped the whole thing in a towel before bringing it over to our table.

"I suppose you could ask your uncle when he's home," she said as she sat down across from me. We both grabbed a croissant from the plate on the tray. Despite the delay in our breakfast, they were still warm.

Almost like magic.

But probably just from Audrey's warming drawer.

"I can ask the next time I call him on the phone," I said.

"What was that sigh for?" Audrey asked.

"What?"

"You just made the most wistful sort of sigh in the world," she said. "When you said the word 'phone.' Do you miss your uncles that much? Or were you thinking of someone else?" She grinned at me slyly. "Because if you're thinking of who I'm thinking of, big magic usually draws his attention."

"First of all, what terrible advice are you giving me? That I should explode my powers just to make him come see me?" I said, and she laughed. "But second of all, if that would even work, he would've showed up when I set the open bar on fire at the Fourth of July party."

"So you *have* thought about it," she said, still laughing.

"He has a lot of answers to my many, many questions," I said a tad defensively. "But, alas, he's also very, very busy. All the time."

"Someone needs to talk to him about work-life balance, maybe," she said as she poured out the tea. "But back to my question from before. Should we go down into that tunnel or not?"

"I don't know," I said. "We also have that list of names that Barnardo gave us. A lot of names. I don't know what to do first."

"Drink your tea," she said, sitting back with her own cup in her hands. The tea had a smoky smell, but all the varieties that Audrey liked best shared that quality, and I couldn't quite tell if this was a Lapsang Souchong or a Russian Caravan. I stirred in a generous spoonful of sugar, then took a sip.

"Ugh. Audrey, that's awful," I said, setting the cup back on its saucer with a clatter. She took another sip of hers with a slight grimace.

"Add more sugar. That will make it tolerable," she said, although she continued to drink hers black.

"Audrey, what am I drinking?" I asked. "I really hope it's not the tea you made last time. As much as it led us right to your grandaunt's killer, it didn't do that in a particularly helpful way. And do I have to remind you that brain damage was the inevitable side effect of that tea?"

"Don't be silly. You can tell by the taste this isn't the same," she said, and gestured again for me to keep drinking it.

I put two more spoonfuls of sugar into the tea and managed another sip. It was smoky. There was no denying that. But I was pretty sure the plant that had been smoked had not remotely been tea.

"What is this going to do to me?" I asked miserably.

"It helps a witch make a decision," she said.

"I never felt the effects of the last tea," I reminded her. "I just followed you."

Audrey shrugged, then finished off her tea and set the cup delicately back on its saucer. "Can I see the list of names?"

"Sure," I said, digging it out of my pocket. She flattened it on the tabletop, then took a pen out of her apron pocket to add something to the bottom of the page. I tried another sip of my tea, but now it was both disgusting and too sweet at the same time.

Maybe a dash of hot sauce was more what was required to get this mess down.

"What are you doing?" I asked her as she pulled something else out of her pocket. It looked like a big jar of iron filings.

"The tea is only part of the spell," she said. "There's a physical component, too."

I pushed the remaining half of my tea away. "I'm not messing with tea with physical effects. You know you really should explain things and get my consent before you pull me into your spells."

"Sorry," she said, not remotely contrite. Then she pulled the top off the jar and set it on the center of the table. I could hear a sort of hum and realized that something, indeed, was about to happen. I picked up the tea tray and moved it to another table so nothing was on our table save the jar of filings and the list of names.

I saw that the word "tunnel" was now on the bottom of the list in Audrey's neat cursive.

"Now what?" I asked, not sure I wanted to sit back down at that table just yet.

"According to what Agatha wrote in her book, the answer will reveal itself in the iron filings," she said. But she was starting to sound a little unsure. The humming was still there, but it had grown no stronger, and nothing much seemed to be happening.

But apparently I recognized iron filings when I saw them. So good job, me.

Then the humming kicked up to a slightly higher frequency, and I could see the jar on the table start to shake.

But I could feel my hair lifting up on end as well. And little shocks of electricity were dancing all over my skin.

"Audrey, I think I have to run," I said as I took two steps backwards, towards the door to the Square. All I could think of was the fireproof rooms my uncles had on every level of the bookshop.

And how far away even the closest of them was.

"It's working," Audrey said, apparently not even hearing me. She leaned in closer as the iron filings started lifting up out of the jar and spilling over to cover the paper with its list of names. They didn't cover the surface evenly. They snaked around in patterns that danced over the page without quite forming any sort of shape or other means of visual communication.

But now it wasn't just electric shocks dancing over my arms. I was starting to spark, showers of sparks that hissed as they hit the cool tile below.

"Audrey—" I started to say as I took two more steps backwards. I was just about to turn and run, the smell of the smoldering denim of my capris thick in my nose.

Then the door to the prosaic world banged open, reminding us both too late that she had opened the shop before we'd had our breakfast. Because I had gotten there so late.

Worse, it was Liam framed in the open doorway. I supposed he had come back for his backpack, but now he just stood there, gaping.

On the plus side, he wasn't even looking at me, who was perceptibly sparking like the cheapest of fireworks.

But only because his eyes were locked on Audrey, and the snaking pattern of iron filings dancing on the tabletop in front of her.

Which would be so easy to explain away as a science trick, really. Magnets under the table. He'd believe it, I was sure.

Or he might have, if I hadn't at that very moment felt a wave of power rush out of me like a sonic boom. It would be great if I could blame the tea, but I couldn't really make myself believe it.

Not when it was the second time that week I shattered every bit of porcelain in the teashop with an earsplitting crash.

Only this time I followed it up by setting every flower in their little vases on the tables on fire. And not little fires, either. These were improbably fierce roaring blazes that licked up towards the ceiling and lit up the teashop interior like a conflagration.

And I didn't know how we were going to explain that away. Or rather, how Audrey was going to explain it. Because I still felt that power building inside of me.

I had no choice. I had to run before I made things so much worse than they already were.

SEVENTEEN

I was going to burn down the Square. I didn't *want* to burn down the Square, but I didn't know how I could even stop it. The power crawling under my skin was building and building, hotter and sparkier than ever.

It was beyond my stunted abilities to contain it, I could feel it. I wasn't going to get to a fireproof room in time. Not when I couldn't run. All I could do was stumble blindly, tripping over everything and nearly passing out from the darkening of my vision.

Even the insides of my eyes were on fire.

"Tabitha!" Houdini called out in the back of my mind. I grasped the corner of a building—I thought it might be the bookshop, but I had no way of knowing—and forced my eyes to open enough to see my dog companion running towards me.

He had come outside. He was terrified, sure enough, but the terror in his eyes wasn't for his own safety. It was all for me.

"I need—" I started to say, when I felt a pressure change behind me, like the air was suddenly displaced and hitting my back like a tiny ocean wave. Then hands were closing on my shoulders even as I slid down the corner of the wall to sit indelicately on the charred grass.

I was burning things already. I could smell the dry July grass smoldering in a ring around me.

But those hands were still on my shoulders, and I realized it was Steph squatting behind me as he spoke close to my ear. All he said was my name, but somehow he imbued that single word, "Tabitha," with all the reassurance I needed in that moment.

I closed my eyes, focused on my breath, and stopped radiating fire.

"We have to get her to the bookshop, to one of the safe rooms," Houdini said to Steph, although his voice was in my mind as well. "We have to get her there without setting the whole building on fire. Can't you teleport her?"

"I don't have that power," Steph said. "But I have something that will help."

His hands left my shoulders, and I felt a momentary panic as the flames once more surged under my skin. But then he was holding my arm and sliding something onto my wrist.

And all the chaos drained out of me. It wasn't instantaneous. It took five or six breaths before I was feeling in control enough to open my eyes again. But the feeling of calm that was all I was left with was perfectly lovely.

"What is this?" I asked, lifting my hand to look at the bracelet on my wrist. It was a simple chain of silver links, each large enough for me to catch a glimpse of some sort of script written along the inside curve of each. It was no writing that I recognized.

"A very old artifact," he said. "The Wizard found it for you. I should warn you, it is technically a forbidden artifact. But you're very unlikely to find anyone, even in our community, who would recognize it as such."

"Forbidden?" I said. It felt cool against my skin, like water fresh from a mountain spring.

Not remotely evil.

"Forbidden by a very obscure law set down by the High Council as it existed eight hundred years ago," he said as he stood then helped me to my feet. "Most of those laws have been overturned in more enlightened times, but others like this one were *so* obscure, no one bothered to dig them up again. I assure you, it's only a technicality. If there were anything dangerous or troublesome about this, the Wizard never would have given it to you."

"What does it do, exactly?" I asked.

"Think of it like a regulator," he said. "It's just there to help you control the uncontrollable. But it's not restricting you from using your power. You're perfectly free to take it off at any time."

"I don't see that coming up," I said, playing with the cool silver links. "Even if I were in danger, using my magic would be unreliable. And, like you said, overkill. Like using a flamethrower to kill the weeds in a garden. Or ants."

"I agree. I just wanted you to know the option was there. No one is shackling you," he said.

"Thank you," I said.

"You're welcome, of course. But you might change your mind about how grateful you are after we deal with the second thing I was sent here to do," he said.

"What's that?" I asked.

"We have to go back to the teashop," he said.

I just nodded mutely. It wasn't like I hadn't seen that coming.

But to my surprise, Houdini followed close on my heels. He didn't say a word, and I could sense the nervousness for his own sake now rising in him, now that I was no longer the source of his worry. But he came all the same.

We went back inside to find Audrey once more standing in the middle of a mess of broken crockery. She had her wand in her hand, but wasn't doing anything with it yet. It was like she was caught in a catatonic state, not sure how to move forward.

Then she saw Steph come in the teashop behind me and she quickly turned away, I was sure so that he wouldn't see her fight back tears.

"I did this," I said to Steph.

"I know," he said. Then his own wand was in his hand. With a few waves of that wand and a few more words of power, all the tea things were back in place, as perfectly intact and sparkling clean as Audrey had left them after the last time I had lost control.

"We need to have a conversation," he said as he tucked his wand away. "But for such a conversation, I bit of tea first would be called for." He crossed the room and placed a single shining gold coin on the counter.

Audrey stared at it dully for a moment. Then she, too, tucked her wand away. She went behind the counter, whisked the coin into a drawer out of sight, then turned to switch the kettle on.

Ten minutes later, we were gathered around our usual table, the three of us plus Houdini sitting with his head barely visible over the edge of the table, each of us humans with a cup of strong tea in our hands. It smelled sweet and had a lovely red color to it, but from the first sip, I could feel the caffeine rush to my tired brain. Assam, I guessed. Not Audrey's usual preference, and yet it felt very necessary in that moment.

Audrey took a single sip of her own tea, set the cup on the saucer, then turned to Steph with her hands neatly folded on the table. As if that sip had discharged her tea-first obligation entirely. "Is this about Liam or about Tabitha?" she asked primly.

"Tabitha has been dealt with," Steph said between sips of his own tea. He alone seemed to be thoroughly enjoying the beverage, his eyes half-closed as he inhaled the sweet steam rising from his cup. That dreamy look on his face and the gentle quality of his voice were enough to take some of the edge off of his statement. But I could tell by the startled look that Audrey shot across the table at me that she had heard the possible threat in the way he phrased those words as well as I had.

"He means he's given me this," I said, and held out my hand so she could see the bracelet.

"What is it?" she asked. She reached out to touch it, but hesitated until I gave her a nod to continue. Then she brushed her fingertips over the silver links. "It's a charm?"

"Of sorts," Steph said. "What happened today shouldn't happen again. At least not by accident."

"It helps me stay in control," I said.

Audrey chewed her lip, but only nodded without a word. I couldn't blame her for being trepidatious. She was the one who kept taking the brunt of it when I lost control.

"So this is about Liam," she said.

Steph drained the last of the contents of his cup, then set it back on his saucer before sitting back in his chair.

"There are three options here," he said. "One, we can keep wiping his memory. Two, we can put him under the control of an oath spell, but that would have to be with his full knowledge, understanding and consent. Or three, the two of you could agree to simply not see him again in any capacity."

"Only three?" I asked. "Did that mean my uncle Frank had sworn to some sort of oath spell in order to be with my uncle Carlo?"

"Your uncles didn't meet in the Square. I don't know the circumstances of their arrangement. They were already married when they moved here and opened the bookshop, and the vows of matrimony were sufficient oaths in the eyes of the inhabitants of the Square," he said. Then he shrugged. "Frank Greene-Baxter has never been a problem."

"But Liam has," Audrey said. Her voice was in a dead zone, and I couldn't really tell if this was a question or a statement.

"Things have gotten messy," Steph said diplomatically. "Now, of the three options I've given you, the safest for Liam would be the third. But since he left this place the better part of an hour ago with clear knowledge that magic exists in the world, I don't see any way forward with that plan."

"I don't think it was workable before, either," I said, trying to send Audrey a sympathetic look. But her eyes were boring holes in the tabletop before her.

"I like Liam Kelly," Houdini offered. "If you ask my opinion, I think he is fully worthy of all your trust."

Audrey jumped, as if only then realizing the little dog was even there. Then she gave him a grateful smile. "Thank you, Houdini," she said.

"As much as I agree with Houdini, that's now how this works," Steph said with a sad sort of smile. "That leaves options one and two."

"But how are we supposed to choose for him? They both sound kind of terrible in different ways," I said.

"They are," Steph agreed. "But you aren't."

"Terrible?" I asked.

"Supposed to choose," Audrey put in. Then she glanced at Steph. "That's what you meant, right?"

"Right," he said, and got up from the table. "The choice is Liam Kelly's. I wanted to explain to you both first, but there is sadly nothing for you to do about it."

"Who—?" I started to ask, but Steph just turned that sad smile full on me. "Oh. You."

"Yes, and I'll have to go now. The risk of him talking to others I considered low enough to speak with you first, but I really can't delay any longer." Then he turned to Audrey with a little bow. "Thank you for the fine tea. I really should stop in more often. Perhaps in the future."

"But wait," she said, getting up from the table to follow him towards the prosaic door. "What are you going to do? Just ask him what he wants?"

"I'll have to explain the situation to him first, of course," Steph said. "It's been done before. Don't worry. There's a protocol."

"So if he chooses to take the oath, we'll be able to talk with him freely about everything?" I asked. The idea was already cheering me up.

But even as Steph nodded to me, Audrey was saying, "But if he chooses the mind wipe, how much are you going to wipe? Just the last hour?"

"I'm afraid not," Steph said. "It's his choice. But if he chooses not to remember, this time I'll have to take all of it. From the moment he met Tabitha until the moment I perform the wipe. Every memory that happened in the Square will be gone."

Then he went out the door, and Audrey ran to the teashop's back room. I could hear her snuffling in great heaves and rushed to follow her.

"I'm sure he's going to choose to remember," I said.

Although I wasn't. At all. The terms of an oath spell were not something I had ever researched before, but I had a general sense that they were quite arduous. Breaking them could be painful, even lethal, depending on how they were worded by the caster. Maybe Liam would decide it was too big an ask just to keep such newly made friends.

But Audrey came back out of the storeroom with a tea canister in her arms, still sniffling but trying to manage a smile.

"I know," she said, her voice all nasally. "It's just, you brought Houdini in here. I wasn't prepared."

"Oh, right," I said.

"I can leave," Houdini offered, although it wasn't hard to guess from his voice that he really didn't want to.

"No, just let me get some of my grandaunt's special tea in me and I'll be just fine," she said.

And indeed, as soon as she'd brewed the medicinal tea, she quickly downed half the cup in one go. Then she brought the rest back to the table to finish.

Only then did she let worry about Liam creep back into her expression. I pulled a chair closer so I could put an arm around her, which she accepted without a word.

But the real measure of just how upset she was was when she let Houdini climb into her lap. He leaned against her chest, tucking his little head under her chin. It was a gesture I had never been able to resist myself.

And even Audrey, as allergic as she was, couldn't help but stroking the little dog's back over and over again as we waited to hear what was going to happen next.

CHAPTER

EIGHTEEN

We waited together in the teashop until long past closing, but Steph didn't return.

And I still hadn't asked him how I could get in contact with him when I needed him. How could I keep forgetting to ask him that?

It was almost like we only saw each other during intense moments of physical danger, and those moments ended all too soon.

Finally, Audrey decided she needed to be alone, and she went up to her apartment on the third floor of the Square. Houdini and I made our way up to the kitchen of my uncles' apartment over the bookshop, and I poured a little kibble into his bowl before opening an empty refrigerator and staring at its lack of contents for entirely too long.

I really had to remember to shop once in a while.

I closed the refrigerator and found what was probably the world's oldest can of beans in the back of the pantry shelves. I heated that up and turned the last of the stale bread in the breadbox into toast and promised I'd find time to hit the Abergavennys' cornershop the next day.

Houdini plowed through his kibble in record time, then hopped onto the bench across from me in the dining nook. He looked at me steadily with his dark brown eyes for a moment, then said, "You should call your uncle."

"It's pretty late where they are," I said. "Which I'm only assuming is still Spain. I'd have to check their itinerary."

"It's still Spain," Houdini said with complete confidence. Based on what, I had no idea. But he just kept watching me steadily as I spooned the last of the beans onto the remaining crust of toast and shoved it in my mouth.

It took forever to tiredly chew it before I could swallow it to ask, "Why?"

"You have to tell him about your mother, I think," he said.

Dogs can't blush. Maybe dragons can; I'm not sure. And there's definitely no way to hear a voice in the back of your mind blushing. I can't even imagine what that would be like.

And yet, I sensed that was what was happening. He felt bad for barking her away.

"Why does he need to know?" I asked. "You already promised not to drive her away if she comes again. What else can be done? What could my uncle do?"

"He should know," Houdini said.

I shrugged, but pulled out my phone.

Again, my uncle Carlo answered, and again on the second ring, in pajamas but with hair that had not yet been mussed by a pillow. "Tabitha?" he said sleepily. "It's late. Is everything all right?"

"Mom was here," I said.

"Oh," he said and blinked. "Well, I suppose it's past time for that, isn't it?"

"You know her schedule?" I asked, trying not to sound too eager.

He laughed drily. "Your mother has never been one to keep to a schedule. But she does try to see you as often as she can. I hope you had an opportunity to catch up. Among other things."

"That's just the thing. We didn't," I said. "She came into my room in the middle of the night, as usual, only this time Houdini was sleeping on my bed with me. He's a bit protective. He barked to wake me up, and I guess she just ran away."

"Oh, dear," Carlo said, and adjusted his glasses.

"Yeah, she never got closer than the doorway. She didn't touch me at all," I said.

"That's not good," he said. "Maybe we *should* cut our trip short."

"Please don't!" I said, then lifted my wrist to jangle my chain at the camera. "Look, the Wizard acquired some ancient charmed thing, and it's really working. My power isn't boiling over all the time, so long as I'm wearing it."

"Well, that explains your hair," he said, then flushed, as if worried I'd take that the wrong way. "I mean to say, your hair is looking quite lovely today. Special occasion?"

"No. I had to stop in the Inanna Salon & Spa for another reason, and Cressida helped me out while I was there," I said.

"That was kind of her," he said.

"Well, Cleopatra charged me quite a lot for the favor," I said, and he laughed.

"Yes, that sounds like Cleopatra."

I chewed at my lip, but opted not to tell him about Delilah Dare and most of my activities over the last few days. If I started all that, we'd be up all night. "Uncle Carlo, do you know of any way for me to get word to my mother? Any way at all? Houdini promised not to drive her away again, but she won't know about any of that if I can't find a way to tell her."

"No, I've never known how to find your mother," he said. Then he adjusted his glasses again.

"No friends from her school days? No distant relatives in the old country? Nothing?" I asked.

"No," he said, a slow slur of a word. And adjusted his glasses again.

"Uncle Carlo, is everything okay?" I asked. I really wished we were in the same room having this conversation. Trying to feel his mood through the screen on my phone was challenging to say the least. But he was clearly upset. Nervous.

Hiding something?

"Everything is perfectly fine," he said, his voice warm and sincere. But then it grew tense again when he added, "I only regret I can't help you with your mother."

That sentence was spoken like it came from a character in a play who is getting one last line of dialogue out before the end of their big death scene. Each word inhabited its own space, each being dragged out from the depths one at a time. Like it was a tremendous amount of work for him to even speak the sounds.

"Did she make you promise not to tell anyone where she was?" I asked, not liking where my own thoughts were going. And maybe it was a red herring anyway, but all the talk that afternoon about oath spells was sitting heavily in my mind. "Did she make you *swear* not to tell? Not even me?"

"No!" he said, suddenly and firmly. "Tabitha, no."

"Did *somebody* make you swear?" I pressed.

"I'm quite sure I can't say," he said, again with the plodding slowness of an actor really chewing the death scenery.

I pulled at my lip, trying to think of a way around the spell. Which would really require a lot of research I hadn't done yet. I should've put this call off until after a long night in the bookshop.

But I had him on the line now. "Uncle Carlo, you've read a lot of books. Do you know much about oath spells? I know they vary by the way they are phrased by the caster, but there must be some commonalities. Are the oath-takers forbidden to speak of them at all?"

"Not necessarily," he said. This time when he adjusted his glasses, I didn't think it was a nervous tic. It was more that he had shifted to academic discussion mode, and that gesture was part of his professorial demeanor. "Many loyalty oaths are open matters. Nothing is forbidden to be spoken about those at all. In fact, they are meant to be public displays. Swearing loyalty to a king or wizard is a public affair."

"Sure, but there are other oaths that *are* about protecting secrets, right?" I asked. "There must be loopholes."

"In order to find a loophole, you'd have to know the text wording of what was sworn," he said. "But usually in such matters, anything written to be recited aloud is burned. In the name of secrecy."

"So someone sworn to secrecy might know the loophole but be unable to tell anyone else about it?" I asked.

"Exactly so," he said.

"So you wouldn't be able to tell me yours?" I said, then held my breath.

My uncle bit down on his lip until it turned white, and I saw a single dot of blood. But then he started grinding out the words again. "If, hypothetically, I had been placed under such a spell under my own free will, then the circumstance you described would, theoretically, govern my actions."

It took forever for him to get all those words out, and I could see sweat shining on his forehead by the time he was done. I was exhausting him, and it was far later there than it was in Minnesota. I should let him go.

But I still had to ask one more time. "Could my mother ever compel you to take such an oath? For a really good reason, maybe?"

Again, his answer to this was swift and sure. "No!"

I nodded, but I doubted I hid my misgivings with that answer.

"Okay. I should let you go. Say good night to Uncle Frank for me," I said.

Then I disconnected the call before he could finish saying good night to me.

I knew three things for sure in that moment.

One was that I was going to be pulling an all-nighter, pouring over every book I could find on the subject of oath spells. By morning, I expected to be as expert as a nonpractitioner could be.

Two was that someone had definitely convinced my uncle to

swear an oath of secrecy. And whatever he had sworn to hide was not something I was ever going to find inside the bookshop, or even in his personal effects. It hid in his mind, what he was hiding, along with what loopholes might free him.

Even whom he had sworn it to.

But three was that, at least in my gut, I honestly didn't think it was my mother. Rationally, she felt like the only possible suspect. Only I didn't think it was her.

But who else could it be? And why? And what was the secret being hidden, even?

I didn't know how to find any of that. But, with Houdini close at my heels, I went down to my nook in the bookshop to work on the first part.

By morning, I would be an expert in the matter of oath spells.

CHAPTER

NINETEEN

By the time dawn eked into my bookshop nook through the Minneapolis-facing window, I had read or at least scanned every book I could find in the shop about oath spells.

I wasn't an expert. Not remotely. The entries were far too varied and vague to be helpful. It was like there wasn't even any boilerplate standard wording for the oaths or the spells. It all depended on the witch—or usually wizard—who was extracting the promise. Some were so loosely worded they were almost benign.

Others felt like the sorts of things only great fools would swear to aloud.

At some point, I had dozed off with the last of the books open on my lap. When the dawn's light reddened the inside of my eyelids, I opened my eyes and sat up a little. The book fell from my perch on the window seat down to the hardwood floor below with a bang, and Houdini woke with a full-bodied jump into the air.

"Sorry, buddy," I said, putting a calming hand on his bristling back. "That was just me. We're okay."

"I didn't bark," he told me. "I'm being more careful about my threat assessments."

149

"Thank you, Houdini," I said. "Unfortunately, I don't expect my mother will try to return for quite some time."

Then I looked down at the cool metal links on my wrist. If it worked the way Steph said it would, I might not need to see her in the same way as usual. But I still missed her. As strange as our relationship was, being only a series of random encounters that happened in some liminal space between dreaming and wakefulness, she was still my mother.

"We should go see Audrey," Houdini said with an enormous yawn. Despite his tiny size, his white teeth looked enormous, to say nothing of his long curl of a tongue. Then he shook himself, his ears slapping loudly.

"It's pretty early yet," I said.

"She's up," Houdini said.

"You can sense her?" I asked, surprised.

"If she'd heard anything from Liam or Steph, she would've come to tell you by now," he said reasonably. "She hasn't called you. Which means she hasn't heard anything. I doubt very much she's been sleeping any more than you have."

"I slept a little," I said. But I couldn't argue with his logic. I was pretty sure he was right.

I went up to my room to take the quickest of showers, then dressed for yet another smothering, smoky, humid July day.

I was sweating even before the two of us had gone down the cast-iron stairs and balconies that led from my uncles' veranda down to the ground level of the Square.

Houdini walked very close to my heels, so close I was a little nervous I might accidentally step on him. And he was shaking a little. But he kept his head up high, as if proving to the world what a brave little dog he was.

The teashop shutters were all still closed, but when I tried the door, it wasn't locked. I went inside, pausing just out of the reach of the morning sun to breathe deeply from the cool Pacific Northwest breeze.

"Oh, hi," Audrey said from where she was leaning at her counter, chin on her hand.

"Houdini guessed you hadn't heard anything yet," I said.

"No," she said. "Tea?"

"I can get it," I offered, but she was already shaking her head.

"It's my one way of being useful," she said, and took the electric kettle into the back to fill it from the sink.

"Well, *that*'s not true," I said. "Your spell yesterday looked like it was working before Liam accidentally interrupted it."

"Oh, it was totally working," she said, coming back out with the filled kettle in her hands. She set it on its base and switched it on, then ducked into her office. She came back with the paper in her hands.

It was scorched.

"I did that," I said regretfully.

"Some of it," she said as she put it on the glass top of her bakery case. Then she smoothed it out with her hands. "But not all of it. See?"

I looked at the paper. The edges were singed. That had been my contribution.

But the list of names was still legible. Untouched.

Except for the last word, the one Audrey had added herself before starting her spell.

The word "tunnel" was now ringed in a glistening halo of metallic dust.

"What happened to the iron shavings?" I asked. I was tempted to blow on the paper, but was afraid that would ruin everything.

"They sort of sank into the paper," she said. "I didn't notice it until everyone left. Not a single name on this list is touched, but all the iron filings had formed a bristling ring around the word 'tunnel.' I shook them back into the jar, but this pattern remained. It's like it's scarred into the paper. You can try wiping it away or blowing on it or anything, but it won't change."

I touched it with a fingertip. As oily and metallic as the halo appeared, none of it came off on my skin. It didn't even smudge.

"Interesting," I said. Then I looked up at her. "That just doubles down on what I said. I didn't even help you with this spell with any kind of research. This is all on you."

"It was Agatha's spell, and her spells always worked," Audrey said glumly. "And anyway, if I hadn't been so eager to showoff, Liam wouldn't be in trouble right now."

"You're the furthest thing from a showoff," I said, although I had to agree it would've been wiser to do that spell after closing, and in her office, if not in the bookshop nook entirely. But hindsight was twenty/twenty, and also not much use to anybody. "And Liam is curious by nature. I think you just moved up the inevitable by the tiniest little bit."

"Maybe," she said, idly rubbing her fingertip over the iron halo. No smudging. "I didn't expect him back so soon. I mean, he was pretty upset. And he doesn't keep anything valuable in his backpack like his wallet or his keys."

Then a sudden thought struck me. "You know what I think?" I asked her. She gave me a confused shrug. "I think his coming back was another part of that spell. I mean, it forced a decision, right? Whether or not to tell him the truth about who you are?"

She chewed at her lip, but didn't say a word, didn't even move. But her cheeks were flushing, and she was blinking a lot. I decided what she needed was a little time to sit with that thought, and looked down at the list again. Mostly just so that I could give her the privacy of not looking at her while she pulled herself together.

But then the questions the list raised started running through my mind. "What do you think this means? That we can write off all these men as innocent?" I asked.

"No, I think that might be too much of a leap," she said, rubbing at her cheeks before leaning in closer to me to also look at the names on the paper. "I think it just means that the next thing to investigate is that tunnel. Or, at least, we can try telling the authorities to do so."

"I'm not sure they'll think this spell was proof of anything," I said. "At least not unless they performed it themselves. I guess we can lure them out here for some of that special tea and recreate the experiment."

"Or we could just check out the tunnel ourselves," Houdini put in.

I looked down at where he stood close beside my ankle. So close I could feel the ends of his upraised hair touching me as he trembled.

But his little dog chin was firmly up.

"Is that a good idea?" I asked them both.

Audrey shrugged. "I don't really want to open up today, to be honest. I'm not good for anything at the moment, and really not in the mood for *customers*." She rolled her eyes at that word, a gesture very far removed from her usual warm and welcoming demeanor when behind the counter.

She really was feeling down.

"Do you really think going down into a storm sewer is going to make you feel better?" I asked.

She barked out a humorless laugh at that. "Well, at least it would be doing something potentially useful. Waiting? Not so much."

I couldn't argue with that.

I looked down at Houdini. "What about you? Do you want to wait here? Or back in the bookshop?"

"No," he said, his voice strong and steady in our minds despite the trembling of his little body. "No, I want to go with you."

"Let's go, then," Audrey said, and headed towards her prosaic world-facing door. I snatched the list of names off the counter and folded it up before stuffing it down the back pocket of my capris.

Who knew? It might still be a clue, that list of names.

Houdini trotted close beside me as we followed Audrey out into the yellowish haze of the morning. She closed the door behind us and locked it with a key before leading the way down the alley towards the crime scene tape. Some of it had come down in the night, but most of it was still twisting and flapping in the barest of breezes that stirred the dumpster-smelling air of the alley.

It felt weird, stepping over that tape. Like we were being watched. Like alarms were about to go off. But we got to the other side, and nothing happened. So we carried on to the very end of the alley, and the grate over the storm drain.

It was not the most functional of drains. The alley wasn't entirely level, but even its highest points were at least an inch or two under the lowest point of that grate. There'd have to be pretty significant flooding for any water to drain away through this egress.

But perhaps that was by design, I decided, as a single tug was enough to flip that grate up like the lid of a box. The various noxious puddles that were scattered around the alley were in depressions too low to reach this higher drain.

Which wasn't to say the sewer smelled great. There was a pretty thick aroma of rotting leaves and other plant matter. But it could've been far, far worse.

There was a ladder built into the wall under the grate, on the side opposite the gap Houdini had wiggled through. I climbed down it about ten feet before reaching a narrow concrete walkway that ran alongside the deeper channel that carried the water towards the Mississippi River. That was what Houdini had fallen into. I turned back and reached up to take Houdini from Audrey's outstretched hands.

"Do you want to walk, or should I carry you?" I asked him.

He took a long time to answer, but in the end he said, "I'll walk. Thank you."

I set him on the concrete, but he once more stayed uncomfortably close against my ankle.

Then Audrey was down at the bottom with us. She brushed the ladder grime from her hands, then looked down both ends of the tunnel. One led back towards the Square, the other led off towards the river.

"Which way?" she asked.

"To the right," Houdini said, meaning towards the river.

I pulled my phone out of my pocket and turned on the flashlight app, and after a moment, Audrey did the same. There wasn't enough room on the narrow walkway for the two of us to walk side by side, so I went first, Houdini close on my heels, and Audrey brought up the rear. The tunnel carried on straight past what I guessed was the length of the building next door to the Square before making a 45-degree turn then widening out to the quay Houdini had mentioned.

And there was a turnstile. Just like under the pub. Only this turnstile was covered in half-rotted leaves mostly on the upstream side. Like the autumn leaves had been washed up this high by a sudden intense storm, and then the water had receded again, leaving this all behind.

But quite some time ago.

"I have a transit card," I said, patting my pockets to make sure I had grabbed it when I had left my room that morning. It was there, with the last of my cash from the box under my bed.

"But it doesn't look like anyone's used this in at least a year," Audrey said. She gestured towards where the card was to be waved to activate the summoning spell, but that area of the turnstile was coated with leaf residue.

"And anyway, the smell I told you about doesn't stop here. It goes on, along the walkway, for ever so far," Houdini said.

"What do you think?" I asked Audrey. "Walk it?"

She chewed at her lip, looking anxiously back in the direction of her shop.

But then she nodded. "Yes. I think we should follow it. Don't you?"

"It's our only clue," I said with a shrug. "Houdini?"

"I will follow you," he said.

We walked through the cool but still humid darkness for what felt like hours, but which my phone insisted had only been about four thousand steps. Then our narrow tunnel ended at a T-intersection with another, larger stream, although our walkway got no bigger. We followed this only for about five minutes before our phones were no longer necessary to light the way.

We had reached another quay, this one with its own magical green lights all around it. The ceiling above was ornate stone arches, almost like an underground cathedral of sorts. And there were five turnstiles, all shiny and giving every indication of frequent use.

There were no people in sight anywhere, or boats out on the water.

And the only way off the quay besides summoning a boat with the turnstiles was a set of art deco elevator doors. The dial over the doors only had a few markers on it, but they almost seemed random. The one on the bottom left said "-4." I guessed we might be about four building stories below street level, give or take.

There was a smooth, unmarked arch to the middle of the dial, which was labelled "33." But the right side of the arch had several notches marked and labelled from 34 to 42.

There was only one place such an elevator could go.

To the hidden levels on top of the Foshay Tower.

I pushed the elevator call button. But I couldn't help giving Audrey a little grin.

The plot was thickening.

CHAPTER

TWENTY

W e stepped out on the 33rd floor of what was, at least in the prosaic world, a 32-story building. The doors opened up onto a gorgeous marble floor that glistened so cleanly it looked like its tiles had just been laid and had yet to be stepped on. The room we stepped into ran the length of the building and half of the width as well, with floor to ceiling windows on the three outer sides.

The view out of the windows was facing Marquette Avenue and showed all of downtown Minneapolis around us. Most of the other nearby skyscrapers were far taller than the Foshay Tower, but having spent at least a slice of my childhood in Manhattan, I didn't find their height terribly impressive.

But the art deco style of everything in the Foshay Tower was quite lovely. And the magical folk who inhabited its secret levels clearly cherished it as much as I did. Everything from the light sconces on the walls to the elevator doors and marble floor below had a geometric, clean line sort of beauty.

"It must be amazing to live here," Audrey said, echoing my thoughts exactly. "I guess it's pretty expensive, though. Every

157

window has such an amazing view, even with all the smoke in the air. Just imagine what it would look like on a clear day."

"I bet you can see clear to St. Paul from the other side of the building," I said. Then I nudged Audrey and pointed toward a gorgeous wood desk that stood alone in the middle of the room against the wall, as if anxious not to block any of those views. No one was behind the desk, but it still looked like the place to start.

Every sound we made echoed around us as we walked, especially the click of Houdini's nails on the marble. For a little guy, he had a heavy step. Or maybe that was a little bit of his draconic nature showing through.

The desk was as art deco as the rest of the reception area, with inlays of different colors and types of wood forming a gorgeous abstract form that hinted at an organic nature in the way its geometry was shaped. Like a cubist sort of tree, I thought. I ran my fingers over the surface and instantly triggered a spell that had been worked into the gleaming wood.

Now the surface was covered in writing: golden letters that spelled out names and numbers.

"I think I found the list of residents who live here," I said to Audrey, who had been looking back out over the city. She turned to see what I had found.

"Check the names," she said, and I pulled Barnardo's list out of my pocket.

Every one of the five names was on it.

So was Cleopatra Manx's.

And, of course, Taurus Vernon.

"Well, we knew Taurus lived here already. He made sure everyone knew, all the time," I sighed. "And I guess it's not a surprise that Cleopatra does, too. My only other guess was more like an apartment in Paris or something like that."

"She does use the portal pretty freely," Audrey agreed. "What should we do about the other five? My spell might have only told us the next best step, which clearly was going through the tunnel. It didn't do anything I would call clearing those names from suspicion."

"No, I agree," I said. "But it's the middle of a workday. They might not be home."

"Let's see," she said, and touched the first of the golden names. This triggered a soft chiming sound, just barely audible to us but enough to tell us a louder one was ringing upstairs somewhere.

But there was no answer.

Audrey checked the list, then pushed a second name. Then a third, fourth, and fifth. But either no one was home, or no one was answering.

"Taurus, then?" Audrey asked, her finger hovering over his name.

"Barnardo said he was definitely gone from the scene of the crime far before the time in question, but I guess it can't hurt to try talking to him," I said. Not that I wanted to talk to him. Ever again. But at least this time I had backup.

Audrey touched the name and the soft chime sounded. Almost at once, there was a whoosh of sound off to my left. I stepped back from the desk to see a second bank of elevator doors there, one of which was now lit up. Or rather, the etched design of two mirror image fairy women holding glass lanterns out towards each other glowed as the lantern parts of the design lit up. Then the doors opened, sliding the two fairy women away from each other to reveal the very lush interior of the elevator car.

I mean, who needs a velvet seat to rest on when going up, at the most, nine floors?

We stepped inside, Houdini close beside me, although he was no longer shaking. Instead, he seemed merely intensely curious, looking around at everything as if he'd never seen anything like it before in his life.

Which made sense. I doubt he had any memories outside of the Square and now the sewer tunnel at all.

There were no buttons on the inside, but once the doors closed behind us, the elevator moved of its own accord, carrying us up nine floors to the very top of the secret levels. Technically, the observation deck the prosaics could visit as well as all the maintenance and antenna equipment were still above us. But powerful magic made it all appear to be nine levels down.

Sometimes magic is really, really cool.

The doors opened, but where I had expected to see a corridor lined with doors, we found ourselves instead stepping into a private entryway to an apartment. There was a rack waiting for coats, a bench waiting for guests to sit on, to slip shoes on or off, and an open doorway at each of the three cardinal points that wasn't an elevator.

"Hello?" I called as we stepped hesitantly out of the elevator. The floor was a lush white carpet, its pile so thick that Houdini's legs half disappeared into it, like an elk standing in tall grass. I remembered too late that we'd come here through a walkway in the sewers and worried what he might track into that carpet, but honestly if you're going to put that sort of carpet in what is essentially your mudroom, you took what you got.

The doors hissed shut behind us, and I heard the whoosh of the elevator going back down to the lobby. And yet there was still no sign of anyone coming to greet us.

"Hello?" I called again as I approached the doorway on our left. It led into a library of sorts. I say of sorts because, while shelves lined both of the long walls that led to the floor-to-ceiling windows on the far side of the room, and every shelf was filled with row after row of books, they all gave me the overwhelming sense of having been bought in bulk sets just to fill the space.

Maybe it was something in the smell of the room that told me that. I could smell the leather from the covers, but nothing of the paper or ink or glue within. As if they had never been cracked open in their lives. None of them looked like actual antiques, but if they had been, I knew I'd find all their pages uncut.

It turned my stomach, the waste of it. Like some people have a visceral reaction to seeing hunting trophies, although I suppose nothing had died to provide this display of hoarding for no purpose. Nothing but a few trees. And the cows for the leather.

Yeah, the waste of it turned my stomach. I wanted to liberate all those books, to find good homes for them where they'd actually be *read*. Or even, if the contents weren't terribly interesting, turned into someone's art journal. I could tell from the doorway they were all made from the highest quality of materials. Someone should get some good use out of all that paper.

"Uh, Tabitha?" Audrey called, snapping me out of my stewing. I turned to see Taurus Vernon standing in the doorway opposite the elevator.

"I rather thought it was you," he said to me. "Although I don't know your friend here."

"I'm Audrey Mirken," she said. "And this is Houdini."

He frowned at her in puzzlement, then belatedly noticed the dog wading through his carpet to stand by my ankle.

"What can I help you ladies with?" he asked when he was done scowling at Houdini.

"I don't like this guy," Houdini growled in the back of my mind and Audrey's. Which wasn't exactly helpful, since Houdini had that reaction to about half the people he met.

"I was hoping to talk to you about Delilah Dare," I said. "And about what happened that night. The Fourth of July."

"It would be a little hard to forget what happened that night," he said. Then he swept his arms towards the library. "Why don't we go inside my study and discuss it there? The view of the river is a little obscured today by the smoke, I'm afraid, but impressive all the same."

I went into the room but didn't cross to the window. I was sure the view was every bit as amazing as he kept promising, but I really didn't want to give him the pleasure of seeing me get wowed by it. Instead, I sank into one of four club chairs that were arranged around a marble fireplace, currently cold and unlit. Then I had to redirect my gaze away from the ornate screen in front of the fireplace, which was a really nice brass piece that looked like a rising sun, and I could feel my appreciation of the workmanship start to glow out of me.

Luckily, Houdini instantly hopped into my lap and butted his head under my chin, distracting me from admiring the decor. I looked instead at Taurus, who swallowed a bit of disappointment as Audrey, too, neglected to admire the view in favor of sinking into the club chair beside mine. But he gave in with good grace, taking one of the seats opposite of us and brushing a bit of lint from the crisp seam of his clearly very expensive trousers.

"I hope we're not interrupting you going to work?" I said.

"I set my own hours," he said with a shrug. "Time is of more value to me than money. Time, and the freedom to spend it as I wish."

"True enough," I said with what I hoped was an equally careless shrug. "The two of us closed our shops to come here today, so we know what you're talking about."

He wrinkled his nose a touch at the idea of comparing running a shop to whatever arcane financial magics he engaged in, but again opted not to say anything aloud about it.

"Tabitha... Greene, wasn't it?" he said to me.

"That's right," I said.

"Tabitha Greene, I'm glad you stopped in today. I was planning to go down to your charming little bookshop this afternoon to call on you, but now you've saved me the trip," he said.

I would scarcely call the immensity of my uncles' bookshop *little*, although *charming* certainly felt appropriate. But all I said was, "Why?"

"Well, I wanted to apologize for my behavior that night," he said. I looked straight into his icy blue eyes, trying to see into his soul. Because while he didn't exactly sound contrite, he also wasn't setting off my creep meter today like he had that night. If anything, my sense was that he wasn't apologizing because he was sorry so much as it was good form to do so. And he always did what was good form, what was proper.

"You weren't the one who started the fire," I said, still watching his face closely. But his expression was giving me nothing.

"Yes, that's true. But I'm not apologizing for the fire. I'm apologizing for... well, using you as a pawn in a game you weren't even playing. That was very inappropriate of me, and I regret it."

"Oh," I said, a bit dumbfounded. This was an actually good apology. Not a waffling "I'm sorry you feel that way" sort of apology.

And I definitely hadn't seen that coming.

"Ah, your reaction tells me everything," he said. "You have very low expectations for my behavior, and that is entirely my fault."

"Well, you were very different that night than you are right now," I allowed.

"I know," he said wistfully. "I'd like to blame the drinks at that party. In fact, I do suspect that the mixologist that Cleopatra hired did a little something extra to whatever she gave me." Just when I was about to check my mental box for "blaming others in the context of apologizing," and downgrade my impression of him accordingly, he went on. "Not that *that*'s any sort of excuse. I knew I felt off. I should've excused myself from that party. Or perhaps spoken to that man with the shop there. What's his name?"

"Abergavenny?" I offered.

But Audrey said, "Bartholomew Bullen."

"Yes, that's it. Bartholomew Bullen. He would know if I'd consumed something untoward. Would likely even have had an antidote. But more's the pity, in that moment, I didn't think of it at all. I thought only of how I could use Delilah's own nefarious methods against her. It was very base of me. I can't expect your forgiveness, but I do ask it."

"He talks pretty," Houdini huffed. But he sounded like he was being won over despite his better instincts.

Or I was projecting my own feelings onto the dog. One or the other.

But Taurus said no more. He just kept looking at me. Expectantly.

"Apology accepted," I said. Because really, after naming what he did and taking—mostly—full responsibility for it, it would be churlish not to.

But getting an apology wasn't why we were there.

"You left the party after the fire?" I said.

"Yes, that is correct. You are well-informed," he said, sitting back in his chair as if relieved at the change of topic. He brushed another invisible speck from his pants.

"And you can prove that you didn't come back again after being seen to leave?" I asked.

"As a matter of fact, I can," he said. "The desk downstairs records the comings and goings of all the residents here. I can show it to you, if you like."

I was about to take him up on that offer when Audrey said, "*All* the residents?"

"Yes, all the residents," he said again. "Why do you ask?"

"It's just, we have a list of names. Other... people we were hoping to talk to," I said. "We rang their bells, but they weren't home."

"If the desk knows they're out, why doesn't it tell us?" Audrey asked.

"Well, people are entitled to a little privacy," he said, crossing his arms as he pinned those ice-blue eyes on Audrey. "They are even entitled to not answer the door if they are not in the mood for company."

"Fair enough," I said. "So if we ask the desk, it's going to tell us it's none of our business."

"Yes, that's what it will tell *you*," he said, raising his eyebrows significantly.

"We would appreciate your help in this matter," I said with my brightest smile. "If it doesn't violate any sort of neighborly bond, of course."

"Of course," he said with a chuckle. "Lucky for you, I'm not overly fond of most of my neighbors. But may I see your list before I agree?"

Audrey and I traded glances, and at her nod, I took out the list and handed it over to Taurus. He scanned it quickly, then handed it back again.

"I see the method to your madness," he said. "You're clearly far more clever than I had thought, compiling these names."

"What do you mean?" I asked.

"Well, most people, including our own investigative authorities, would look at men with whom Delilah Dare had actually been involved. Not the ones she had completely fail to get on with," he said airily.

"That makes it sound like you think we're taking the wrong track," I said.

"Not at all," he said, and motioned for the two of us to get up and follow him back to the elevator. He pressed the ornate brass button to summon it, then turned to look at me again. "No, not at all, my dear. I mean, it *is* madness. All of it. But, like I said, there is a method to it."

"You think someone would reject Delilah's advances and then kill her?" I asked.

"Oh, very much so," he said, just as the elevator doors whooshed open. We all stepped inside the elevator. Houdini hopped up on the velvet seat and curled up, as if intending to nap for the entirety of what we already knew was going to be a very short ride. "Yes, that is just what I think. But you are missing all the middle bits."

"The middle bits?" I asked.

"Yes, exactly," he said, beaming at me like a teacher whose student has just accidentally said something brilliant. "First, they attempt to reject her. Then she makes an enormous nuisance of herself. *Then* they kill her."

"But not you?" I said, trying really hard not to make it sound like a challenge. Although I was pretty sure I failed at that.

But he didn't take offense. "That's correct. Not me," he said as the doors opened and we were once more in that magnificent lobby. It was a short walk to the desk, but when he got there, he only leaned an elbow on it to look down at me with that thing that was queasily close to fondness. "Not me, because, you see, I never rejected Delilah Dare. I think that's where I went wrong, by the way. Not rejecting her. If she didn't have to chase after it, to fight for it, she didn't really want it. I figured that out a bit too late."

"I think realizing that would quickly lead to realizing you never wanted such a person in the first place," I said.

But he just laughed. "A wiser person would likely do so. Yes, a wiser person than I."

"So you're sorry that she rejected you, but you don't seem sorry that she's dead," I couldn't help but saying.

"Well, I suppose if she'd been hit by a car or died of some disease, I *would* be sorry that she's dead," he said ponderously. "But while I had no reason to wish her dead, I know many who *did* have reason. I don't wish to speak ill of the dead, and so I won't give you details, but if you call on those five men of yours, they'll all tell you stories that will make it very clear to you just how terrible a person she could be when crossed. The things she did... but I said I wouldn't speak of them, and I won't."

"She didn't do anything to you?" I asked skeptically.

"If she had, I would be free to tell you. But she didn't, and so it's not my place," he said. Then he tapped the surface of the desk, his fingertips zooming about in a complex sort of spellwork that he had clearly done before. When he was finished, the surface of the desk was once more covered in golden lettering, but instead of names and apartment numbers, these were names and times.

"Here I am," he said, drawing our attention to a point midway down the lefthand column. "This is when I came back from the party, well before the time of death, I'm sure. And here is when I left again, late the next morning. Now let me see that list again."

I took it back out of my pocket and handed it to him, but it wasn't exactly surprising that ten minutes later, when we were watching the elevator doors slide shut between us in the lobby and Taurus on his way back up to his penthouse apartment, every name on that list now had an alibi. They had all been home from hours before until many hours after the murder had taken place.

"Do you believe it?" Audrey asked as we headed back to the elevator that would take us back down to the quay.

"I suppose we have to," I said. "What else can we do? The only person we know who can hack into things is Liam, and he definitely can't hack into that."

"Liam," Audrey said wistfully.

"You're going back to the teashop," I guessed.

"I think I should," she said, tucking her hair behind her ears. "Just in case he shows up. I want to be there."

"Of course," I said, forcing a little more heartiness into my voice than I actually felt.

"Are you going to open up the bookshop?" she asked as we stepped inside the elevator. "You can just hang out in the teashop with me if you'd rather."

"I appreciate the offer, but I think I want to see just where the other end of this tunnel goes," I said. "Past the alley grate. It looks like it goes to the Square, but I think I want to be sure. What do you think, Houdini? Do you want to stay with me or go back to the teashop with Audrey? Or back to the bookshop?"

He gave it a long moment's thought, but when the elevator doors opened to let us out onto the quay, he looked up at me with those intelligent brown eyes and said, "I want to say with you."

I smiled down at him in gratitude. As pointless of a side quest as I was sure it would turn out to be, it was still nice not to have to pursue it alone.

CHAPTER
TWENTY-ONE

The path alongside the running storm sewer beyond the alley grate was pretty much the same as it was from the grate to the Foshay Tower. The concrete walkway was high enough above the water to be dry now, but watermarks on the walls and the occasional drift of half-rotted leaves spoke of wetter times in the not too distant past. The lights that had dotted every arch or so behind me were gone here, and I had to take out my phone and turn on my flashlight to see more than the dimmest of outlines.

I confess I didn't do as thorough a job of investigating the sewer tunnel as I had intended to. Houdini was so nervous, trembling when he walked and outright jumping into the air on more than one occasion. There was never anything there, but it still took a couple of minutes each time it happened to calm him down enough to continue walking.

And it didn't even seem to be worth the anxiety for him, because the tunnel led exactly where we assumed it would: to the quay under the pub where I had taken the boat under the river to downtown. This was a smaller side passage, lost in shadows under what had appeared to me when I was here before to be a decorative arch off the end of the quay.

"I guess it's just what it looks like," I sighed as I looked around the quay in the greenish light from the lanterns overhead. "A smaller channel that the boats just don't use anymore."

"So we can go upstairs from here?" Houdini asked, a little too eagerly. He was eyeing the wooden staircase that led up to the pub cellar.

"You can if you want to," I said. "I'm going back one more time to give it all one last, more thorough look."

"But why?" Houdini asked, not quite a whine.

"I don't know. I just have a bad feeling that I'm missing something important," I said.

"But you don't have that kind of divination magic, do you?" he asked.

"I don't have any kind of magic, as you well know," I grumbled. "Call it woman's intuition if it makes you feel better. Look, you can go up to the bookshop or go find Audrey if you'd rather. I can do this alone."

"No," Houdini said, and made a visible effort to stop his little legs from trembling. "I go where you go. We're companions."

"That doesn't mean we can't split up if we need to," I said.

"I'll go with you," he said again, more firmly.

"Only if you're going to be some help," I said. "Otherwise, honestly, I'd rather go in alone. It's a short walk. It will only take me ten minutes to look as hard as I'd like to. I can find you topside when I'm done."

"No," he said again, and turned his back to the staircase. "No, I'm going with you. I'll be good. I mean, I'll be helpful."

"Are you sure?" I asked, giving him one last out.

"Positive," he said. "I have senses you don't. There is almost no point in you going without me, really."

I didn't think that was true, but I opted not to argue. I really didn't want to go back in alone, even though I was sure it was perfectly safe.

I mean, nothing had jumped out at us the first time.

Houdini walked close at my heels as we started back away from the quay, leaving the greenish light behind for the darkness of this lesser-used tunnel. But having been through here once before, he was calmer now. And more focused, as he sniffed the air and peered into the shadows around us.

I kept my phone up high and constantly moving, panning over every surface. The reflection of that light off the surface of the water was too intense to get more than a vague sense of what the shapes were that were floating along its surface. Branches for sure. Some bits of paper and plastic straws. A few other things that didn't bear thinking about their origins too much.

"Wait," Houdini said. We'd only passed three archways since the quay, about twenty or so feet. But I stopped and looked down at him, shining my light near him without blinding him. He was standing ramrod straight, sniffing at the air. Then he took a step closer to the stone wall to our left. And then another.

"What is it?" I asked.

"Something here isn't right," he said. "I didn't notice it the first time. It's very subtle. But I'm sure something here is being actively hidden from us."

"Something in the water or on the ground?" I asked, shuffling my feet in case I was about to trip over some invisible object.

Or body. I tried not to think that word, but it kept pushing itself back to the front of my mind. An invisible body, maybe left under an invisibility spell, never to be found.

"Neither," Houdini said. "There's something about the wall."

"A clue?" I asked, reaching out a hand towards the stone wall. But I couldn't quite summon the courage to touch it. I could see the sheen of moisture that coated it reflecting the light from my phone. I knew this was a storm sewer, not a sanitary one, but still. The miasma that had created that moisture wasn't something I was eager to have all over my fingers. Not when I had not so much as a tissue to wipe it off with after.

"Can you tell what it is?" I asked him instead. "Like blood spray or scratch marks that might have DNA in them or something like that?"

Because if it was that kind of clue, I definitely didn't want to touch it.

But Houdini made a low growling sound in the back of my mind, one that was decidedly negatory.

"Okay, so what is it?" I asked impatiently.

"It's... nothing," he said, sounding confused by his own words.

I waited for a moment. But when he said nothing further, I screwed up my courage and reached out with my fingers splayed wide.

And felt nothing. Or rather, no stone wall. But I did feel a definite chill, like touching metal in the heart of the coldest January.

Then the wall before my eyes rippled, like I was looking at the surface of a pond that someone had dropped a pebble into. It rippled, then warbled and then fell away all together. The cold feeling left my fingers, although they still felt numb to the bone. I tucked my hand under my armpit, then shone my phone's flashlight straight ahead.

At first I saw nothing but a dark void. Then I realized it was another tunnel, a narrower, darker one. The walls here were still stone, but not the grayish stone of the sewer behind me. They were completely black. And not even natural stone. These were all finely hewn stone blocks, but hewn from no stone I had ever encountered before.

They reflected absolutely nothing. Even with the light hitting them head-on from inches away, it was hard to discern there was a wall there.

But when I touched it, I could feel cold, dry, smooth stone.

"Where do you suppose this goes?" I mused aloud.

It was rhetorical—no matter what the answer was, I was still going to follow it to be sure—but Houdini answered me, anyway.

"The heart of the Square," he said with complete confidence.

"How can you be so sure?" I asked, looking down at him. Neither of us had quite stepped inside that new tunnel yet. The numbness was easing from the hand I had stuck into it, but I wasn't sure if that meant it was safe to go in. I suspected the cold and numbness were an effect of the concealing spell, and I had dispelled that by touching it.

But it might be a protective feature of the tunnel itself.

I mean, black, nonreflective stone that is all but invisible even under direct light? That totally felt magical to me.

"That's the direction it's heading," Houdini said. "It goes straight ahead of us. Straight, and ever so slightly uphill. I suppose it's meant for runoff, given that channel down the center of the floor. But it doesn't look like it's been anything but bone-dry in ages."

"I don't see any of that," I confessed, aiming my phone light straight ahead. Nope. All I saw was blackness that went on forever.

But when I tipped the phone down, I did see the channel down the center of the floor that Houdini had mentioned. It continued on into a crack between two stone blocks that ran between my feet and then behind me towards the sewer water. There were a few faint lines on that stone, not as prominent as the watermarks on the walls, but there all the same.

"We should follow it," Houdini said.

"Really?" I said.

It was a little embarrassing how our roles had reversed. But now he was the one all bravely eager to investigate more, and I was the one too scared to press on.

It was just so dark in there.

"I can lead the way," Houdini said. "You'll be able to see me in the light from your phone. And I can see well enough on my own to follow that channel."

"Someone did go to a lot of effort to hide this," I admitted.

"It might run to some point in the Square, or it might run past it, to some other place," Houdini said. "We should really be sure."

"You're right," I said, and straightened my shoulders. "Lead on. I'll be right behind you."

Despite his brave words before, he hesitated with one paw in the air just outside that tunnel. But then he pressed on, finishing that step and then taking another and another.

"It's very cool in here, but not too bad otherwise," he said to me without looking back.

I bit my lip but forced my own feet to get moving. Passing through the tunnel mouth gave me another blast of intense cold, but nothing like before. And once I was through it and into the tunnel proper, it faded away to a tolerable chill.

I mean, I wasn't remotely dressed for it. But it didn't feel like a magical effect. It was just a drier sort of cave chill.

Houdini kept a steady pace, walking with the dry channel in the floor always between his paws. I followed behind him, occasionally panning around with the light but never able to see anything clearly save Houdini, even black as he was, and that channel in the floor.

I never saw a light ahead of us until we were standing in it, and I blinked at the startling transition. It wasn't even a bright light, really. It just felt like the first real light I'd seen in days. And it was coming from directly above me.

I tipped my head back and found myself looking up a long shaft. The bottom half of the shaft was the same strange black stone as the tunnel I was standing in, but then it gave way to a more usual gray stone. I could see metal rungs in that stone, leading up to another grate. And through the bars of that grate, I could see just a sliver of the afternoon sun between wisps of hazy wildfire smoke.

"I can't climb that," Houdini said.

"Do the rungs come all the way down?" I asked. "Because I only see them starting about twenty feet above me, and I definitely can't jump that far."

"Yes, if you reach out to your left, you'll touch the bottom rung," he said.

"Right," I said, shutting off the flashlight and tucking my phone into my back pocket. "This might be a little awkward, but I think I can carry you inside my shirt. You'll have to be careful not to squirm, though. I'll need both hands to climb, and I'd hate to drop you."

"I'll be perfectly still," he said.

As confident as those words had sounded, when I picked him up, I could feel that he was trembling again. I took a minute just to hold him close and pet him until he calmed a little. Then I put him inside my shirt and tied the bottom ends together, then tucked them firmly into the front of my pants.

I sensed Houdini about to say something, but he seemed to change his mind. In the end, he just tucked his head against the side of my neck. I think he even closed his eyes, but at that angle I couldn't tell.

I reached out blindly, nearly jamming a finger into the front of the ladder rung, but it skidded over the top of it without real injury. Then I started to climb. I stopped every five feet or so to take a hand off the ladder and put it under Houdini to be sure he was still secure.

He was trembling, but he wasn't slipping.

I hadn't really considered how difficult it might be to try to open a storm grate from this angle until I was nearly at the top. What if I couldn't budge it? What if it had rusted shut? My arms were already aching from the forty-foot climb. Would I even be able to lift Houdini so that he could scramble through? It looked like there was a gap wide enough for his little body to fit.

But I was seriously worried about dropping him. This was a lot of athletic work for someone like me who, honestly, never worked out.

But when I reached the top, I felt that warm sunlight directly on my face, and it was rejuvenating. I gripped the top rung tightly with my left hand, then raised my right hand to touch the bottom of the grate.

And it swung open with perfect ease. Like it was hinged, and those hinges were well-oiled, and also there was some sort of counter-weight working with me to get that metal grate up to a 90-degree angle.

Yeah, it was clearly too easy. Like someone used this path a lot.

But whoever had cast that concealing spell at the other end of the tunnel was clearly someone who could work a little grate-opening magic with no problem.

If only I knew for sure how old the spells were. But for all I knew, these spells had been in place since Prohibition times. Stranger things were found in forgotten magical places, that was for sure.

"You're going up first," I said to Houdini just before I hoisted him up and out of my shirt, up into the sunlight. Then I followed.

And found myself laying on my back, arms trembling with exhaustion, looking up into that hazy July sky.

And framing that view was the tops of the topiaries that formed the walls of the hedge maze. We were indeed in the heart of the Square.

TWENTY-TWO

I sat up and looked around. Houdini and I were in one of the hedge maze alcoves, but it wasn't one I had ever seen before. The fountain in the center was an open oyster shell spraying water high into the air, and the benches to either side were cast-iron that had once been painted white but were now almost entirely rusty iron.

The fact that I didn't recognize where I was wasn't entirely remarkable. The maze was—like almost everything else in the Square—bigger on the inside, and was prone to moving around on its own at random times. The path to the portal that allowed magical travel to other parts of the world stayed consistent, but the rest of the maze was constantly shifting.

"Do you see any clues?" I asked Houdini, who was sniffing aggressively all around the alcove. He poked his head in and out of the shrubberies and made a concentrated search pattern around the fountain. But in the end, he sat down on the grass with an air of defeat.

"Nothing," he said.

"Well, if our murderer brought Delilah through here, I doubt they left any sign," I said. "He took her things, and anyway, she was definitely killed in that alley."

"This feels like an abandoned place," he said, and I had to agree. The shrubberies around us were overgrown, barely holding their proper shapes as walls. And then there was the state of the paint on the benches.

"If we can get the authorities to come in here, they can use their magic to reveal who has passed through here before us," I said.

But that would mean they'd have to believe that this crime was their jurisdiction, and worth their valuable time to follow up on.

I briefly wondered if I could find a similar spell in the bookshop, something I could craft to suit Audrey's talents. The two of us could come back here and see what we could see.

But first I had to find a way out of the maze.

"Do you know which way to go to get out of here?" I asked Houdini.

He sniffed at me as if his feelings were hurt. "Of course," he said. "I have a perfect sense of direction on top of my perfect memory. What more does one need to navigate a maze?"

"Let's get to the teashop, then," I said.

Houdini led the way. We took a few bad turns, Houdini reminding me that perfect memory is for not repeating mistakes, not for not making them in the first place. I heartily agreed, although it was irritating to backtrack each time and try a different path. I was soaked in sweat, and the sun was still high enough in the sky where the topiary walls offered no shade at all. But, with the humidity level as stifling as it was, there would be little relief even if we found a some shade.

Also, the water in the fountains was all uncomfortably warm when I put my hands in it. As thirsty as I was, I had only wanted to wet my hands and maybe slosh a little on the back of my neck to cool off. That water wasn't quite jacuzzi-warm, but it was close.

But finally we reached the stone arch that was the portal at the heart of the maze, and from there we both knew the path that led out to the open meadow between the maze and the storefronts of Violenta Court's Boutique and Bartholomew Bullen's Potions & Magical Sundries.

By that point, we were both too exhausted from the heat and dehydration to even bother trying to quicken our steps to the teashop. It was just one plodding step after another through the smoky air until we finally reached the cool interior of the teashop.

Audrey wasn't alone. I sensed that more than saw it as I stood inside the doorway, blinking in a vain attempt to hasten the adjusting of my eyes to the dimmer interior after the full sun outside.

"Tabitha!" Audrey said. She started my name in a happy sort of tone, but by the final vowel, an edge of anxiety had worked its way in. "Where have you been? You look dreadful!"

I wanted to say something quippy in response, but my mouth was too pasty-dry to form words. I felt someone's hands on my shoulders—not Audrey's—guiding me to the nearest delicate teashop chair and pushing me down in it. Then a marvelously chilled glass of something was put in my hands and I took my first cautious sip of an Arnold Palmer.

"Get something for Houdini," I croaked as soon as I could speak. I still couldn't quite see anything around me, nothing but the beautiful golden hue of the beverage in front of me. I took another, longer sip.

"Not too cold, you'll cramp his little belly," I heard someone say.

I was pretty sure that was Liam.

I took another, longer drink, and it was like the sugar and caffeine finally hit me and my brain woke back up from its stupor.

It was, indeed, Liam. He was sliding into the chair across from mine with that familiar sheepish grin on his face. "Hey," he said.

"Hey yourself," I said, my voice still a little on the frog end of the spectrum. I looked up to see Steph standing over my shoulder and guessed it had been his hands that had guided me to the chair. He was watching me closely with a worried frown on his face, and gestured for me to drink more of the Arnold Palmer. I took another sip, then said, "I guess I was in that hedge maze longer than I thought."

"Time can run funny in some of the more obscure parts," he said. He was still studying me intensely, like he was afraid I was about to pass out and he might have to catch me.

"I noticed it," Houdini said in my mind even as he drank greedily from the bowl Audrey had set on the floor in front of him. Or as greedily as he could with his inefficiently small tongue.

The minute he spoke, I saw Liam across from me jump.

"You heard him?" I said. "You heard Houdini, didn't you?"

He flushed and stammered, but before he could get a word out, Houdini said, "Of course he can hear me. He's part of your little group now, isn't he?"

"Is he?" I asked, craning my neck to look up at Steph again.

He took pity on me and left his hovering position to sit down at the table. "He is," he said. "He has taken an oath to keep our secrets, and the Wizard himself has given his approval to the wording of the oath. He is free to come and go between our two worlds as he wishes."

"And he can help with our investigation?" I asked.

"Can and will," Liam said. "But I also have *so* many questions."

"For me?" I asked, surprised.

"Well," Liam drawled, not quite looking at Audrey. The color of his cheeks looked redder than mine felt, and that was saying something.

"Of course. For Audrey," I said, and quickly took another drink of my Arnold Palmer. Which turned out to be the last. There was nothing left in the glass but ice.

"Do you want another?" Audrey offered.

"Yes," Steph answered for me, and she nodded briskly, then hustled into the back room. I heard the refrigerator door open, then close again.

"I'm going to help," Liam said, and bolted from the table.

Houdini grumbled something about watching where people stepped, although he was far enough away from the door in the counter to never have been in any danger. I was sure he knew that, since he never stopped drinking even as he spoke that complaint into our minds.

It took him a long time to drink, really. It was like watching a hummingbird feeding, little bursts of activity that didn't seem to yield him much. But he kept at it.

I turned to Steph the minute I was sure Liam was out of earshot and whispered, "Can you tell anyone else the wording of the oath that he took, or is that secret?"

"That's up to Liam," he said. "But I promise he understood completely everything he was agreeing to before I accepted his vow. I'm no Mephistopheles looking to trick him into something."

"No, of course not," I said. Now I was the one blushing. Although I was still so borderline heat-stroked, I was pretty sure he couldn't tell.

"You can tell him anything, answer any of his questions, without worrying about breaking the rules that protect the Square," Steph said. "The two of you are completely safe. And so is Liam, now."

"Thank you," I said. I picked up my glass again, forgetting it was empty. There were a few more drops in there now from the melting ice, but not enough. I set it back down, but when I did so, the bracelet on my wrist jangled just a bit. Enough to catch the light.

"How is this working out for you?" Steph asked, brushing a fingertip over the silver chain.

"So far, so good," I said. "And thanks for that as well."

He brushed my thanks away with a careless wave of his hand. "I will tell the Wizard. He'll be pleased." Then he got up from the table.

"Wait," I said, catching his wrist. He looked back at me.

"Yes?"

"I wanted to ask you something," I said, but I could hear Audrey and Liam's voices growing louder as they came back into the main room. I kept hold of Steph's wrist, pulling him with me as I headed outside to stand on the patio, where there was a modicum of shade.

But, again, in that kind of humidity? Didn't make much difference. I was sweating again pretty much instantly.

"Perhaps we should go up to your nook," Steph said.

"No, I have a feeling this is going to be a quick conversation," I said.

He raised an eyebrow at me. "Now you've roused my curiosity. What do you want to ask me about that you are already so sure of the brevity of my answer?"

"I think my uncle has sworn a magical oath," I said.

"Indeed?" He didn't *quite* sound skeptical. But he was definitely skeptical-adjacent.

"Is there any way for me to confirm that?" I asked.

"Besides asking him?"

"I think he's not allowed to talk about it," I said. "In fact, I think there's a bunch of stuff he's not allowed to talk about. And I have a sinking feeling it's all about me."

Now he was frowning in a worried sort of way. It wasn't until I could literally feel my heart sinking that I realized how desperately I had hoped he would tell me I was just being silly. Or that it was nothing to worry about.

But judging from his face, there was a lot to worry about.

"That would be a very powerful spell," he said. "Do you know of anyone your uncle interacts with who has that kind of power?"

"I've spent maybe fifteen days all told in his company in my entire life," I said miserably. "I have no idea who his friends and acquaintances are, let alone his enemies."

"I can ask around for you," he said. "But, no promises on getting an answer you'll like."

"I appreciate that, truly," I said. "He comes back home at the end of August, and I'd really like to know by then if maybe he'd be safer if I weren't here."

"I can see why you'd feel that way," he said. "I won't tell you that you have nothing to worry about. I have no idea if that's true. But I will say that your uncles aren't the only ones in the Square who are eager to help you."

"Even though I set fire to our Fourth of July party?" I asked.

"Even though," he agreed with a twinkle in his eye. "Now, I've let a lot of work sit while I was working with Liam, and I really do have to get back to it." He gave me one last questioning look, as if to be sure I didn't have anything else for him before he left.

"Wait!" I said for the second time. And he raised that eyebrow at me again. "Look, do you even have a cellphone?" I blurted out.

"Not currently," he said.

"Have you ever?" I asked. Completely irrelevant, actually, but something I had to know after *that* vague answer.

"No," he admitted with a little laugh. "What's this about?"

"Well, it would just be handy to have a way of contacting you when I need you. Or just want to talk to you," I said.

That blazing redness was back in my cheeks for sure.

But he was looking at me in a bemused sort of way. "Why, Tabitha, I know your magic has never been reliable, but you've still lived among magical people your entire life. You really don't know how to summon me?"

I shrugged then shook my head. "I never had a lot of friends."

Any. The word I actually meant was *any*. As in, I had never had any friends. Until Audrey. Who had a cellphone.

Which reminded me. "Audrey and Agatha used to communicate through scrying mirrors. She has both parts now, and no real use for them—"

But he held up a hand to stop my words. "Not necessary. We live in the same neighborhood, not hundreds of miles apart."

"So how do I call you when I need you?" I asked.

"You just call my name," he said. "Just call out to Stephanos Underwood, apprentice to the Wizard of St. Anthony Square. Although just 'Steph' will do if said with real, urgent intent."

"That's it?" I asked, trying not to sound as doubtful as I felt.

"That's it," he agreed. Then I thought I saw the beginnings of a flush on his cheeks before he leaned close to my ear to say, "Your own control of magic doesn't matter for this. I'm always listening for your voice. I'll hear you."

I pulled back to look up at him, but my eyes blinked as I did so. And in that eye blink, he was gone.

CHAPTER

TWENTY-THREE

The next morning dawned as hot and hazy with smoke as all the days before, and I could already feel how cranky I was after a night barely sleeping in the stuffy attic room.

I was definitely going to have to find a way to enchant my French window with some of that Pacific Northwest breeze magic.

But in the meantime, I settled for a shower under water as cold as I could stand it. Then I got dressed and went down to the teashop for breakfast. This time, Houdini went with me. And he wasn't even eying every patch of shadow for potential threats as we walked. He was finally getting comfortable leaving the bookshop. Perhaps our little trip through the sewers had helped emboldened him.

I really hoped nothing happened to change his newfound confidence.

After my customary pause inside the teashop doors—eyes closed as I drank in the cool forest air with every pore of my body—I noticed that Audrey wasn't alone. Bernardo was there, with Miss Snooty Cat in his arms.

And so was a radiantly grinning Liam.

"Group meeting, right?" he said to me as I approached the table where they were all gathered. He got up to pull over another chair for me, and Audrey quickly poured out a cup of tea for me and pushed the plate of fresh-baked scones a little closer.

"I guess I missed the memo?" I said as I settled into my chair. Houdini jumped up to sit on my lap even before I had gotten down far enough into the chair to *have* a lap. He narrowed his eyes at Miss Snooty Cat, who kept her head carefully turned away in a show of ignoring him. But to my relief, he didn't start growling or barking at her.

"We nearly always meet in the mornings," Bernardo said as he stroked his cat.

"That always felt like a coincidence of timing to me," I admitted.

"It is pretty much every morning," Audrey said as she tucked her hair behind her ears before buttering the scone on her plate. "I didn't think you'd mind adding Liam to the mix."

Liam gave me an anxious, expectant look.

"Not at all," I said. "I guess I never thought of it as a meeting, though. That sounds like something with minutes and an agenda."

"Oh, we totally have an agenda," Bernardo said. "And the first item on it is that list of names I gave you."

"I already told him about the records in the Foshay Tower," Audrey said to me.

"Yeah, they all seem to have alibis," I said.

"None of them were seen anywhere near the Square on the night in question," Bernardo said. "Believe me, I've asked *everyone*."

I didn't doubt that.

"What about on the prosaic side of things?" I asked, looking at Liam as I took my first sip of Audrey's signature blend of strong black tea. I quickly added more sugar.

"That's me," Liam said, almost beaming with pride. "I'm afraid the situation is pretty much the same. Anyone she had any known connection with has been ruled out as a suspect. They can all prove they were nowhere near here at the time. That, plus the security cameras not showing anything at all, makes this pretty much on a straight path to becoming a cold case sooner rather than later."

"Delilah knew such a wide range of men," I mused as I stirred the sugar into my tea. "I doubt our two lists cover them all. It's possible we're not even looking in the right place at all."

"What do you mean?" Audrey asked.

"Well, there are people with magical capabilities who aren't part of our society," I said. "You know, prosaics who have developed magic are rare, but not unheard of. And there are witches who drop out of the magical community to live alone in the prosaic world. Maybe she crossed paths with one of them. It would be very hard to trace one. They basically live off of every grid. And they tend to practice a lot of nondetection illusions."

"Do they?" Audrey asked. "I've never heard of anything like that. But I guess it sounds plausible."

"I've read a lot," I said. "It's part of the territory, not focusing on one course of study and sticking to it. You become Random Facts Girl."

"Sounds handy to me," Liam said. "But then again, I suppose I'm the prosaic corollary to that. Random Facts Boy."

Audrey gave him a fond smile, and his ears reddened. But then he looked back to me again. "Obviously, I've never heard what you're talking about with these hermit magician types. But I thought the problem with the cameras was because of the effect of having that thing called the Tower so close?"

"That's right," Bernardo said with a nod.

"Oh, that's right!" I said, slapping my own forehead. Houdini made a little protest at the jostling motion, then settled back down to his nap. "In all the excitement yesterday afternoon, I never even told you what Houdini and I found in that tunnel."

"You found something?" Audrey asked, sitting up straighter. "I assumed it had just dead-ended, or ended at the quay under the pub. You actually found something?"

"Yeah, we found a hidden tunnel that led from that sewer line to a grate in one of the more obscure parts of the hedge maze," I said.

"That explains why you looked so frazzled when you came in," Audrey said. "Just how long were you wandering that maze in the middle of the afternoon?"

"I doubt she could even tell you," Bernardo said between sips of tea. "In the lost parts of the maze, time runs at any rate it wants to. It could've been hours and felt like minutes, or minutes and felt like hours. Or—and this is the real mind-bending one—been minutes outside the maze and felt like minutes inside the maze, but actually been hours inside the maze."

"Huh?" Liam said.

"Ditto," Audrey said.

"I think I get it," I said. "I had my phone on me. I saw the time, and when I came into the teashop, it was still synched correctly. Houdini and I parted ways with you about an hour before we came into the teashop, and that *feels* like how long we were gone, traveling through the tunnels and then finding our way out of the maze. And yet I was so thirsty and so tired and... I don't know, sun-dazzled, when we got back to you, it kind of feels like my *body* was in there a lot longer."

"Wizards have studied the phenomenon," Bernardo said. "I don't pretend to understand any of that myself. But I know it's something they've measured. Most people who go into that maze stay on the popular paths. Those who aren't just hustling to the portal and back, that is. I assumed you'd been warned."

"My uncle mentioned something about that," I admitted. "I didn't remember at the time. And anyway, when we came up through that grate, all I knew was that we were in the maze. Although it *did* look like no one had been there in years and years."

"And yet someone must have," Audrey said. "You think it's how someone got from the Square to the alley to kill Delilah without being seen."

"It could just be a coincidence," Bernardo said. "Magic places always have more paths and rooms hidden away than anyone could possibly remember. It's practically part of the magic."

Liam was grinning again, and I could almost see his fingers twitching, longing to pull out a notebook and write all this down. I would be willing to bet by the end of the month he'd probably know more about magical communities and their infrastructure than the average witch.

"But nothing about this extra tunnel points to the kind of off-the-grid mage like you were talking about," Audrey said, drawing my mind back to the moment.

"Except for the way that tunnel was hidden," I said. "There was an illusion covering the entrance of that tunnel into the main sewer line. Even though that was a forgotten side-passage, entirely in shadows, since the magic lights didn't extend down that branch. It was a powerful spell, too. It numbed my whole hand when I put it through the surface of that spell. And I don't know if most witches would've even known it was there."

"How did you know?" Liam asked, then flushed. "I mean, Audrey explained about how you're... not like other witches."

"She told you I can't do magic," I said, and by his deepening blush, I knew I was right. "No, that's a fair question. And the answer is Houdini."

Houdini heard his name and opened one of his eyes briefly. Then he realized we were all just talking and settled back into his nap.

"Because he's..." Liam started to say, then aggressively shoved an entire scone into his mouth. His eyes watered as he chewed. And chewed. And chewed.

I was pretty sure we were all gaping at the result of the oath spell he had submitted himself to. And I instantly wanted to summon Steph so I could give him a big, crushing hug.

Because it had never occurred to me to include Houdini's secret among all the secrets of the Square as something Liam should both know and swear to protect. But it had occurred to Steph. And, of course, spending all of his time with the two of us, it wouldn't take long at all for him to realize there was something different about Houdini.

"You knew, didn't you?" I whispered down to Houdini.

He opened that one eye again to gaze at me levelly. "Obviously. Why else would I allow him to hear me?"

"Is he all right?" Bernardo whispered, looking at Liam with mild alarm. Bernardo who knew about the Square, obviously, but not about Houdini.

"He really likes these scones," Audrey said as Liam finally managed to swallow down the last of his massive mouthful.

"Sorry," he said, then downed half his cup of tea in one long swallow. "I knew better than to try that."

"Savor little bites at a time," Bernardo said, bemused. I was pretty sure he sensed that there was more going on than he knew, but being Bernardo, he was happy to be left on the outside of such things.

"You'll get used to it," Audrey told him, putting a reassuring hand on his shoulder.

"Houdini is a very perceptive dog," I said, and picked him up to nuzzle around his ears. He allowed this, but made a show of not really enjoying it. Although I knew he did.

Miss Snooty Cat turned her head to regard Houdini intently, then turned away again. Her opinion on the matter was abundantly clear even before she lifted her nose into the air disdainfully.

"I suppose it's the sense of smell," Bernardo said. "He has rat terrier in him, doesn't he? Those are good sniffers."

"Agatha said he was a rat terrier and chihuahua mix," I said. Although I was suddenly curious why she had chosen that kind of dog for Houdini's disguised form. Had she seen one once and liked the look of it? I suspected the fact that he was, even fully grown, under ten pounds had been the main factor. No one would suspect such a tiny little thing was, in fact, a dragon of—probably—immense size. But had she considered things like sense of smell or hunting ability too?

I had no idea. I hadn't known what Houdini really was until some time after Agatha had died. I had never gotten the chance to ask her.

"You broke the spell when you moved through it?" Audrey said, and I heard the twinge of disappointment in her voice.

"Regretfully," I said. "I didn't know we couldn't just move through it."

"I wonder if the caster could?" Bernardo mused. "Maybe that's a feature of the spell. Now he knows someone has found his secret tunnel."

I hadn't even considered that. But he was totally right.

"Great," I grumbled.

"I was only thinking that if it were still up, it would be something the authorities would be willing to come down and investigate, maybe," Audrey said.

"Were there any clues besides the spell itself?" Liam asked.

"We searched the alcove in the maze where the grate came up, but we didn't find anything," I said. "I was pondering working out a ritual spell that you could do, Audrey. The kind of thing the authorities do to play back the events in a space."

"I don't know," Audrey said. "I mean, I believe you could write a spell I could cast to do it, absolutely. Only when the authorities did that after Agatha was murdered, it didn't really help them much."

"They didn't realize they were dealing with an entity from the under realms," I said. "That's a level of deceptive power they weren't prepared for. I doubt we're dealing with anything so powerful this time. I mean, Delilah Dare wouldn't be anywhere near as hard to kill as Agatha was."

"My worry would be that nothing you found would be admissible as evidence," Bernardo said. "The authorities need to perform these magics themselves. And if they thought your spell had contaminated the scene before they could perform theirs, that could cause problems in the investigation."

"So, what can we do?" Audrey asked helplessly.

I felt just as frustrated. But I wasn't really capable of throwing up my hands and doing nothing.

"I'm going to text Deputy Fluellen everything I saw yesterday, just on the off chance it matters," I said. "I mean, he did tell me he was keeping a case file, just in case. Maybe this combined with something he knows, but we don't, means something. I don't know. It's better than nothing, right?"

"I can touch base with my contact again, see if there's any progress on the case on this side," Liam offered.

"Good idea, thanks," I said. Then I downed the last of my tea and pushed away from the table. Houdini hopped down to the ground, then shook his whole body vigorously, his ears slapping loudly and his little feet sliding apart on the tiled floor. Then he looked up at me with those strangely intelligent brown eyes.

"We're going back into the maze, aren't we?" he said in my mind.

I gave him a little nod. Miss Snooty Cat's head whipped around, as if she, too, had heard Houdini speak. But Bernardo didn't notice as he gently nudged her to one side to reach for the teapot and pour himself another cup of the now tepid tea.

"I have my phone if you need me," I said to Audrey.

"Be careful," she said. Bernardo gave her a questioning look before turning his attention back to his teacup. Liam gave me a half-wave/half-salute, and I knew he also had heard Houdini say where we were going.

"It's perfectly safe inside the Square," I said, with more surety than I felt. Then I pushed my way back out into the already hot morning, Houdini trotting close beside me.

CHAPTER

TWENTY-FOUR

Houdini and I wandered around the hedge maze for what felt like an hour, although now, with Bernardo's words in my head, I realized it was likely far longer.

The sunburn prickling over my skin certainly said that it had been.

And yet we were no closer to finding the alcove we had been in just the day before.

Finally, we stopped in one of the other alcoves to rest in the shade, for as little as that was worth. But at least there was a little bit of a breeze. A hot breeze, to be sure, but we sat downwind from the fountain. The spray of water was warmer than I would've liked, but was better than nothing.

"I suppose we should've just come up through the tunnel again," I sighed as I petted Houdini's head.

"I did think with my perfect memory and sense of direction that I could find it again," he huffed unhappily.

"Well, you do realize the hedges move around when they want to," I said.

"Oh," he said, straightening up a little taller. "No, I didn't realize that."

I was glad that made him feel better. But it didn't really help our current problem. How were we ever going to find that alcove now? We could wander around forever and never stumble across it.

And yet the only way this path to the sewers was usable to anyone was if there *was* a way to find it at will from this end. There had to be one.

But with my limited skill, I was terribly unlikely to discover it. Unless we got very, very lucky.

Which was its own kind of magic.

"We should probably just head back out and try coming in through the tunnel," I said.

"Let's," Houdini readily agreed.

This time we wandered for far less than what felt like an hour, but far longer than the point where we both had the same suspicion we were too afraid to voice to each other. Finally, I just had to stop walking and blurt it out.

"Face it, we're lost," I said.

"I'm so sorry!" Houdini said. He turned back as if to face me, but he was hanging his head so low I couldn't make eye contact with him. His radar dish ears were down flat against his neck, and his usually curly-queued tail drooped in the dry grass.

"I'm not blaming you!" I said, dropping to my knees. I avoided his ears since he was clearly in a sensitive place and just rubbed his doggy shoulders vigorously.

"But I shouldn't ever *be* lost!" he moaned.

"I know, buddy," I said. "I should've warned you about the hedges before."

"I should've felt it happening," he said. "But I don't feel that time thing Bernardo was going on about, either. This whole place is making me feel like a dog and not a dragon."

"Hey, we're both at the mercy of the elements here," I said. I sat down on the grass and let him climb into my lap. Walking around wasn't doing us any good, anyway.

"What do we do now?" he whimpered.

"I think the maze will let us back out if we keep walking," I said. "It did yesterday."

"I know my senses are not to be trusted in here, but something is different from yesterday," he said.

"What's different?" I asked.

"I don't know. It's subtle. But something is different," he said. He buried his nose under the palm of my hand. "I'm sorry I can't describe it better."

"Don't worry about it. You're being too tough on yourself," I said.

He started to relax under my hand as I stroked his back, but then we both heard the sound of footsteps approaching and froze stiffly. Houdini sniffed the air, but I had nothing to rely on but my ears. And the sounds were echoing around as if we were in a fog. Those steps could be coming from any direction, and be at any distance. It kept changing from instant to instant.

I still had my hand on Houdini's back, and I could feel the bristling of the hairs all up and down his spine. It was almost like they were all twitching, like he could sense things through them like thousands of tiny antennas, and he was constantly redirecting their efforts to different areas.

Then he stiffened up entirely. I was looking back behind us at that moment, at the nothingness of the maze corridor between the hedges, but I immediately turned to look ahead, to see what he was reacting to. Before I had quite gotten all the way around, I felt him relax. Then I saw the shape approaching, a man with his hands up in the age-old show of "I mean you no harm." The sun was behind his head, so bright it almost shimmered like a halo. I guess that's why it took me far longer than it had Houdini to recognize who was there.

Then he stepped closer, and the sun was out of sight behind his shoulders, and I finally recognized Taurus Vernon.

"I hope I didn't startle you," he said, stopping six feet away from the two of us. I got to my feet, Houdini in my arms.

"No, we heard you coming," I said.

"I didn't expect I'd ever find anyone in here, to be honest," he said, giving me a relieved sort of smile.

"What do you mean?" I asked.

"Well, I've been wandering around in here for quite some time. I guess I was warned about certain parts of this maze, but I confess I didn't take those warnings too seriously. I was pretty sure I was capable of getting myself out of anything. But, well..." he trailed off, rubbing at the back of his neck with a chagrined look. Then he winced, and I realized he was as sunburned as I was.

"Something is different today," I said.

"You're lost too?" he asked, sounding almost relieved at what was, honestly, kind of bad news for both of us.

"Yeah," I said. "What are you even doing in here, anyway? I mean, I live in the Square. This is kind of my backyard."

"Oh, sure," he said. Then he thrust both of his hands deep into his pockets. Again, this felt like a demonstration of having no ill intent. I would've trusted it more if I hadn't felt that "demonstration" part of it so intensely. "To be honest, after our conversation yesterday, I was curious myself what happened to Delilah. I checked the usual news feeds, but there didn't seem to be any breakthroughs in the investigation on either side of the veil. So I thought I'd see if I could find anything. Stupid, I know."

"Well..." I drawled, and despite myself I could feel my cheeks flaming.

"Oh, of course. You're doing that already," he said. "Sorry, I didn't mean it was a stupid thing to do. I guess I get the impulse. It doesn't sit right, knowing justice isn't being served. Not that I was fond of Delilah in the end. But that doesn't mean she deserved what she got. No, it just doesn't sit right with me."

"I get it," I said. "But why are you here specifically?"

"Well, this maze was the last place anyone saw Delilah alive, right?" he said.

"Cleopatra saw her here," I said. "I guess she was the last one. Well, except for the murderer, of course."

"Of course," he said. "I was hoping I could find some sort of clue. Not to break the case, necessarily. Maybe just enough to get the authorities to take the investigation seriously. It just feels like they're going to drop the ball, doesn't it?"

"It kind of does," I said. I pulled my phone out of my pocket and glanced at the screen. I had full bars, but no texts from Deputy Fluellen. If he had gotten my five long texts at all, he hadn't responded to them.

"So are you here just to enjoy the afternoon in your backyard, or are you looking for clues too?" he asked. There was a teasing glow to his eyes, and I knew he already knew the answer to that one. But I just shrugged noncommittally. "Well, if you were," he went on, "perhaps you'd be interested in joining forces?"

"To find clues or to find a way out of this maze?" I asked.

He laughed at that. "Frankly, either. But one and then the other might be optimal. Provided we don't both get sunstroke first."

"It is a pretty uncomfortable day," I admitted. "But I don't see a better one in the next two weeks of weather forecasts. And we're here already."

"So that's a yes?" he asked.

I looked down at Houdini. His ears were still flat against his head, but at this point, that could be as much about the heat as about his emotional state.

"I don't think we need his help," he mumbled in my mind. "But I guess it would be cruel to leave him in here alone. He looks pretty helpless."

I didn't think the two of us looked much better, but I stroked the back of his head in a gesture of agreement.

"Sure, let's see what we can find. Although honestly, I don't know how to find the alcove where she was," I said.

His attention perked up at that. "You know where she was?" he asked.

I bit my lip. It must be the impending heat stroke, making me say more than I ought to have done. But there was no taking it back now. "Well, she must've been somewhere she and Cleopatra could've had a fight, right? So I assumed they went into one of the alcoves."

"We're standing in the middle of a corridor right now, talking," Taurus said.

"Sure, but we ran into each other here," I said. "They went into the maze specifically to have a conversation. I would think they'd take that into an alcove."

"Right, but then, why not one of the more accessible ones?" he asked.

"If you think that, why are you this far in?" I countered.

"Look, I already admitted I got lost," he said. "And, sure, I'm playing devil's advocate with your investigative theories. But isn't that how it's done? We have to poke holes into every theory to figure out which ones are sound?"

"I suppose," I said.

"I'm not trying to take over your investigation," he said, hands out of pockets in that surrender gesture again. "I've heard that's kind of your thing. I'm not trying to step on any toes." Then he noticed me glaring at his hands and put them back in his pockets. "And I'm not trying to make you feel bad about what happened the other night. I know that wasn't something you do all the time or on purpose."

"You seem to *know* a lot about me," I said. I was still holding Houdini close to my chest, or else I would've air-quoted those words.

"People have come around to talk to me," he confessed.

"Who?" I asked at once.

"Lots of people," he said vaguely. "Look, are we going to look for clues or not? Because standing and debating under this hot sun is at the bottom of my list of things to do right in this moment."

"We'll follow you," I said. Houdini, in my arms, lifted his head to give Taurus a piercing gaze. Despite the fact this was coming from a small dog, I couldn't help noticing when he took half a step back, almost in reflex. Like he could sense the dragon.

Then he turned and led the way through the maze. He was making selections at random, something I would normally object to. Only Houdini and I had already tried choosing every righthand turn, and then every lefthand turn, for quite some time, and neither method had led us anywhere. Might as well try random.

I lost all track of time, just plodding along after Taurus with Houdini in my arms. I was getting dizzy and disoriented, and a quiet voice in the back of my mind was whispering something about maybe this really was heatstroke. That voice was also worried about how listless Houdini was. He *never* wanted to be carried this much.

But that voice was so little, and so quiet. It was easier just to keep walking and wait for this all to be over.

Then suddenly, I was nearly colliding with Taurus's sweaty back. He had come to a dead stop in the middle of yet another crossroads in the maze, with three choices before us.

"Honestly, I can't keep doing this," he said to me in utter defeat. "I don't know where to go. I just know all my choices are wrong. Do you want to take the lead for a while?"

"Sure," I said dully. He stepped back, as if I needed an unimpeded view of three identical paths through ratty, unkempt hedges that grew far taller than the top of my head. But I looked down each anyway.

"What do you think?" I whispered to Houdini.

"Don't care," he said. "Left, I guess."

I turned to the left. This path only went a few yards before turning yet again to the left.

Great. We were going in circles already.

Then it turned to the left yet again, this time ending in a very familiar-looking alcove.

I stood there staring at the water shooting out of the oyster shell for entirely too long before finally dropping my eyes to the ground at my feet.

And the grate that stood there, still open from when Houdini and I had come out of it the day before.

TWENTY-FIVE

For a long moment there was nothing but the heat, the humidity, and the constant droning of the midsummer insects in the hedges around us.

Then Houdini moved restlessly in my arms. It was really warm, holding onto his hot little body. And he was probably even more miserable, with my arms completely around him. But he wasn't trying to tell me to put him down. He was just adjusting himself to a more comfortable position. He left itchy black hairs all over my sweat-soaked arms, and I was about to object to his fidgeting when he promptly went still, his nose resting on my shoulder without being pressed up against my even sweatier neck.

Then Taurus was standing beside me, looking around the alcove in a confused manner. "Why did you stop here?" he finally asked me.

"That's it," I said, nodding my head towards the open grate. "That's where the secret tunnel begins."

"Secret tunnel?" Taurus said. I watched as his facial expression morphed from genuine surprise to something like dawning realization. I could almost hear the pieces clicking together in his head.

"Delilah went from here to the alley through a secret underground passage?"

"It leads to a mostly unused water channel off the quay under the pub. I'm guessing that's how you get downtown," I said. He nodded. "This leads to a channel that branches off of that one, and passes under the end of the alley before also heading downtown. Although it lacks a view from under the falls. I'm guessing it goes deeper."

He still looked genuinely surprised by all this information as he stood looking down into the darkness beyond the open grate. I guessed he hadn't been trying to find this opening specifically as I had. He had just been looking for any kind of clue at all. Kind of a hopeless quest, really.

"I guess we should go down then," he said.

But I was looking at Houdini.

He was shaking like never before. As if he were in that cold already.

"What's wrong, buddy?" I whispered to him.

"I can't go back down there," he said to me.

"But that's what we came here to do," I said.

"I know, I know," he said, still trembling like crazy.

"Did something change? I mean, besides the whole maze," I said.

Houdini said nothing. He just kept shaking in fear. He also seemed to be avoiding looking at Taurus, who had stepped past me to inspect the open grate.

"What's wrong?" I asked Houdini, taking half a step back, out of the alcove. "You don't trust him?"

"No, he's fine," Houdini said. "I just... I don't think I can go back into that alley. Not today," he said, and buried his nose under my arm so that I couldn't meet his eyes.

"That's all right," I assured him. "But I don't know what else you're going to do. We're lost in here, remember?"

"I'll wait here," he said miserably. "When you're done looking for clues, you can come get me again."

"I don't like that plan at all," I said. "What if something happens to you? What if I can't find you again?"

"I can't go in there, Tabitha. I just can't," he said.

I didn't have it in me to try to talk him into it. I just didn't. I turned to tell Taurus of the change of plan. He wasn't facing me, just standing with his hands in his pockets, looking down at the open grate. I couldn't see the expression on his face because the sun was behind him again, glowing like a hazy halo and keeping his features in shadow.

He was waiting for us to go down that hole. And after all the work it had taken to find it, it would be foolish to back out now that we were finally here.

"All right. I'm not going to make you," I said to Houdini. "Maybe I should call Steph for help. He can get you out of here and safely back to the bookshop."

"No, that's not necessary," Houdini said with an air of wounded pride. "I'll be quite all right. I'll wait here. And if you don't come back soon, I'll call Steph myself. I know he can hear me."

"You do?" I asked, surprised.

"Yes. I've done it before," he said.

"You have?" This was news to me. What on earth had the two of them spoken about when I wasn't there?

"Don't worry about me. But Taurus is getting impatient," Houdini said. "And you really should get out of the heat. You'll feel better down there. It will clear your head."

I didn't doubt that. It was so hard to think, and I was so very thirsty. Not that there was any drinkable water down there. But the sooner we were done, the sooner we could go back to the teashop.

"All right. We'll be quick as we can," I said, and set Houdini on the ground in the shade under one of the benches. The spray from the fountain was too warm to be entirely refreshing, but he turned his face toward it, anyway.

"Ready?" Taurus asked as he mopped the sweat from the back of his neck with a silk handkerchief. It was the sort of thing I would expect Bernardo to have on him, but not Taurus. He saw me looking at it and tucked it back into his pocket with a nervous chuckle.

"Houdini is going to wait here. He's sort of a lookout," I said.

Taurus looked past me to where Houdini was still trying to catch the warm spray from the fountain on his long curl of a tongue. A hard look passed over his face, there and gone before I quite grasped what it was. Then those ice-blue eyes were on mine again.

"Are you sure? He's all black hair; he must just be absorbing all the heat," Taurus said with real concern.

"He'll be all right in the shade," I said.

I wasn't going to approach anything like explaining to Taurus that Houdini was afraid. That was too close to his real relationship with that alley, a relationship that had nothing to do with Delilah and what happened to her there. I didn't want to risk misspeaking, not when my brain was so very groggy from the heat.

"If you say so," Taurus said. "Shall we?"

I nodded, and he went first down the hole. I started to follow, but paused when my eyes were level with Houdini's under the stone bench.

"Are you sure you're okay?" I asked him.

"I am," he said. But his voice in my mind sounded so very tremulous. Maybe the heat was getting to him worse than it was to me. Hopefully, a break in the shade and warm spray from the fountain would help.

Then I was down in the cool darkness. I found my way down the long ladder by feel, but once my feet were both on the ground, I pulled out my phone and turned on the flashlight.

Taurus was right there, far closer than I had sensed, and I made an involuntary yelping sound.

"Sorry. Didn't mean to startle you," he said, taking a step away from me. "I didn't think to bring any light, but I'm glad you did."

"It's this way," I said, and led the way down the passage of eerie black stone walls towards the sewer. He followed along behind me, but not too closely. He kept touching the stone with his fingertips or looking back behind us into the impenetrable inky darkness.

It wasn't quite natural, how quickly the light from the grate above was no longer visible once we were more than a few yards down that passage. It was like the shadows down here just consumed that light.

"This is where she was killed, do you think?" Taurus mused as we walked.

"No, that was definitely in the alley," I said.

"So, was she dragged through here, or was this her secret tunnel?"

"I don't know," I said.

The tunnel ended, and I stepped out onto the sewer walkway. The concealment spell was definitely gone, so there was no icy numbness as I passed through the archway this time.

Taurus emerged behind me, still touching the walls and trying to look everywhere at once. "I didn't see any kind of clue in there. I'm guessing you didn't either." I shook my head that I hadn't. "Yeah, but that doesn't feel like it rules out anything, does it? It's like that tunnel hides things. If Delilah had left some clue behind about who her attacker was, I'm not sure we even could've found it. Don't you think?"

"It does feel like that darkness devours things," I agreed with a little shiver. The sweat on my skin had dried, but my clothes were still damp and clinging to me coldly.

"At least we can see in here somewhat," he said. "Can you shine your light around a little?"

I let him take the lead, since I'd been up and down this dark sewer twice already. He would occasionally think he saw something, but every time he asked me to train my light into one shadowed corner or another, there was never anything there but water-logged branches or rotting leaves.

Or garbage. There was a disturbing amount of plastic garbage. But it was disturbing in a way that had nothing to do with Delilah.

"Which way to the alley?" he asked in a resigned voice.

"The quay under the pub is that way, and the alley is this way," I said, pointing each way with the light on my phone.

"Let's go to the alley," he said. But he sounded no more optimistic than before. Not that I didn't understand the desire to be thorough, even if you were sure it would prove useless. That was pretty much why I was down here in the first place, after all.

I led the way to the lighted part of the sewer, then up to the grate in the back of the alley.

I was sensing the presence of the Tower more strongly today, like a pressure on my mind that was steering me away from noticing its existence. After climbing out of the grate, I crouched just out of the way while I waited for Taurus to join me, and I wondered why that was. Maybe it was a side effect of the grogginess from the heat? The cooler air underground had been a pleasant change, but the hoped-for clearing of my mind hadn't happened. I felt as foggy-headed as ever.

Or maybe it was because this time Houdini wasn't with me?

I wasn't sure what that could mean, but I mentally filed it away as something to ask Steph later.

"Ugh. The smell," Taurus said the moment his head came into view.

The dumpster smell was stronger than before, but there was also a coppery undertone to it that I didn't remember from before.

"Is that blood smell?" I asked out loud.

"I thought she was strangled," Taurus said as he clambered the rest of the way out of the sewer.

"I thought so too," I said. "I guess that could cut the skin, if the killer used some sort of tool and not just their hands."

"Is that how it was done? Do you know that for a fact?" he asked, his icy blue eyes boring into me.

"I'm not sure how it was done, actually," I said. "I didn't think to ask."

"Well, that's probably to be expected," he said smoothly. "You're not a professional investigator, are you?"

"No," I said. But I suddenly felt like I wanted to take a few more steps away from him. His vibe was changing in a way I didn't like. Or was my brain fog clearing? Was I noticing things now I should've been noticing all along?

I was suddenly very—but belatedly—suspicious of Houdini's fear of going back underground. What had changed? When he'd looked back over my shoulder for that bare instance, what had he seen?

Taurus had been behind us. But Taurus was no wizard. What could he have done to put a whammy on a *dragon*?

And what hope did I have if he tried it on me?

Then a cold chill ran up my spine. He *had* tried it on me. Tried and succeeded. I had gone done a dark hole with him.

And I'd left my companion behind. I'd gone alone.

My brain fog had nothing to do with the heat.

I weighed my options as I backed away. But I already knew I wasn't on any security cameras, and no prosaic witnesses could see past the Tower.

"No, I'm sure there are many things you didn't think of," Taurus said, matching me step for step until he was once more standing over me. All the charm was gone from his voice now. He wasn't the cad from the Fourth of July party, and he wasn't the apologetic, bumbling try-hard of the last two times I'd interacted with him. He was someone else now.

Someone whose true calling wasn't finance.

I didn't want to look up at him, but it was like I couldn't help it. And those eyes bored into mine again.

"Many things," I repeated his words. Why did my tongue feel so thick? Was it just the dehydration? I glanced down the alley, towards the teashop. I could really use an ice cold Arnold Palmer.

"So many things you didn't think of," he went on, his voice almost hypnotic in its warm, slow tones. Like what he was really meant to be doing was audiobook narration. And he was smiling down at me, just as warmly as he was speaking. If I ignored the look in his eyes, the rest of it was quite soothing. "So many things you didn't think of, it would be easy to forget all of it. Don't you agree?"

I started to nod. But a sudden flash of clarity washed over my mind.

"I thought to call the deputy," I blurted out. "He knows I'm here. I told him all about that secret tunnel into the hedge maze and everything."

"Did you?" The warmth was still there, but it had an edge to it now.

"I gave him enough to open the investigation," I said. "I was just coming here to wait to meet him."

"Why don't I believe you?" he asked me.

"I don't know. It's all true," I said. I took two more steps back, but found myself with my back pressed against the wall of the alley. Or, rather, the exterior wall of the Tower. It was buzzing in my mind, shouting at me to ignore it. It was over-whelming.

Then Taurus took another two steps to stand over me again. Only now he had something in his hand. But I couldn't look away from his eyes long enough to see just what it was.

"You're right," he cooed at me. "I should believe you. Yes, it's safer if I believe you."

"Safer for whom?" I asked, but my voice squeaked out the last syllable. Because in that moment he leaned closer to me, his nose almost touching mine. His head was haloed by the sun again, but there was something wrong with the way it glinted around him this time.

Then I sucked in a breath. No, what had been wrong had been how it had glinted the first two times. That glint was not natural. That glint had been a spell.

And the moment when Houdini had frozen in my arms, right before he had started trembling, had been another.

Taurus Vernon might work in finance, but his magic was nearly as forbidden as mine.

He was working mind control magic.

And he was very good at it.

"What did you do?" I asked, even as my hands closed into fists.

"I think you know what I did," he said. Then he raised his hand into my line of sight, and I saw a strip of white silk dangling from his grasp. For one confused moment, I thought this was his handkerchief again. I almost gave in to a sagging relief.

But then he caught the other end of it with his other hand and snapped it tight. I could see the tight knot in the center of the scarf between his two hands.

I could see the reddish-brown stains dotted over that silken knot. He had strangled Delilah violently enough to make her bleed. And he hadn't used piano wire or fishing line or anything fine like that. He had used a silk scarf. A silk scarf, and his own angry strength.

I glanced towards the teashop again. I could see the door to the comic book shop, much closer.

But I could see no sign of any other human beings. Not even on the usually busy road at the end of the alley.

I was totally alone.

"You know how this is going to end," Taurus said with what sounded like regret. "If you hoped there would be an easy way and a hard way and that I'd offer you the choice, I'm afraid that's not how I do things. There's only the one way."

I swallowed hard, but I had to keep him talking. At some point, Deputy Fluellen would read my texts. He would come. It was my best hope.

It was my *only* hope.

"I know why you have to kill me, since I know what you did. But why Delilah? I mean, she was Cleopatra's pale shadow. Why did you care so much that she didn't want you?" I asked.

He scoffed but said nothing. He just took another step closer with that scarf in his hands.

"I mean, if you were mad that she rejected you, couldn't you just consider every man in the magical and prosaic communities both rejecting *her* karma?"

Now he sneered at me. He didn't say it, but I could see he was disappointed that I hadn't put something together.

"Wait, you *made* those men reject her? To get revenge? And then, when that didn't work, you tried using me?"

"Every time I almost destroyed her, left her a whimpering emotional sack, and every time Cleopatra would put her back together again. I was never going to *win*."

I had no answer to that. I'm not sure why I ever thought his motive would make sense to me. But this went beyond deranged jealousy.

I was still reeling from feeling sympathy for Delilah Dare and grudging admiration of Cleopatra Manx when Taurus took another step closer with that scarf raised at the height of my throat.

"Don't touch me with that," I hissed at him. "It's evidence."

He laughed at that, a sudden bark of laughter like my attempt at a joke had taken him off guard.

But then he was leaning in again, and I could feel his hot breath on my face even before the brush of silk made contact with my skin.

I ducked down, dropping to my knees in one of the fouler-smelling puddles. That got another chuckle out of him before he grabbed for a fistful of my hair to drag me back to my feet.

But I had a half-second to slide off that bracelet. I didn't need more than that. I already knew what my power could do.

Only the bracelet didn't budge. If anything, it felt like it tightened around my wrist, the chain links digging in, hugging me in a way that was not remotely comforting.

Being dragged up by my hair was just as horrific as it sounded. Then I was pushed back against the stone wall again, the Tower once more buzzing in my head with its overwhelming urgency to just be ignored.

It was really hard to ignore that call to ignore.

But then another sensation was tickling my mind. Just a tiny wave of emotion. It didn't have words like when Houdini spoke to me, but I could sense a question.

It was the charm in the bracelet, gently querying whether I was sure I wanted my control back. Or lack thereof, I suppose. But the charm wasn't as judgy as I was.

As Taurus's silk scarf once more touched my skin, I sent that charm a resounding YES.

I could still feel the weight of the bracelet on my wrist, but that cool, calming sensation fell away.

And I instantly started to spark. An arc of electricity shot from my skin to Taurus' hands. He fell back with a hiss, but only momentarily. He glared at me angrily as he shook feeling back into his hands, then started to come towards me again.

But this time, he never even got close enough to touch me. The next electric arc I summoned didn't even come from my own body. It came straight down out of the hazy sky above, an enormous bolt of lightning that struck his entire body. I could smell singed hair even before I heard his scream. His arms and legs were out straight like he'd become a starfish, only they were shaking worse than Houdini in the heights of his anxiety.

Tinier bolts were shooting out of him all over, from every finger and from the toes of his expensive shoes. They arced all around the alley, bouncing off the stone walls and striking the fetid pools in hissing bolts that added yet more smells to the already over-ripe air.

My concerns about just what were forming those pools were justified when many of them caught on fire. Then lines of that fire started snaking along cracks on the pavement, seeking each other out.

But that all stopped when the rain came, a heavy torrent of drops the size of buckets pounding down on everything. I was soaked to the skin within a second, and every fire was out within two.

Only then did Taurus's charred body stop shooting sparks and fall to the ground with a thud.

But my body thudded down right after it. I was still sparking. Despite the plastering rain, I was still shooting sparks I couldn't control.

Great, we were back in "high risk of burning down the Square" territory.

Worse, I could feel my consciousness slipping away. It was all I could do to form a thought outside of the relentless ordering to ignore the existence of the Tower.

But I only needed one thought.

I swear I tried to say his whole name, but all I know I got out for sure was a single, barely audible syllable.

"Steph."

And then the blackness took me.

CHAPTER

TWENTY-SIX

When I finally came to, the first thing I was aware of was the cool feeling of that charmed bracelet against my wrist.

Then I felt the warmth of Houdini, curled up behind my knees, just where he liked best to sleep at night. And I started to put together that it was my own pillow that my head was resting on, and I was wearing one of my sleeping T-shirts. Houdini and I weren't under the covers, but the afghan that usually sat folded at the foot of the bed had been pulled over both of us.

I could hear the sound of a gentle rain outside the French window, and a cool, misty breeze was blowing in from time to time.

And I was definitely clean. The gross feeling of dried sweat was gone from my skin, and I didn't smell even a hint of the alley dumpster aroma coming from any part of me.

Or the smell of charred Taurus.

I opened my eyes and heard three people suck in a breath as one. I carefully sat up without jostling Houdini, but I was suddenly being assisted by too many pairs of hands. It took a moment to sort out that it was Liam who had lunged to pick up a protesting Houdini while Steph was propping the pillows up behind me.

Then Audrey was pressing a mug of sweet-smelling tea into my hands.

"Drink that first," she said in a no-nonsense sort of voice. I took a sip of the warm but not hot tea. There was a grassy taste to it that wasn't great, but it had been almost thoroughly drowned out by great quantities of lemon and honey. And it slid down my raw throat like a welcome balm.

Why was my throat sore? Taurus had never succeeded in his attempts to strangle me.

No, this had more the raw feeling of having screamed too much the day before.

I took another sip then pushed it back into Audrey's waiting hands so I could slump back against the pillows. I pushed a chaotic mass of curls out of my face and felt a stab of genuine sorrow that all of Cressida's hard work on my hair had been undone. It didn't crackle with static electricity, but it was definitely as untamed as ever.

"Put me down, boy," Houdini groused, and Liam set him back on the bed. He lunged into my lap, but rather than settling down there, he jumped to nip at my nose again and again. I couldn't get my coordination working well enough to catch him, but I managed a few pets-in-passing as he jumped about.

"Houdini, you agreed she needed rest," Steph chided him as he sat down on the edge of the bed to catch the little dog in one hand.

"I did, and she did," Houdini said. "She's awake now."

"Awake, but not recovered," Steph said. "She still needs rest."

"And food," I said, my voice coming out like a froggy croak. "I feel like I haven't eaten in days."

There was an awkward silence at that, and three pairs of eyes nervously trading glances.

"It's been days?" I said, trying not to panic. "I've been here for days?"

"Just two," Audrey said, then thrust the tea at me again. "You really shouldn't speak until this tea has had a chance to mend your voice."

"But we all pretty much agreed that wasn't likely to happen," Steph said.

"I brought paper and pens," Liam offered, and dug them out of his bag sitting on one of the chairs by the open French window.

I shook my head before he could thrust them at me, then took three more sips of the soothing tea. Then I said, "As shredded as my voice is for whatever reason, my hands are even shakier. I think I'll just try to keep my questions short."

"You don't remember calling my name?" Steph asked, reaching out to brush the hair back out of my face. Uselessly, as it just fell right back into my eyes.

"I only managed a 'Steph.' But you said that would be enough," I said.

"It was," he said, but he looked amused for some reason I couldn't fathom.

"Everyone with any kind of magical senses at all in the entire Midwest heard you say 'Steph,'" Audrey said, and tipped the mug in my hands up to my mouth again so that I had to take another swallow.

"I've already taken the blame for that," Steph told me. "It was my mistake, after all. I told you to call out with intent. And you certainly did."

"But if it was a magic calling, why does my throat hurt?" I asked.

"You yelled too," Audrey said. "Liam and I heard you inside the teashop."

"I heard you, from whatever hell dimension that hedge maze had sunk me into," Houdini said petulantly.

"What?" I asked, nearly choking on the tea that Audrey was still forcing on me.

"Not literal hell," Steph assured me.

"But how did you get out?" I asked Houdini.

"By my own power," Houdini said, lifting his chin at me.

"He went through the walls," Steph said. "Those hedges won't allow a human to do that, but Houdini, being both small in size but large in power, managed to have his way." He sounded genuinely impressed.

"My sense of direction was all I needed to get to the teashop," he said. "I didn't bother with the doorways out of the hedge maze at all."

He puffed out his chest, exceedingly self-satisfied, but I couldn't blame him.

"And Taurus?" I asked, then dutifully took another drink of the tea before Audrey could take over again.

"Dead," Steph said.

"Dead, and found by the authorities on my side of things," Liam said. "Killed by a freak bolt of lightning out of a clear blue sky. Well, it would've been a clear blue sky if not for the smoke. And the rainstorm that blew in right after."

"It's been raining for two days," Audrey said. "It's been perfectly lovely, at least after the first intense minutes passed. Just a gentle pattering of drops and cooler air."

"And no smoke," Liam put in.

"You're both looking at me like that was my doing," I said.

"Rain wasn't in the forecast," Liam said with a shrug. "And you made the lightning, didn't you?"

"I think so," I said. "The bracelet asked if I wanted my power back under my own control, and I said yes." I swallowed reflexively, and my dry throat still burned, but not as badly as before the tea. "Of course, that really means no control at all."

"Oh, I don't know," Steph said. "You dealt with the threat, and then you channeled the rest into something we all desperately needed. There are worse ways to lose control."

I didn't say anything, but inside I had nothing but doubts about that rain. Nothing I had done had even been reaching out for rain. If it had followed the lightning, I could scarcely take credit for that. All I had wanted was to stop Taurus from touching me again.

And I had achieved that by turning him into a charcoal briquette. I couldn't even remotely make myself feel good about that. I could remember the smell too vividly.

I doubted I would ever forget that smell.

"I wasn't kidding when I said you needed more rest," Steph said as Audrey took the now-empty mug out of my hands. "We can talk about everything later, when you're a little more recovered."

"But I'm going to be close by with more tea, whenever you wake up," Audrey promised me.

I *was* feeling pretty epically tired. But my mind was whirring with still unasked questions.

One of which Liam, at least, seemed to sense. He had gone to retrieve his bag from the chair by the window when he suddenly spun back around to say, "We should at least tell her about the scarf."

"You know about the scarf?" I said. "I assumed that was nothing but ash now."

"No, you had it in your hand when I found you," Steph said. "I had to pry your fingers off of it one by one before I took you out of the alley."

"He got you out just before the local police arrived," Liam said. "There wasn't enough of Taurus Vernon left for anyone to ID, not by fingerprints or dental records either, even if he existed in prosaic data bases."

"Which he doesn't," Steph put in.

"Right. But that scarf had Delilah's DNA on it, and they did get enough DNA from the corpse of Taurus to match what was found under her fingernails. So they don't know who he is, but they know enough to close the case," Liam said.

"He put a spell on me, didn't he?" I said, touching my own fore-head as if there was somehow evidence of what felt now like a pretty grievous assault there. But the skin felt totally normal. Only my mind had been touched.

"He worked in finance, but when he went to school he was studying charms," Steph said, his voice suddenly grim. "He was supposed to be under the influence of certain restraining spells under the terms of his employment."

"Why?" I asked.

"No one wants to hand their finances over to a company who employs charm mages and mind controllers," Audrey said. "How could you trust them, ever?"

"He was a con artist?" I asked.

"It doesn't seem so," Steph said grudgingly. "But he was still holding out. He must have been very clever to outmaneuver the intent of the vows he swore to. The bank he works for has been doing a thorough audit, but so far, it seems like he never used his charms for work."

"Only in his... well, I don't want to call it a love life," Audrey ended in a mumble.

"But Cleopatra?" I put in.

"Cleopatra Manx has too much power to be trifled with like that," Steph said. "Whatever Taurus' faults were, and it seems there were many, he knew better than to attempt to charm her."

"I don't think he even tried with Delilah, honestly," Audrey said. "Or if he did, that's what happened just before she died. He tried, and he failed."

"No," I said. "I didn't think he ever even tried with her. But he charmed all the men she was interested in. That's why they all rejected her."

"Oh," Audrey said. "That makes sense. The kind of stalking that Barnardo has been telling me about, that Delilah was never charged with but apparently was always doing? It sounds a lot like someone trying to figure out what kind of spell someone else was under."

"Breaking into their homes to look for cursed items, following them around to see who they were meeting that might be putting them under a spell," Liam said, nodding along. So I guessed this had been breakfast conversation while I had been sleeping.

"Anyway, I don't think he ever charmed her," I said again. Then added with real bitterness, "I don't think that would've been *fun* for him."

I still couldn't believe I was feeling sympathy for Delilah, but there it was. She had been living a wretched life, and she didn't figure out what was happening to her until it was too late.

"We'll never know for sure, but that does seem like the likeliest scenario," Steph agreed.

"But he charmed me," I said glumly. "He knew he could get away with it with me."

"You broke free in the end," Audrey said.

I glanced up at Steph, but I could see in his eyes that he already guessed the truth before I even shook my head. "No, I didn't. He dropped the charm. I told him that Deputy Fluellen was on his way, and he dropped the charm before he tried to kill me."

Liam's eyebrows drew down in a confused expression, but when he started to ask me something, Audrey just caught his arm with a stern shake of her head.

"We'll let you rest now," she said, then dragged Liam out before he could say a single word.

"You're not powerless," Steph said as he fussed with the afghan, drawing it up around me even as I found myself sinking deeper into the pillows. Houdini ducked under Steph's arm, diving under the afghan to curl up by my knees once more.

"I'm not sure having no setting between minimum and maximum is doing me any favors," I said sleepily. I suspected something in the tea was kicking in, but I was too tired to care.

Steph laughed softly. "No, but that's the other thing I was going to say. You're not without control, either. You just need to learn how to work with that charmed bracelet."

I lifted my wrist to look at the silver bracelet. A bit of the light from the lamp on my nightstand caught it, reflecting into my eyes with too dazzling a brightness.

And then I was back in the world of sleep.

CHAPTER
TWENTY-SEVEN

I woke up again, certain it was a different day, although the same gentle rain continued to fall outside my window.

This time, the only other person in the room with me was Audrey. I heard her moving towards the bedside before I had done more than open my eyes, so she must have been keeping a very close watch on me.

"Here," she said, putting another mug of warm, but not hot, tea in my hands.

"This is making me sleep, isn't it?" I asked.

"Yes, but you need it," she said, pushing the mug closer to my mouth. I took a swallow, at first just to humor her, but the honeyed, lemony, grassy tincture once more soothed a throat I hadn't realized was still so damaged. "Wow. That must've been quite a shout I made, huh?" I said.

"It was," she agreed, smoothing down my covers before sitting on the edge of the bed.

"What time is it?" I asked before taking another sip of tea.

"Three in the afternoon, pretty much," she said.

"You closed the teashop to be here with me," I said.

"It's been three days," Houdini put in. He was curled up at the very foot of the bed, not under the covers, and I hadn't noticed he was even there. "I've been told to give you more space," he said huffily, as if reading my mind.

"Why?" I asked.

"You've been a bit restless at times," Audrey said vaguely.

"Nightmares. Which is why you need me close," Houdini said. He lifted his head out from under his back knee to give me a steady look.

"You knocked him off the bed," Audrey said. "That's why Steph thought it would be best if he slept downstairs."

"Why didn't you just wake me up?" I asked, alarmed. I hated even the thought that I might have hurt Houdini, however accidentally it had been.

"It's not always possible," Audrey said, motioning me to drink more of the tea. But I set it down on my lap quite deliberately.

"Tell me what's happening here," I said, hoping I sounded more firm than exhausted. But I kind of doubted I did. "You're drugging me with tea. Why?"

"It's not my recipe, or Agatha's either," Audrey said. "It was something Steph gave me from the Wizard. He's very worried about you."

"Steph, or the Wizard?" I asked.

"Both," Audrey and Houdini said at the same time. They gave each other a nervous glance.

"You channeled a lot of power, and without the proper training," Houdini told me. "That's what Steph says, anyway. You need to rest, or you risk damage to your psyche, he says."

"The Wizard says," Audrey corrected him.

"Steph was here about an hour ago, and he reckons you're about halfway to recovered," Houdini said.

"Three more days?" I said, pressing a weary hand to my forehead. The worst of it was, I felt like I needed three more days of sleep. My whole body hurt. But mostly my throat.

My mind seemed okay. But if that's what they were mostly worried about, maybe I couldn't trust my own senses on that?

I decided I didn't want to dwell on those thoughts.

"Taurus charmed me," I said instead, looking glumly down into the mug of tea.

"We said we'd talk about this later," Audrey said.

But I ignored that. "What about when we went up to his apartment? When he apologized. Was he charming us then?"

Audrey chewed her lip uncertainly. But I was pretty sure it wasn't the answer that was doubtful in her mind, but whether it was her place to give it to me.

"You should drink that tea," she said instead.

"Ugh," Houdini growled in frustration, a strange sound to hear inside your own mind. He didn't quite roll his eyes, but the feeling was there as he looked at me. "Listen, Steph figures that he didn't dare do that kind of magic anywhere that it could be detected. Definitely not at his office, and definitely not in his home. He only tried to nudge you a little at the Fourth of July party, mostly because he thought you'd be an easy target. He didn't push harder, even though he could see you had resisted his attempt."

"But the alley was fair game?" I asked.

"We don't think he ever tried to charm anyone that close to the Tower, actually," Audrey said.

"It was in the wilder parts of the hedge maze. That's certainly where he put enough fear in my mind to force me to part from you when you needed me most," Houdini said mournfully.

"He charmed me there too," I reminded him.

"Right. And then, in the alley, he knew the magics of the Tower would obscure what he was doing from prosaic witnesses. But it's likely he didn't want to risk any magic so close to the Wizard's abode. Which was why he didn't try to charm you again there," Audrey said.

"Hence the silk scarf," Houdini said. "He didn't use his own magic to kill. He just piggy-backed off of the Tower's own protections."

"That's pretty loathsome," I said. "I guess that's why the Wizard is so involved in all this."

"No, that's pretty much just you," Houdini said, then tucked his nose back under his leg again.

"You need to drink that tea," Audrey said. "Three more days, and we can talk again about the rest of it. Like how the authorities found Delilah's purse and phone in Taurus' apartment as well as a secret staircase in the back of his bedroom closet that led all the way down to the quay underground, which is how he bypassed this own building's security. But the only important thing is we're all safe now. And the Wizard is adjusting the spells around that part of the Tower. This can't happen again. Thanks to you."

"Yay me," I said, and downed the last of the tea. I handed the mug back to Audrey, then laid back on the pillow. I was asleep again within minutes, but this time, it felt like it would be a restful sleep without nightmares.

Houdini must have thought so too, because as I started to drift off, I felt him nosing his way under the covers to curl up behind my knees.

I came out of that duped slumber again, uncertain of how much time had passed, but willing to bet it was once more measured in days.

It was night now, and the rain had stopped. Steph was gone, and Audrey and Liam hadn't returned.

But I wasn't alone. Houdini was still with me, deep under the sheets and blankets, closer to my feet than my knees now.

And my mother was there, standing in the doorway. I could barely sense her silhouette, the room and hall beyond were both so dark. But I knew it was her.

I had that feeling again, like I wasn't sure if this was a dream or if I truly were awake. My brain was too fuzzy to sort it all out.

But then I felt a throbbing question coming from my wrist.

Again, this was a question without words, nothing more than a feeling.

Did I want to know? Did I want to be truly awake?

The minute I formed the thought of YES I was sitting up. I had never felt so awake in my life as I did in that moment.

"Mom?" I called.

But she was already sliding away from the door. "Oh, Tabitha," she whispered even as she slipped away. "You really shouldn't have done that. You've made everything so much harder."

"Mom!" I called again, throwing back the covers and stumble/running towards the door.

But she was already gone. I looked down the darkened staircase to where a single light burned at the bottom of the stairs. The light came from a tablet, and it was shining up into Audrey's face.

"Tabitha? Are you all right?" she asked, half-sitting up out of the chair.

"I'm fine. I... just a dream," I finished lamely.

"Do you want more tea?" she asked uncertainly.

"No, I'm going back to bed," I said.

And I did. Houdini made a protesting sound when my feet slid back beside him, but he didn't quite wake up. Almost like he was under a sleep spell. One that my bracelet had generously broken for me.

I wasn't supposed to be awake when my mother came. She had adjusted for the presence of Houdini this time, but I had still messed it up. Somehow, I didn't think she'd try a third time.

I had a thousand more questions to ask Steph when I saw him again, but in the end, none of those answers really mattered. I knew in my heart that my mother was now lost to me, even more than she had been before.

I was on my own with managing my power now. The grounding visits I had half-thought were only dreams wouldn't be happening again. I would just build and build sparks of chaos forever now.

But the bracelet on my wrist snugged a little closer around me, like a hug. And I was pretty sure that I would be okay.

TWENTY-EIGHT

The whole Square turned up for Delilah Dare's wake and interment in the vaults in the catacombs under what was the comic shop in the prosaic world. I had been down there before, for Agatha Mirken's interment, but back then I hadn't yet explored much of the area around the Square. This time around, I was admittedly distracted. The catacombs were like tunnels in an ant farm, going in all four directions but up and down as well. I didn't feel free to wander, especially during the ceremony itself, but every corridor I looked down was well lit, and yet I never saw the end of any of them. They all went on forever, or so it seemed.

And yet surely the sewer and hidden tunnel and quay under the pub were all crossing this same space?

In the end, I had to let those thoughts go. Clearly the catacombs the weird woman Volumnia oversaw were their own pocket dimension, bigger on the inside, just like the hedge maze.

And the bookshop.

I was still thinking about that the next morning when I opened the shop for business, then sat behind the counter, Houdini sleeping in the dog bed at my feet. The dog bed that had once been his personal space in Agatha's teashop. I had thought about putting it in my nook on the fourth floor, but he had already picked the chair at the head of the table for his own, so it made more sense to put the bed down here, where I spent the other half of my days.

I still felt physically worn out, as much from the two days spent lost in the hedge maze under the intense July sun as from the last blowout of my power before the storm. It took actual effort to chew food, let alone move my whole body around. But I owed it to my uncles to keep the shop open, especially after putting the *closed* sign out so many times over the last week.

Not that there were any customers. The rain had stopped, but the cool, smoke-free air had lingered. I could guarantee that all the customers, magical or prosaic, were out enjoying the sunshine without fear of heat stroke. It would only last for a few days, though. By the weekend we were due to have another heat wave, and then they would all be back seeking the cool interior of the bookshop and the many books within.

I was sitting with my ankles wrapped around the legs of my tall stool, chin on my hands, trying to summon up the effort to go upstairs to do a little more research. But, like chewing, that felt like a lot of effort. And there was a sort of subliminal hum I could just barely hear, like the books themselves were trying to lull me to sleep.

"Hey," Steph said suddenly, and I snapped awake, sitting up so abruptly I nearly pitched myself off my stool.

"Hey yourself," I said, smoothing back my curls. I had fallen asleep sitting up and leaning my chin on my hands, but that didn't mean I didn't have bedhead. Stranger things happened. But the cream rinse I had bought from Cressida and used diligently every time I showered was doing its job. It didn't look as nice as when she styled it, but it was still soft and electricity-free.

"I have some answers for you, and I sensed you were alone in here. Houdini excepted, of course," he added.

"That's right," Houdini mumbled sleepily in our minds, then lapsed back into his nap.

"Answers about what?" I asked.

"First of all, how Taurus managed to charm you," he said. "That's a little bit my fault. An unforeseen complication." Then he touched the bracelet on my wrist lightly.

"The bracelet?" I said, closing my other hand over it almost defensively. "Do I have to give it back?"

"No, most assuredly not," he said. "But now that we know it leaves you exposed, we'll add compensating to that to our training regimen."

"We have a training regimen?" I asked. He had mentioned something before, but most of my memories of the times I had woken after collapsing in the alley were a fog. A medicinal tea-associated fog, I suspected, but I couldn't argue that I had needed to rest. I was *still* wiped out.

"We will, when you're ready," he said.

"Aren't you a little busy for that?" I asked.

"No," he said with more firmness than I had expected. I blinked at him. "Sorry, but once I'm done telling you the rest, I think you'll understand why the Wizard feels this is important enough to make part of my duties."

"Now you're kind of scaring me," I said.

"I don't mean to. But I'm not surprised you feel uneasy," he said. "But first, the bracelet. It needs more time to bond with you properly. I'm guessing you don't yet have an understandable intercourse with it?"

"It doesn't talk to me, exactly, but I know when it's asking me things," I said. "It asked if I wanted it to give me control of my powers in the alley. Not in words, but it was a strong feeling. And when I said yes, I felt it release me."

"When you finish bonding with it, your dialogue with it will be clearer," he said. "Probably not as clear as when you speak to Houdini, because the bracelet is not exactly intelligent, but clearer. In the meantime, it is going overboard protecting you."

"But you said the fact that I was charmed was a side effect. I don't understand how both can be true," I said.

"It is trying to protect you by suppressing all of your natural power. Even your protective power," he said.

He was looking at me intently, like he was encouraging me to finish his thoughts for him. I wanted to give up and ask him to just tell me, because I was still so tired that thinking was too much effort.

But I knew that this was definitely worth the exhaustion. So I closed my eyes and puzzled it out.

"Taurus must have charmed me the minute we met in the hedge maze," I said after some thought. "He was standing with the sun behind him, and there was a kind of halo or sparkle or something. I was already feeling some symptoms of heat stroke, so I didn't think anything of it. But that was the charm spell kicking in, wasn't it?"

"You know it was," he said. "You've read as much about such things as I have. And now you've experienced it for yourself, which I have not."

"That feels right to me," I said.

Then I remembered the Fourth of July party in the Square. Taurus had come up to me then, completely out of the blue. His assumption of his own attractiveness and how I should be responding to it had been annoying at the time. But now that I was really thinking about it, there was something more.

"The first time I met Taurus, he tried to charm me too," I said slowly, eyes half-closed as I remembered that moment. "There had been a sparkle to his eyes that wasn't quite natural. But it didn't work."

"He must've been confused and frustrated by that," Steph said. "I don't think with his level of skill he'd ever had anyone shake off one of his spells before."

"And with my reputation for having no magical ability, that must have been doubly puzzling," I said.

"But you don't lack magic," Steph said. "You just haven't been taught how to channel the magic you have."

"I've studied every branch of magic at every academy in the world, even the most obscure," I said. "I've never done a single thing that was an intentional use of magic. I can set things on fire, but not at will."

"You have a lot of innate power, as I'm sure you'll agree," he said. "After what you did to the being that was possessing Nell Bloom, and then what you did to Taurus Vernon, I don't think you can argue otherwise."

"But I can't control it," I said. Then I looked down at my hands. My left hand was still closed around the bracelet on my right wrist, like I was afraid Steph was about to take it away from me. I released it and looked down at the silver charm. "Not without this."

"That's just what I'm telling you," Steph said. "I gave you the bracelet to help suppress the power you didn't want channeling through you. But as a side effect, it damped down what were very powerful protective magics. Your innate ability to not be charmed by spells, for one. He couldn't charm you until I put that bracelet on you."

I looked at it, its silver surface catching the warm glow of the bookshop light, even as it felt distinctly cool against my skin.

"But once I can properly dialogue with it, I can stop it from suppressing my defenses?" I asked. Steph nodded. But it still felt weird. I had never realized I even had those defenses.

I had never needed them before, I guess.

"You've studied every branch of magic that is being taught in the world, even the most obscure," Steph said, echoing my own words back to me. "But what you haven't studied is any of the forbidden ones."

I couldn't help but shiver at those words. "I'm not sure I want to plunge in to a bunch of studies of forbidden magics. That sounds like a straight path to really big trouble."

"Of course not. Most of those are forbidden for good reasons," he said.

"So it's just chaos magic, then," I said with a sigh. "But isn't that also forbidden for good reasons?"

"Some of the reasons are good. But not all. At least I don't think so. And neither does the Wizard," he said.

"How can you be sure?" I asked.

He rubbed at his chin for a moment as he mulled over his response. Then he gave me an awkward grin. "Okay, I can't. But what I can tell you is that mages with chaos magic as their only calling are still being born. Like you. And what good is it doing you forbidding you from learning how to control your power? Let alone forbidding you from even knowing what it is that's happening to you."

"There are others?" I asked.

"It's rare," he said. Then he chewed his lip as if debating going on. But he clearly decided to, when he added, "Most die before they reach twenty-five. It's a lot of power to tap and not know how to control. And a lot of them, they don't die alone."

"I could burn the whole Square down," I said, and realized I was gripping that bracelet tightly again.

"The official position is buried deep in the archives where only those who are looking for it specifically could ever stumble across it, and even then the odds are against it," he said. "But the Wizard and I found it. The council contends that all born with the chaos calling are found when they are young and trained in some other field of study without ever realizing what they were truly born for."

"So I was found and..." But I trailed off, uncertain where the council had ever been active in my life at any point. "Why was I constantly changing schools and changing courses of study if the council was directing me to some specific, safer end?"

"Well, you see, that's how we know the official position is a lie," Steph said with a warm kindness that made the knowledge bombs he was dropping on me just barely survivable.

"They *want* me to flame out and die?" I asked.

"I don't think it matters now what they want," he said. "The Wizard and I are protecting you now. The council has political power, but the Wizard has real power. They will find diplomatic ways to make it seem like it was their decision, I'm sure, but in the end, they will do whatever the Wizard tells them to."

I fidgeted with the bracelet, spinning it around my wrist. It felt so familiar, like I had worn it forever, even though it had only been a few days. It was almost as much a part of me as the glasses my uncle had made for me.

"My uncle," I said. "He can't talk about things. Like I said, I think he's under a spell."

"I haven't found anything out about that," he said.

"I know. But I'm just thinking, maybe this is why. And maybe it's why my mother only comes at night." I closed my eyes and tried to summon another of the dream-like memories from my time spent in bed over the days of rain after my fight in the alley. "My mother came again. She had done something to keep Houdini sleeping, so he didn't know she was there."

Steph sucked in a breath, and I stopped talking.

"Sorry," he said. "It's just, I can't imagine the power it would take to make a dragon sleep."

"I don't know what she did," I said. "But the bracelet asked me again what I wanted. This time, if I wanted to be free of her soporific spell. And I said yes. And I was awake. She left at once, but before she was quite gone, I heard her say I had ruined everything. That everything was going to be much harder now."

"There's something I haven't been telling you," he said, and now he was the one fidgeting, with one of the pens from the cup on the counter by the computer. He turned it over and over in his hands, as nimbly as he worked with his own wand.

"What's that?" I asked, taking the pen out of his hands and putting it back in the cup.

"I've tried to find information about your mother," he said, not quite looking at me. "But I can't. As far as I can tell, she doesn't exist. I mean, not officially."

"I see," I said. "That, with what's going on with my uncle, and me constantly moving from place to place. It feels like it's all related."

"It would be a heck of a coincidence if they weren't," he admitted.

"Maybe it was to protect me from the council," I said. I could feel a glow of hope in my chest. Like my lack of a real relationship with my mother might have had a very good reason. Like she had only done it to keep me safe from... something. "Maybe she believed the official thing about being found and forcibly trained in another branch of magic. Or maybe she knew something we don't."

"Here's the thing," Steph said, and reached out to take both my hands. My heart sank. The only reason for that gesture was that the next thing he was about to say was going to be even a bigger bomb than the others.

But I swallowed hard and managed to eke out a quiet, "Go on."

"The Wizard and I can help you learn to work with this bracelet, and we can teach you some very good general techniques for channelling magic as powerful as yours," he said. But then he trailed off uncertainly.

"But?" I prompted.

"But what you really need is a mentor. A master in exactly the sort of magic that's been forbidden for centuries," he said. "And so far, our search has turned up exactly no one."

"Except my mother," I said.

"Well, we don't actually know if she shares your magic or not," he said. "It's hereditary, but it could come from your father's line, and not your mother's."

"And I don't know a single thing about my father. Not even his name," I said with a sigh.

"Also, it might skip a generation or two. Like I said, it's an exceptionally rare magical calling," he said.

"Well, for now, I'm willing to settle for being able to control it," I said. "I never wanted to be a wizard, anyway. Working in a bookshop and living a quiet life is enough for me."

"I think we can achieve that much for you," he said. Then he seemed to realize he was still holding my hands and quickly released me, thrusting his hands deep in his pockets. "Anyway, there is still one last hope."

"What's that?" I asked.

Then he was grinning at me again. "Well, books," he said. "Granted, we haven't been able to find any yet. But there are rumors of texts. The practitioners of chaos magic have been rare across time, but books live practically forever. They can be found. They can be acquired."

"And they can be learned from," I finished for him.

And we shared that grin. As impossible as this quest sounded, it was better that not having a goal to work for at all.

There had to be a book out there, somewhere.

And it was just waiting for me to find it.

ABERGAVENNY'S CORNERSTORE
THE VIOLENTA COURT BOUTIQUE
BARTHOMEW BULLEN'S POTIONS & MAGICAL SUNDRIES
THE SQUARE PUB
THE WIZARD'S TOWER
LEBEAU'S FRENCH BAKERY
VOLUMNIA'S STAIRCASE
COMIC SHOP
PORTAL
THE BITTER BREW COFFEESHOP
VACANT STORE FRONT
INANNA SALON & SPA
THE WEAL & WOE BOOKSHOP
THE LOOSE LEAVES TEASHOP

CHECK OUT BOOK THREE!

Tabitha Greene knows more about magic than most. She might not be able to cast a workable spell to save her life, but she has read every magical tome and text in existence.

Or so she thought. But then she hears of another book. A rare volume delineating an even rarer type of magic. A type of magic that just might be Tabitha's real calling.

But when she tracks down the magical bookseller who owns the only known copy, she finds only a dead shop owner and no sign of the book.

Maybe a random robbery gone wrong, but Tabitha doubts it. But either way, if she wants that book, she has to find the murderer first.

With the help of her friends, she intends to do just that. But if the thief who stole the book killed the bookseller in order to hide the truth the text contained, Tabitha and all her friends face a dangerous threat.

THE BOOKSELLER BLUNDER, Book 3 in the Weal & Woe Bookshop Witch Mystery series. Available December 12, 2023 direct from RatatoskrPressBooks.com or January 16, 2024 in stores everywhere.

THE WITCHES THREE COZY MYSTERIES

In case you missed it, check out Charm School, the first book in the complete Witches Three Cozy Mystery Series!

Amanda Clarke thinks of herself as perfectly ordinary in every way. Just a small-town girl who serves breakfast all day in a little diner nestled next to the highway, nothing but dairy farms for miles around. She fits in there.

But then an old woman she never met dies, and Amanda was named in her will. Now Amanda packs a bag and heads to the big city, to Miss Zenobia Weekes' Charm School for Exceptional Young Ladies. And it's not in just any neighborhood. No, she finds herself on Summit Avenue in St. Paul, a street lined with gorgeous old houses, the former homes of lumber barons, railroad millionaires, even the writer F. Scott Fitzgerald. Why, Amanda can practically hear the jazz music still playing across the decades.

Scratch that. The music really, literally, still plays in the backyard of the charm school. Because the house stretches across time itself. Without a witch to protect this tear in the fabric of the world, anything can spill over. Like music.

Or like murder.

Charm School, the first book in the complete Witches Three Cozy Mystery Series!

THE VIKING WITCH COZY MYSTERIES

In case you missed it, check out Body at the Crossroads, the first book in the Viking Witch Cozy Mystery Series!

When her mother dies after a long illness, Ingrid Torfa must sell the family home to cover the medical bills. Her career as a book illustrator not yet exactly launched, Ingrid faces two options: live in her battered old Volkswagen, or go back to her mother's small town in northern Minnesota.

The small town that still haunts her dreams more than a decade since she last visited it. Or rather, not the town but the grandmother.

All of the drawings she fills notebooks with witches and the trolls that do their bidding? Not as whimsical in her nightmares as she sketches them in the bright light of day.

If not for her beloved cat Mjolner, living in the Volkswagen just might tempt her.

But the cat wants four walls and a door, so north she goes. And finds trouble in the form of a dead body before she even finds her grandmother's little town. How much can a town of stoic fishermen possibly be hiding?

As Ingrid is about to find out, quite a lot.

Body at the Crossroads, the first book in the Viking Witch Cozy Mystery Series!

ALSO FROM RATATOSKR PRESS

The Ritchie and Fitz Sci-Fi Murder Mysteries starts with Murder on the Intergalactic Railway.

For Murdina Ritchie, acceptance at the Oymyakon Foreign Service Academy means one last chance at her dream of becoming a diplomat for the Union of Free Worlds. For Shackleton Fitz IV, it represents his last chance not to fail out of military service entirely.

Strange that fate should throw them together now, among the last group of students admitted after the start of the semester. They had once shared the strongest of friendships. But that all ended a long time ago.

But when an insufferable but politically important woman turns up murdered, the two agree to put their differences aside and work together to solve the case.

Because the murderer might strike again. But more importantly, solving a murder would just have to impress the dour colonel who clearly thinks neither of them belong at his academy.

Murder on the Intergalactic Railway, the first book in the Ritchie and Fitz Sci-Fi Murder Mysteries, available everywhere books are sold.

FREE EBOOK!

Like exclusive, free content?

If you'd like to receive "A Collection of Witchy Prequels", a free collection of short story prequels to the Witches Three Cozy Mystery and Viking Witch Cozy Mystery series, as well as other free stories throughout the year, go to my website CateMartin.com to subscribe to my newsletter! This eBook is exclusively for newsletter subscribers and will never be sold in stores. Check it out!

ABOUT THE AUTHOR

Cate Martin has written stories which have appeared in the **Mystery, Crime and Mayhem** quarterly magazine as well as in the annual **Holiday Spectacular** Advent calendar of holiday stories. She is also the author of three witch mystery series: **The Witches Three Cozy Mysteries**, and **The Viking Witch Cozy Mysteries** and **The Weal & Woe Bookshop Witch Mysteries**. She currently lives in Minneapolis, Minnesota. You can learn more about her work at Cate-Martin.com.

Also by Cate Martin

The Witches Three Cozy Mystery Series

Charm School

Work Like a Charm

Third Time is a Charm

Old World Charm

Charm his Pants Off

Charm Offensive

The Witches Three Cozy Mysteries Books 1-3

The Witches Three Cozy Mysteries Books 4-6

The Viking Witch Cozy Mystery Series

Body at the Crossroads

Death Under the Bridge

Murder on the Lake

Killing in the Village Commons

Bloodshed in the Forest

Corpse in the Mead Hall

Slaying on the Lake Shore

Bones by the Forest Road

Sacrifice Behind the Falls

Body Under the Café

Assassination in the Glade

Bewitchment After the Storm

Predator in the Lanes (available January 14, 2025 direct from me or February 11, 2025 in stores everywhere)

The Viking Witch Cozy Mysteries Books 1-3

The Viking Witch Cozy Mysteries Books 4-6

The Weal & Woe Bookshop Witch Mystery Series

The Teashop Terror

The Salon & Spa Scandal

The Bookseller Blunder

The Entrepreneur Enigma

The Novelty Shop Nightmare

The Courtyard Conundrum (available December 10, 2024 direct from me or January 14, 2025 in stores everywhere)